RONNIE O'SULLIVAN

THE BREAK

MACMILLAN

First published 2018 by Macmillan
an imprint of Pan Macmillan
20 New Wharf Road, London N1 9RR
Associated companies throughout the world
www.panmacmillan.com

ISBN 978-1-5098-6401-0

1 3 5 7 9 8 6 4 2

A CIP catalogue record for this book is available from the British Library.

Typeset by Palimpsest Book Production Ltd, Falkirk, Stirlingshire
Printed and bound by CPI Group (UK) Ltd, Croydon, CR0 4YY

THE BREAK

August 1997

To Frankie James,

*By the time you read this, I will be dead. And shortly
after, you might wellwish you were an all.. Haha.*

*We had ourslves a little agreement now didnt we? That
you would keep zipped about certain things you know
or think you do about me and mine. And me in return
I would not hand into the police the weapan used to
murder that witnes – which as you know full vbloody
well is all covered in your sticky little fingerprints.*

*Well you will be glad to hear that even here in death I
intend to honor my part of our bargain . . . . I have not
handed over the pistol to the filth. No that is because i
Have intead handed it over in a nice little platsic bag to
my son Dougie.*

*Now you might think that the ifnormation you had on
me means that you and Dougie are even and that he
cant hand that pistol in to the cops and get you done
fro murder without you then telling the cops what you
know about me.*

*BUt I am ~~doead~~ DEAD now see? So you can tell them
what you want and it wont make no diffrence to me.
bUt you are still royally screwed with that gun.*

*I have told DOugie too that you are full of shit and he
shouldn't lisen to any bollocks you try telling him to
wriggle out of him having one over on you like this . . ..*

1

But i have told him an all that you are resorsful &
might prove useful to him or maybe he will just decide
to give the cops that pistol anyway ? ?! And if he does
then when they bang you up make sure you remember
my face wherever you are cos i will be grinning at you
frm ear to fcking ear.

Yours sinceerely laughing at you from my grave,

Terence Hamilton

cc Douglas Hamilton, my son & heir

1

'I'll tell you what I want . . .'

For the Spice Girls, the answer to this little philosophical conundrum bopping out through the boozer's tinny sound system couldn't have been any easier.

But for Frankie James, sitting here at the bar with his heartbeat drumming like Keith Moon on amphetamines, things were a bit more complex. Because what Frankie really, really, really wanted was to be anywhere but here . . . in this part of London . . . today . . . for the reason that he was.

The pub he'd taken refuge in from the thunderstorm pelting down outside was called The Paradise by Way of Kensal Green. A quote from some G. K. Chesterton poem about a jolly old Victorian piss-up, according to a bar girl Frankie had once chatted up in here on his way to his first ever Notting Hill Carnival a few years back when he'd just turned eighteen.

Nothing much jolly or heavenly about it in here today, mind. Even the whopping great stone angel's head leering down at him from the wall looked like it was up for a ruck. Not the only one either.

Frankie pulled his black trilby down even lower over his brow and risked another glance up past his stubbled reflection in the chintzy bar mirror. Early doors it might have been, and Sunday to boot, but it was already well busy in here.

Two distinct tribes. First lot were a bunch of Jarvis Cocker and Elastica wannabes. Most of them mid-twenties like him, but Christ they made him feel old, him here in his suit and tie, and them all heroin chic eyes, sloganed T-shirts, too-tight jeans and Aviator shades, like extras from one of those Christmas Diesel ads. Probably locals, or whatever passed for locals round here these days anyway, since West London had got itself so hip.

But it was tribe two that had Frankie's ticker clacking like the maracas. Gangsters. Not the semi-friendly sort either. Not Tommy Riley's boys, who'd at least warn Frankie before maiming him if he ever pissed them off. Nah, this lot were way worse. The Hamiltons. Riley's rivals for the grisly Soho Crime Family of the Year Award. A bunch of kneecappers, face slashers and vertebrae stampers, all of who would happily give Frankie a proper bleedin' beating on sight, given half a chance.

They even looked like old-school gangsters today. Blacksuited and booted. Clean shaven. Freshly barbered too, judging by the spanked arse red tan lines showing at the backs of their fat-muscled necks. They could have been extras from *The Godfather*, the lot of them. Except their Marlon Brando was nowhere to be seen.

But that was the whole point, wasn't it? Why they were

here. Why Frankie was here. Why he was so totally and utterly screwed. All because the Hamiltons' boss man was dead.

*

Word had first reached Frankie on Sunday night two weeks ago, back down Soho in the Ambassador Club, when Jack had come bursting in, nearly sprawling headfirst over the snooker table nearest the door. It had just gone half ten, with the last couple of punters finishing up on table four, and Frankie had been on the point of shutting up shop and calling it a night.

'Don't tell me,' he said. 'You're training to be a samurai?'

'You what?'

Frankie nodded at the poxy little ponytail his kid brother had tied his hair back into, black hair like Frankie's, Sicilian, like their mum's.

'Piss off.' Jack grinned back at him. From the colour of his face, he looked like he must have sprinted the whole way here from the James Boys Gym the other side of Oxford Street. 'You haven't heard, have you? I knew you couldn't have, or you'd have rung.'

'Heard what?'

Jack was already behind the bar, pouring himself a Guinness, and one for Frankie too, even though he knew damn well he'd quit. 'Terence Hamilton,' he said.

'What about him?' Even the name sent a shiver down Frankie's spine.

Jack slowly pulled his forefinger across his throat.

'What, *killed*? Bloody hell! By who?' Christ, if Riley's

5

mob had got anything to do with it, it would be like Sarajevo round here before the night was done.

'Not who. What.' Jack took a long, greedy slug of his Guinness, without even waiting for it to settle. 'Cancer,' he said. 'Couldn't have happened to a nicer bloke.'

Cancer . . . *Flash*. Frankie remembered Terence Hamilton's face. Two years ago now in that filthy basement only a few short streets away. Terence telling Frankie he was dying. Skin like ivory. Black shadows circling his eyes. So he'd been telling the truth, had he? All that hadn't been just another of his sick bloody games?

'Cause for celebration then, eh?' Jack said with a wink, nudging Frankie's pint towards him.

And, yeah, Frankie was tempted. He'd already got himself a gobful of saliva just looking at it. And nearly enough cause too, right? Because Hamilton was a bastard, cubed, no doubt about that. Someone whose death deserved a bloody good toast.

Flash. Frankie pictured him again leering down at him in that basement. *Flash*. Those ropes cutting into Frankie's wrists. *Flash*. Frankie's bloodied, broken teeth. *Flash*. That blood-soaked corpse at his side. *Flash*. The blade of Hamilton's Stanley knife glinting. *Flash . . . flash . . . flashflashflashflashflashflashflash . . .*

Frankie had been lucky to get out of there alive. But not just lucky, smart, right? Because he'd tricked Hamilton, hadn't he? Into thinking that Frankie had something on him. A tape recording connecting Hamilton to a whole bunch of bad shit he never wanted coming to light. Enough to get Hamilton not to kill him. Enough to get him to help clear

Jack's name too after he'd been set up for the murder of Susan Tilley, that poor girl who'd been due to marry Terence Hamilton's only son.

'I mean, just thank fuck he's gone,' Jack said. 'Because I don't reckon he ever really did believe I was innocent, you know. I reckon he kept on blaming me . . . wanting me dead.'

'Yeah . . .' But Frankie still pushed the pint away. Because, dead as Terence was, his son, Dougie, was still very much alive. And, judging by the beating Frankie reckoned Dougie had secretly ordered on Jack last year, still hated Jack and blamed him for whatever part he thought he'd played in his fiancée's death every bit as much as his dad ever had.

Meaning Frankie and Jack's real trouble with the Hamilton gang might have only just begun.

*

'The thing is, I felt I knew her.'

It was the barmaid in the Paradise talking. Jet-black eyebrows. Bleached, cropped hair. A treble clef tattoo stamped on her neck. All very Gwen Stefani.

'Yeah, well, we all did, didn't we, dearie?' This from a stick-thin, squiffy older bird sitting hunched down next to Frankie with a fag in her hand. 'Cos she felt like one of us . . . like a friend . . . you know? That's why everyone's so upset . . . because we all know we could've helped her . . . when she went through her dark times, like . . . if only our paths had crossed . . .'

Rolling news of Princess Di's death was playing on the muted TV screen above the cigarette machine. Flowers piled up outside Kensington Palace. The people's princess wearing baby blue on the steps of Buck House the day she'd got engaged – 'like a fawn in the headlights', some commentator had just said. Her with her kids. Her in minefields. Her with Elton John.

Her being killed in a car crash in a tunnel in Paris last night was all anyone had been talking about all day.

'D'you know what I heard?' the stick-thin bird went on, swilling the last of her gin and bitter lemon round her glass.

'And what's that, Doris?' asked the barmaid.

'MFI did it,' Doris said in a whisper.

Silence. Then a snigger. This from the barmaid, but Frankie couldn't help smiling too.

'What, the furniture store?' asked the barmaid, giving Frankie a little conspiratorial glance – not the first one she'd slipped him either, he'd noticed, this last half-hour since he'd walked through the door. Had even asked him if he was Italian when he'd come in. Had said he had something of the young Bob De Niro about him.

'No, the bloody spies,' snapped Doris. 'And it's not funny either, it's true. It's because she was going to marry him . . . that Dodo she was with . . . because he's the son of that Arab what runs Harrods, see . . . and the Royals, well, they could never have stood for *that* . . . and so *that's* why they sent in the MFI.'

'I think you mean MI5, love,' said Frankie. 'Or MI6, they're the spies.'

'You've got a nerve, showing your face in here,' another voice – male, all bleedin' testosterone – growled.

'What?' The old girl looked round, confused.

'Not you, *you*,' the wheezing voice said.

A chisel-hard finger thudded into Frankie's back, in case there was any doubt left over who was being addressed. Frankie looked up past the barmaid into the mirror. A brick wall with a balding head spattered with ginger stubble was standing right behind him, glaring back through bloodshot eyes. A Soho face. Jimmy Flanagan, AKA 'The Saint'. So called not because of any passing resemblance he had to Ian Ogilvy. But on account of how many people he'd put into A&E in Paddington's St Mary's hospital over the last few decades he'd been professionally kicking arse.

George Michael's 'Older' had just started playing through the speakers. Yeah, well, Frankie needed to be wiser too. He stayed sitting. No point rising to the challenge. He might be six foot two himself, with a couple of teen kickboxing medals in a box under his bed, but The Saint was nearer seven and chewed people like Frankie up for laughs. He was one of the Hamilton gang's top enforcers, meaning any lip from Frankie here today, and all he'd have to do was click his Bowyers sausage-sized fingers and the rest of Hamilton's crew would pile in sharpish and bury Frankie like an avalanche.

'All right, Jimmy,' Frankie said, opting for a friendly tone instead. He turned round to face him, nice and slow.

'Don't you fucking Jimmy me, you little scrote,' said The Saint, wiping his bulbous, blood-vesselled conk on his suit jacket sleeve. 'The only reason I haven't kicked your head halfway up your bumhole already is because I still remember your old man from school.'

The Old Man, Frankie's dad . . . along with Terence Hamilton, Tommy Riley, Jimmy Flanagan and half the rest of the senior hoods in London, they'd all gone to the same East End shithole of a School for Scoundrels back in the sixties. Had split into warring factions since, mind. Wolves scrapping over the same rotting London carcass. But some of them at least still trod a tad softly around each other's families, just for old times' sake.

Paddington, that's what Frankie's dad had always used to call The Saint. Not because of the St Mary's connection, mind, but because of those ginger patches of hair he'd had since he'd started going bald back in his twenties. Made him look like he'd just pulled a marmalade sandwich out from under his hat, the Old Man had always said. Though probably best not to mention that now.

'You'd better have a bloody good reason for being here,' said The Saint.

'Burgers.'

'You what?'

Frankie nodded from the chalkboard on the wall to his empty plate. If you were going to have a last meal, this was as good a place as any was what he'd reckoned on his way past here from the tube station to the cemetery just now. Had got itself a nice new rep as one of the leading gastro pubs that were springing up around this part of West London. According to the *Time Out* review Frankie had spotted in the window, at least.

'Organic Hereford beef patty with Monterey Jack cheese,

lamb's leaf lettuce and heritage tomatoes in a lightly toasted brioche bun,' Frankie explained.

'Toasted brioche what? Speak English, you prick,' said The Saint.

'All right, fair enough,' said Frankie. 'The truth is I was hungry and I didn't think you lot would be in here. Thought it was too far from the cemetery for well-off gentlemen like yourselves to walk. Thought it was more likely you'd be gathering down the William the Fourth. Or else I'd have steered clear. And especially if I'd known you were all setting out from here an' all.' He nodded through the rain-spattered window at the blurry outline of the horse-drawn hearse that had pulled up ten minutes ago, the same time a bunch of other cars had pulled up and the Hamilton crew had piled out and into here.

'Yeah, well, it might not be the nearest pub to the cemetery, but it's the nearest one that does a decent pint,' said The Saint.

A fair point and one that Frankie would probably have picked up on quicker if Dr Pepper hadn't been the strongest thing to pass his lips these last six months.

The Saint let out a horrible, wet sneeze. 'Hay fever,' he muttered, wiping his nose on the back of his paddle-sized hand, looking Frankie up and down, taking in the black bespoke suit, black tie and white shirt that Frankie was wearing under his old-school beige Hanbury raincoat.

'Good God,' he said. 'Don't tell me you're out this way because you've come to pay your respects?'

'In a way . . .'

'Yeah?' The Saint smiled – something he could have done

with more practice at, because his crooked teeth looked like they were about to take a bite out of Frankie's head. 'Because the way I heard it,' he said, 'there was no love lost between you and Terence. Even though, for whatever reason, we were told not to tread on your twinkly little toes these last two years.'

For whatever reason . . . The Saint was fishing, wanted to know exactly what deal it was that Frankie had struck with Terence Hamilton. But Frankie knew better than to be drawn into that.

'Not that it matters any more anyhow,' said The Saint. 'Not now there's a new boss in town. Because all bets are off, or hadn't you heard? We're on the up, son. The Hamiltons are back.'

The *new boss*. He meant Dougie. All kinds of rumours had done the rounds this last couple of weeks since Terence had carked it. That the Hamiltons were over. That Terence's wife had seized the throne. That the Albanians, then the Triads, then the Poles had moved in. But it was Dougie who'd come out on top eventually. Exactly like Terence had planned. The king of Soho East was dead. Long live the bleedin' king.

'So it seems,' Frankie said, looking past The Saint at the thirty or so thugs gathered in the bar behind him. There was a cockiness to them, all right. An air of expectancy, like all they were waiting for now was their orders on what – or more specifically *who* – to do next.

Frankie couldn't help wondering what Tommy Riley would make of all this. How was he going to react? The same as everyone else, Tommy had clearly seen the Hamiltons on the wane and him on the wax. He'd been steadily nibbling into their territories these last two years, no doubt thinking the whole of Soho would soon be his, and no way would he be giving an inch of it back now without a fight.

'But all you really need to know right now, son,' warned The Saint, 'is that the new boss hates you and your weasel brother like a rash.' The Saint chuckled at this, a horrible, phlegmy sound. 'And whatever protection Riley's giving you down town, that don't count for shit here. Especially today.' The Saint stared at him, unblinking, through emotionless grey eyes. 'So if I were you, I'd get the hell out of Dodge before Dougie finds out that you're here.'

A woman's voice interrupted. Like butter through concrete.

'It's all right, Jimmy. Relax. It was Dougie who asked him.'

Her . . . Frankie looked right, sharpish. Because, oh yeah, he remembered this voice, all right. *Her* . . . Last year in that top-of-the-range Merc with the bass thumping out. *Her* . . . with the same short, bobbed black hair and heavy kohl make-up she was sporting now. *Her* . . . like some modern-day Cleopatra, leaning out of that Merc as it had cruised by Jack's new flat to tell him she had a message for him. *Her* . . . strong enough to keep a grip of Jack's collar as the car had pulled away and dragged him down the street.

Her . . .

If Frankie hadn't been there to pull her off of him, Jack's head would have been rammed smack into that metal electricity junction box. *Clunk*. Lights out.

'You,' Frankie said.

13

He was already on his feet, eyeballing her. Forget The Saint. This one didn't give warnings. She liked hurting people for fun. He'd seen that for himself. His hands were already curled up into fists.

'You've got a good memory,' she said, looking him over the same way boxers did each other down Jack's gym.

'You don't deny it then? That it was you?' *And Dougie* . . . because, oh yeah, Frankie reckoned he'd glimpsed that posh prick too in the back of that Merc . . . there to watch his nasty pet tiger play.

'Why should I?' Her blue eyes flashed.

Her accent, what was it, Dutch? Afrikaans? Something Frankie had puzzled over last night when he'd heard her message on the phone, telling him to be here today. *Or else.*

'Because the way I see it,' she continued, 'there's not much you can do about it here . . . or anywhere . . . ever.'

A fact, not a gloat. Not even the trace of a smile on her cold shop dummy of a chiselled face. And fair enough. Because she was right, wasn't she? Dougie had Frankie over a barrel. Because of what Terence had given him. Because of that gun. Terence's handwritten letter telling Frankie he'd given it to Dougie had only reached Frankie last night. Delivered by hand. By some courier who'd insisted on giving it to him personal, like, and had told him to read it right away. About ten minutes before this one had then left that message on his phone, ordering him to be here today.

'Dougie asked me to tell you to wait at the cemetery until after the interment,' she said.

'The *what*?'

'Interment. In the family mausoleum.'

Yeah, posh, all right. Like sodding royalty. A simple coffin in the dirt wasn't good enough for the likes of Dougie Hamilton. Unlike his father, who'd grown up in the stuff and wouldn't have given a shit.

'You got a problem with that?' said the woman, like she was reading his mind.

Frankie just glared at her. Or tried to. Because that was the messed-up thing. He *wanted* to hate her. Because of what she'd tried doing to Jack. And yet . . . there was something about those big blue eyes of hers, a flicker of amusement there that wasn't reflected in the rest of her face, like him and her were somehow connected, somehow in on some kind of grim joke that only the two of them got.

'Just be there,' she said – turning and walking back to the door, the crowd parting before her without her even needing to ask.

'Best not get on the wrong side of that,' said The Saint.

'Yeah?' Frankie watched her turn up her black coat collar as she stepped out into the rain. 'She got a name?'

'Viollet. Viollet Coetzee. Dougie's right-hand man . . . woman, attack dog, whatever.' The Saint's lips peeled back to reveal another sabre-toothed smile. 'Ex-South African copper, word is. Nobody fucks with her, a fact. No one at all.'

Frankie tracked her outside. Watched her opening the door of a sleek black Daimler parked up directly behind the horse-drawn hearse. He thought he clocked Dougie Hamilton lurking in the back. Did she lean over and kiss him as she slid up beside him? It certainly looked that way to Frankie as she pulled the door shut.

2

Frankie locked eyes on her again an hour later down in Kensal Green Cemetery, as her and the rest of the Hamilton mob trudged back in slow procession through the rain towards their line of black limos, Beamers and Mercs.

The last mausoleum Frankie had been near was the massive one him and some of his old school muckers had once tried breaking into in St James's Church, Piccadilly, after watching *Indiana Jones and the Last Crusade*. They'd been hoping to find a bit of Templar gold or whatever, to buy themselves some new BMXs with, but instead they'd got chased off by some crazy old vicar who'd heard them all fumbling about.

Terence Hamilton's final abode here looked more like a bungalow. A big fat rectangle of black granite. Hard. Soulless. Frankie grinned. Much like its new occupant. Hah. Must have cost Dougie a bomb. Well, hopefully it had a nice deep lift shaft in it too. To get Terence safely down to hell where he belonged at the foot of Old Nick.

'Viollet said to give this to you.'

Frankie turned to see a boy looking up at him. Or a bit of a boy anyway, a sliver of face peering up out of a baggy black hoodie. A headphone wire hanging out one ear. Couldn't have been more than ten. He was holding out a folded piece of paper.

'Did she now?' Frankie opened it and read.

The Cobden Club, 170 Kensal Road.
2.30. Staff entrance.

Staff, eh? Frankie checked his watch. A Rolex, kosher. His dad's name engraved on the back. The Old Man had given it him to look after seven years ago, the same night he'd got arrested for armed robbery.

It was still only two o'clock. Thirty slow minutes, then, until he found out whatever the hell fate had planned for him. A tad melodramatic? He bloody wished. Because whatever reason Dougie Hamilton had summoned him here for today, it certainly wasn't a nice cuppa and a chat.

'She said you'd give me a tenner for delivering it,' said the boy.

The bloody cheek. Frankie stared across the cemetery to where Viollet was standing under a black brolly next to Hamilton's car. And, yeah . . . even over that distance, he could have sworn he saw her staring right back at him, with that same 'in on it' look as before.

Viollet . . . He reckoned the name suited her. Half violin, half violence, right? Both playful and deadly all at once.

'And who the hell are you, then?' Frankie asked the kid.

'Little Terry. After my uncle.'

Terence Hamilton's nephew, then. Dougie's little cousin. 'You don't look so little to me.'

The kid held his stare. 'I'm second tallest in my class.'

And first hardest, if your rellies are anything to go by.
Frankie shivered. It was still pissing it down and he was
half-soaked, raindrops dripping off the brow of his hat and
running down his coat. He folded and stuffed Viollet's note
into his pocket and took out his silver money clip. Peeling
off a twenty, he handed it across.

'Looks like you're in luck, Little Terry,' he said. 'Unless,
of course, you've got change?'

'Nah,' the kid grinned.

'Didn't think so. You can owe me then,' he said.

'My cousin, Dougie, told me never to owe anyone anything.'

'Good advice.' And easy to give too, if you had thirty
thugs standing by to take anything you wanted off anyone
you wanted whenever you saw fit. 'What you listening to?'
Frankie could hear the tinny sound of music coming out the
earphone.

'The Notorious B.I.G.'

'Yeah? That good, is it?'

'He's my favourite. Him and Puff Daddy.'

Sounded more like a cereal than a singer. Frankie just
nodded. The kid might as well have been speaking a foreign
language. He really did need to start getting out a bit more.

'See ya, then, Frankie,' said the kid.

'Yeah, see ya, Little Terry.'

Frankie. So she'd told him his name as well, eh? Not
that man. Not *that prick. Frankie.* He watched Little Terry
running back through the rain to the Daimler. Viollet opened
the door as he reached her and the two of them climbed in.

*

18

'Sit.'

Frankie looked round the small room on the top floor of the Cobden Club. A stink of paint. Fresh white emulsion on the walls. Cloth draped over the only window. A single bare light bulb glaring down from the ceiling. Relaxing. Welcoming. Not.

But other than the solitary red leather armchair Dougie was uninvitingly staring at him from, there was nowhere *to* sit.

'But . . .'

'Yes, yes. Come on. Chop chop. Right there.' Dougie jabbed a manicured forefinger at the bare floorboards halfway between him and the door. His expensive and fashionable black-rimmed glasses glinted, as he smoothed down the lapels of his tweed suit jacket and pushed his long black fringe back behind his pointed ears.

'Are you –' Frankie started to say.

'What? Serious? I don't know.' Dougie pointed at his own face, all pale and ghostlike in the gloom, apart from his beady little eyes that glinted darkly, like a rat's. 'Do I look like I'm joshing?'

Joshing? 'Er, no,' Frankie said.

'Then bloody well *sit*.' Colour flared into Dougie's cheeks.

Spoken like Barbara bleedin' Woodhouse . . . like Frankie was his mutt . . . his junior . . . a servant . . . some scum . . .

'Go fuck yourself,' Frankie said.

Boom. Big mistake. A creak of floorboards. A shadow fell. Something smacked Frankie hard in the back of his kidneys. He sank gasping to his knees. All he could do not to puke.

19

'There, now. Much better. Who's a good boy?' Dougie leant forward and rubbed his hands together like he was warming them in front of a fire. 'Now *stay*.'

Frankie couldn't have moved if he'd wanted.

'If I had a biscuit or a chew, I'd give you one,' said Dougie. 'But I don't.'

A wrinkle stretched at the right side of his mouth. The closest this bastard ever got to a smile? Yeah, that was Frankie's guess. Dougie stroked his square, clean-shaven jaw. He might have been handsome, if he hadn't been such a prick.

'If he swears at me again, Barry,' Dougie said, 'split his head open with that bat of yours and then bring a real dog in here to lick up whatever muck dribbles out.'

Barry . . . Frankie was guessing he meant the same hulking Sasquatch in a suit who'd been standing sentry outside the room with a Louisville Slugger baseball bat propped up beside him when Jimmy Flanagan had led Frankie up here just now and shown him in.

Frankie felt the hard end of the bat pressing up against the base of his skull, just to remind him it was there. He heaved in more breath. *Keep your shit together. If Dougie really wanted you dead, you already would be, right?*

Dougie gazed down at him with the kind of expression that stared out at people through DHSS hatches, letting them know they were about as important as a piece of shit on a shoe. The kind that let you know they were totally in charge.

And, Christ, it couldn't have been more different, could it, to the first time him and Dougie had properly met?

20

Because that had been outside the Ambassador after Jack had been arrested for the murder of Dougie's fiancée . . . after Dougie had lost control of his sky-blue Merc and had rammed it into Raj's newsagent, before trying and failing to stove Frankie's face in with his fists, a drunken, distraught bloody mess, more boy than man.

Frankie would never forget what he'd screamed at him: *Your bastard brother. He fucking killed her . . . he's ruined everything that I had.* He'd never forget either how Dougie hadn't given up struggling, even after Frankie had bested him. Making him the very worst kind of bastard there was – one who didn't know when to quit.

And all that when Dougie had still been a civilian . . . a lawyer, a man with a career and a family and a civilized life ahead of him, before he'd been sucked into his father's gang on the back of his fiancée's death.

God only knew what kind of resistance he'd put up now.

'Of course, today should be the worst day of my life,' Dougie said, his voice calm again, businesslike. No harsh East End vowels like his dad's on show here. Word was Dougie had gone to some posh private school. Then off to read law at uni, then into the City. A right little Thatcher's child, he was. 'Because that's what they say, isn't it?' Dougie went on. 'How it feels to lose a parent. But not for me. Not by a long shot.'

Frankie already knew where this was going. Nothing he could do to stop it.

'But then you'd know that, wouldn't you?' Dougie said. 'Because you were there, weren't you? Not when she died, not when she was killed, not when she was clubbed to death, not when she was sexually molested – but there outside your club when I drove there to . . .' He pressed his fingers hard to his brow. '. . . to *what*? I don't even recall now. Stress does that to you. It makes you forget. My psychiatrist told me that. Did you know I had a psychiatrist and that he charges me over a hundred quid an hour to doctor my head to make me feel good about myself?'

'Er, no,' Frankie answered. Something he'd learned from his dealings with Tommy Riley, this. When in the presence of a quite possibly verifiably psychopathic personality, it was always best to assume they weren't being rhetorical and really did want an answer to every single crazy question that they asked.

'They even tried putting me on that trendy new medication everyone's taking . . . Prozac, because it numbs you,' Dougie said. 'It detaches you from your anxieties. It calms you down and stops you getting upset about the things that hurt. But do you know what?'

Again, Frankie dutifully replied, 'What?'

'I don't want to be numb. I don't want to forget. I want to remember everything about her. Everything that happened to her. It's what drives me, do you understand?'

Frankie nodded.

For a second, Dougie looked pleased. Genuinely. His whole expression seemed to soften. But then it tightened again and he stared at Frankie so long that Frankie started hearing his own heartbeat. Only all messed up. In his neck. In his bloody ears. Shit. What if he just ran? How far behind him was that door? Could he make it past Barry the Sasquatch? Could he fuck.

'You look different,' Dougie finally said. 'Shorter.'

Another tight little twitch at the corner of his thin-lipped mouth. Another joke? Well, sod him. Frankie had had enough. Just how screwed was he? He might as well find out and get this done with. Whatever *this* was.

'Just tell me what you want,' he said. He'd hoped to sound businesslike, even defiant. But instead he just sounded beat.

'Oh, I think you already know. I've invited you here today because of the letter my father sent you. The one I had couriered round to you last night. Do you have it with you?'

'No.'

'Is that because you've destroyed it? Because it incriminates you?'

'Yes.'

'Are you always this monosyllabic?'

Ha-bloody-ha. Frankie didn't answer.

'Do you even know what that means?'

'Yes.' The prick.

'Good, because that's what I heard. That you're smart. Half-educated. A rarity for a member of your family, I'd have thought.'

I could say the same for you. This time, Frankie kept the words to himself.

'Which means you'll no doubt have realized,' Dougie said, 'from the fact that I was cc'd in on that letter, that I have a copy of it myself.' Another smug twitch. 'And, of course, you'll also know that's not all I have. I also have the pistol that was left to me by my late father. A Browning Hi-Power. Quite classy, according to Dad, not that I really know much about these things – although I am trying to learn. A pistol with your fingerprints all over it. That was used to kill Mario Baotic, who as I'm sure you're aware, was the chief police witness to the murder of my fiancée, Susan Tilley.'

The way he said it . . . these last two words, her name, soft, that faraway look in his eyes . . . it was the same way you heard religious people talking about their saints and their gods. But that wasn't what put the shits up Frankie. It was the switch in Dougie that came with it. No longer expressionless, his whole face was clenching up. Redder and redder, like he'd started burning up from inside. Like he was about to go exo-fucking-thermic. Christ, maybe this bastard really was planning on watching Barry the Sasquatch crack Frankie's head open with that bat after all?

'I didn't do it,' Frankie said quickly. 'I didn't kill Baotic. The only reason my prints are on that gun at all is because your father –'

'Enough.'

But *no*. It *wasn't* enough. Frankie might not be able to prove any of this, but he might as well at least try to tell Dougie the truth. And Dougie was still a lawyer, right? Meaning maybe he still might listen to reason. ' . . . *is because your father . . .*'

Dougie clicked his fingers, once.

The bat came smashing down. Pain ripped through Frankie's shoulder. He groaned. Slumped. Nearly fell flat on his face. Barry's shadow was all over him, shifting, ready to lamp him again, even though, Christ, he'd just nearly popped Frankie's collarbone clean out.

'You will *not* interrupt me again,' Dougie said. 'Do you understand?'

'Yugh-guh,' was all Frankie could manage. He squeezed his eyes shut. *Breathe, just breathe, do it . . . breathe through it, through the bleedin' pain . . .*

'My father warned me you'd try lying your way out of this,' Dougie hissed, 'that you'd try blaming someone else for Baotic's death.'

But I'm telling you the truth! Frankie bit down on his lip. The shadow of that tosser behind him was still swamping him. Bat up. Ready to strike. And Dougie would let him too, wouldn't he? Because he'd already been poisoned so much against Frankie and Jack. He didn't understand that Terence Hamilton was still pulling everyone's strings, even from beyond the bloody grave.

'He said you might even try telling me some nonsensical story about a recording you had of him and threaten me with giving it to the police.'

Which of course would have been fine. Just bloody dandy. If that sodding recording existed. But it didn't. Because it never had. Because it was just something Frankie had invented to plea bargain his way out of that cellar.

No, he'd got nothing to prove to Dougie that the real truth about his fiancée's death was anything but what his bastard of a dead father had said.

'He said you'd try all kinds of tricks, but you're not to be trusted,' Dougie went on, 'just like the rest of your family. Not without an extreme threat hanging over you . . . but fortunately that's exactly what I've got here with this pistol.' The redness in his face was fading now, growing more corpse-like by the second, like he was somehow getting control of himself, pushing the devil inside him back down. 'Because, you see, whether you did actually pull that trigger on Baotic is irrelevant. All that matters is that the prints on the gun say you did. Then there's the fact that, according to my sources, the police already suspected you were messing around with their investigation into your brother . . . and were already looking into you even before Baotic died.' He smiled, watching this sink in. 'And that, of course, alongside the pistol, would pretty much cement your guilt in their eyes, wouldn't you agree?' That posh accent of his getting stronger by the second, like some brief's closing statement, when he knew he had the opposition beat. 'In fact, even without the pistol, I'm guessing it wouldn't take too much pressure to get that investigation into you started again.'

His *sources*? Meaning who? That scumbag DI Snaresby had headed up the murder investigation. So what did this mean? That he'd been on not just Tommy Riley's payroll back then, as Frankie had suspected, but on Terence Hamilton's as well? And what the hell was all this about the cops having been pursuing Frankie as a suspect too? On what grounds? What did they think they knew? Really enough to maybe fit Frankie up for something even without the prints on that gun?

'Now I still don't know exactly what involvement your nasty little brother had in my fiancée's death,' Dougie said. 'The way I've heard it, he's a coward and an incompetent, and so it's probably likely that he didn't actually kill her himself. But was he part of it? Was he there? I don't know.' He glanced up at Barry like he was about to give him another order, but then his eyes flicked back down to Frankie's instead. 'But one day,' he said, adjusting his silk tie knot against his spotless white shirt, 'and you can take this as fact, I *will* have myself a little chat with young Jack . . . no, not now, not with him being so closely under Tommy Riley's protection, and no, not now, not when the police still know how much I want to talk to him . . . but, one day, I *will* get to the truth –'

A sharp knock at the door. Frankie turned to look.

'Ah-ah.' Dougie clicked his fingers at him. 'Eyes front. There's a good boy.'

The shadow around Frankie rippled. He did as he was told.

A click of the door opening. The shadow pulled back. Footsteps. Someone coming in? Someone going out?

'Your mother's asking for you.' A woman's voice – *hers* – Viollet's. Had she come in to see what was happening? To join in? To *play*? It took all Frankie's will not to turn.

Dougie checked his watch and sighed. 'Yes, of course. Please tell her I'll be there in a minute. And tell the manager to make sure she's given Tanqueray No. Ten and not Gordon's. Neat, with a slice of lime.'

More footsteps. The door clicked shut. The shadow returned and Dougie's eyes settled back on Frankie.

'Did you know I trained as a lawyer?' he said.

Frankie nodded.

'And worked as one too?'

Another nod.

'Right here in London,' Dougie said. 'Property law. That was going to be my thing. My speciality. My métier. And

27

I was getting very good at it too. So good that I'd been headhunted by an American firm. You see, I didn't plan to live my life out in places like this . . . in the shadows, with grubby little people like you . . . I was moving to New York to start a new life. A better life. Away from my family. With my new wife. Can you imagine how excited I was? How excited *we* were? And how it then felt for that all to be snatched away?' Dougie leant forward in his chair, his eyes boring into Frankie's. 'Can you?'

'Yes.'

'No. No, you can't.' That same faraway look was back in Dougie's eyes. 'But you soon *will*.'

Frankie's heartbeat spiked, but Dougie only slowly wagged his finger at him, as though reading his mind. 'Oh no,' he said, 'I don't mean soon, as in *now* soon. Not today soon. Maybe not tomorrow either. Or the day, or the week, or the month after that. But soon enough, Frankie. Because that's just it, isn't it, my little doggy? I've got you on a lead now, haven't I? A choke chain, if you will. And you're going to do exactly what I tell you for as long as I tell you. You're mine now. I own you. Understand?'

Frankie said nothing. Because what *could* he say? Because Dougie was right.

'There now.' Dougie smiled flat and wide. 'I'm glad it's sinking in, who's in charge . . . Because that's the main reason I brought you here today, so you could learn . . . who's boss, who your new owner is . . . *me*.'

Frankie gritted his teeth.

'Of course, you might think you already have an owner,' Dougie said. 'A Mr Tommy Riley. And you're right, you do.

But do you know what one of the most important aspects of property law is?'

'No.'

'Due diligence.'

Due *what*?

'Yes, I can see from your expression that this means nothing to you. So listen, little doggy. Allow me to explain. In layman's terms. So you can understand. Essentially due diligence means finding out everything you can about the other side before entering a negotiation and going to deal. In the case of a property deal, this might mean finding out if the person or persons you are buying a property from actually own it in law and whether the property itself is in the condition as advertised. Are you following me so far?'

'Yeah.'

'Good boy. Now in the case of a dog-owning deal such as this, I made it my business to discover exactly what your connections are with your current owner, Mr Tommy Riley.'

Here we go . . .

'There's the Ambassador Club, for one. Insofar as he owns it and you just lease it off him – unless I've been misinformed?'

'You haven't.'

'I never am. Then there's your little snooker tournament, the Soho Open. Taking place in less than two weeks, over the twelfth, thirteenth and fourteenth of September. And it's my understanding that Riley's got a twenty per cent stake in that too.'

Correct again. Even though that was meant to be confidential. Someone had been talking. Someone in Riley's organization. *Who?*

'In other words, Mr Tommy Riley must feel like he has you on a nice tight leash too . . . am I right?'

'Yes.'

'Good.' Another thin smile. 'And I want to keep it that way. Because even though you *are* very much *my* doggy now, for reasons I've explained, I don't want your other owner to be aware yet . . . of your . . . *disloyalty* . . . at least not until I want him to be.'

Frankie just stared.

'That's right, Frankie. You get it,' Dougie said. 'You keep on working with Tommy Riley for now. But in reality, you're mine. And you'll jolly well come to heel when I call.' He cocked his head to one side. The muffled sound of bass was thudding up now from downstairs. Sounded like Elvis's 'Burning Love'. Surely better suited to a cremation than a burial? Way more suitable for a party than a funeral too. He got up and stretched out his arms, smoothing down his suit jacket, before walking past Frankie and patting him gently on the head. 'Take him back out through the staff entrance,' he told the Sasquatch. 'This meeting's over. I've got a wake to attend.'

3

Monday morning and Frankie was up with the larks. Or less larks. More like tarts, drunks, junkies, gamblers and whatever other lost souls were still left reeling home from whatever dirty little frolics they'd been up to in Soho last night.

He gazed out at them blurry-eyed, stumbling in ones and twos down Poland Street, from the bedroom window of his flat above the Ambassador Club. Sirens wailed in the distance. A bin lorry clattered past. Its cabbagy reek mixed in with the sweet smell of freshly baked baguettes and croissants rising up from the French deli over the road bringing him close to retching even as his stomach growled and his shoulder and kidneys throbbed.

He normally loved it up here, just watching the world go by. His big fat mess of a city. His perfect view of it, with all its happiness, sadness, ugliness and beauty rolled into one. Christ, how many hours had him and Jack spent perched outside here on the windowsill as kids, smoking nicked roll-ups and catcalling the punters ducking in and out of the peep shows, cafés and bars below, while the Old Man had been working downstairs?

Happy bloody days. But, Christ, it all suddenly felt so long ago. The urge to smoke a cigarette was almost overpowering. Just to somehow . . . get back, feel young again, free of responsibility . . . like yesterday at the Cobden Club had never happened, like his whole life hadn't just been turned to shit.

He sighed, letting the window blind drop back down with a rattle. But now that he'd got the idea of a cigarette into his head, he couldn't get it out. And not just that, but worse. Just as well he'd cleared out his drawers of all the half-smoked packs of Marlboros and half-drunk bottles of Jack Daniels. Because he could have quite happily got stuck into both right now. Just hole up in here and get hammered. The first time he'd felt that way in months.

But routine . . . yeah, he had to stick to that instead, right? The only way to keep his head straight and keep the old demons at bay. But forget his usual fifty press-ups and sit-ups. No way would his shoulder handle that. He made his double bed, and put his dirty clothes in the laundry basket. But then he spotted the half-empty blister pack of diazepam on the bedside table and picked it up.

He'd forgotten he'd even taken any last night, but, yeah, now he remembered. He'd cadged them off Spartak, who'd popped round for a couple of frames after he'd finished his shift on the door at the 100 Club. Not that Frankie had been able to play, with his shoulder being so wrecked. He'd had to tell Spartak he'd had a fall while out running, or else his old Russian mucker would have started baying for the blood of whoever had done it. And not even Spartak was hard enough to take on the Hamilton gang alone.

Frankie stared at the pills, half scrunching one out into his hand. Because wouldn't it be nice, yeah? Just to switch off the stress already building up in his chest, and evict that little Lord Snooty wanker Dougie Hamilton and everything he'd said from his head?

But ah-ah. Naughty, naughty. One pill led to two, led to booze and on to gear, and no way was he letting an arsewipe like Hamilton derail him like that. He hit the bathroom instead. Shit, shower, shave, deodorant, teeth, gargle, spit. He stared into the mirror. Christ, his shoulder looked like something that should be hanging in a butcher's window. His face didn't look much better either. Haggard as hell. Not exactly fair, considering that these days he had the liver and lungs of a monk.

He got dressed into one of his four black suits and listened to Mark and Lard on Radio 1, as he ate his Crunchy Nut cornflakes in the kitchen. He normally liked all their bollocks banter, but this morning even they seemed a bit low. The music they were playing didn't help much either. Lots of cheery little numbers like 'Karma Police' by Radiohead and 'Bitter Sweet Symphony' by Verve. And then, of course, there was more stuff about Princess Di, with the French cops now saying her driver had been drunk. Misery upon misery. The perfect soundtrack for his mood.

More routine. He cleared up the crumpled remnants of last night's Chinese takeaway that he'd snaffled in the lounge while watching *Mission: Impossible* on DVD. He felt bad about it now. Not just the film, which he'd been way too blurry on those pills to follow. Or the bloody theme tune, which he'd got stuck in his head on a loop. But the food. Because it hardly exactly matched his new healthy lifestyle, did it? And there'd been plenty of fresh salad in the fridge he could have nibbled on instead.

But then special fried rice and sweet and sour pork balls had always been his go-to comfort food, hadn't it? It was what the Old Man had always used to order in when Frankie and Jack had first started living here full time in '88. And, anyway, it wasn't all bad, was it? At least while he'd been slumped in here in his diazepam MSG-induced coma, watching Tom Cruise prancing around on screen, he'd felt happy as the proverbial pig in shit, and hadn't thought about Dougie Hamilton once.

He carted his dirty plate and tins through to the kitchen and opened the window. It was a bit of a tip in here from yesterday and so he gave it a quick spruce and got stuck into the washing-up. Oh, yeah. Keeping it clean. All part of his Goody Two Shoes routine.

He banged on the Rolling Stones' *Forty Licks* CD from the Old Man's collection on the rack on the wall for good measure, and clicked through the tracks to '19th Nervous Breakdown'. Always cheered him up and got his feet tapping. He even started whistling while he worked. Yeah, come on. He could do this. Not let that scumbag, Dougie, get him down. Keep positive. Keep his head straight and he'd think of a way round it, right? Just the same as always, yeah?

Ten minutes later in the flat's little hallway, with his notes for today's Soho Open meetings already tucked up in his jacket pocket, he touched his fingers to his lips and pressed them to the face of the woman in the framed photo hanging on the wall. His mum, with him and Jack as kids in '85, taken a year before her and the Old Man had broken up, and three years before she'd vanished from all of their lives altogether. He'd found it under the Old Man's bed, hidden. She looked beautiful, she did. No wonder he hadn't wanted it up. It would have reminded him of how much he'd lost.

'I love you, Mum,' Frankie said, the same as he did every day he went out.

He was still sure in his heart he was going to see her again one day. Especially after tracking her as far as Mallorca last summer. Especially now he knew she'd made it out of London alive.

*

The James Boys Gym on Hanway Street was already bustling by the time Frankie got there just after lunch. It had been totally fixed up since he'd first brought Jack here a year ago to discuss him taking over as manager, after the previous manager had taken an unexpected – well, for him, anyway – nosedive through an upstairs window.

Past the snazzy new reception, the gym's vast and echoing *mildew-à-la-mode* walls and double-height ceiling had been painted over with pristine white. Its once sagging, frankly bloody terrifying, viewing balcony looking down onto the two boxing rings below had been widened and reinforced to allow for tiered seating.

The rings themselves had been refurbished to competition standard and all the equipment had been replaced or modernized, from the free weights, kettle bells, jump ropes, punch bags and speed bags currently being battered by a platoon of focused fighters in the training area, to the multi-gyms in the side rooms out back.

But some things never changed. The smell of sweat and Ralgex still hung heavy in the air. Along with every swear word under the sun. Capital Radio was still blasting out bass-thumping anthems, with Daft Punk's 'Around the World' being the current club classic that was assaulting Frankie's delicate ears. And, of course, GoGo JoJo was still right here at the centre of it all, conducting the show, and taking matters not one iota less seriously than he had done when he'd been Muhammad Ali's blood man back during his visit to Great Britain in '63.

'Morning, kiddo,' he said, somehow catching sight of Frankie out of his peripheral vision, while keeping his gaze fixed on the two lithe boxers currently circling one another in the ring nearest the door.

Oh yeah, and that was another big change since last year. The women. Frankie's idea, that one, presented via Jack in his first week as official manager here. Of course, Tommy Riley, who owned the place, had been resistant at first. Women were good for two things, according to him, or two places anyway, being the kitchen and the bedroom. But even Tommy had come round to the idea, once he'd seen how many of the women going to the exercise classes in the done-up studios upstairs had then signed up for boxing and kickboxing down here too.

Yeah, the ghost of the old Rope-a-Dope club had been well and truly exorcised. *Viva la* James Boys Gym.

'Morning, JoJo. How's tricks?' Frankie asked.

'All good, kiddo.' JoJo was still concentrating on the ring, dragging a comb back through his thinning grey hair. He looked Frankie's black suit and matching Chelsea boots and briefcase over, but clocked the gym bag on his shoulder too. 'You here to talk with your jaw or your paws, then?' he said.

'A bit of both. But jaw first.'

Frankie wanted to have a quick catch-up with Jack before he got changed and hit the bags. He'd been trying to get hold of him since the funeral the day before yesterday but without any luck. What with all this shit going down with Dougie, he needed to check that the Hamilton boys hadn't been sniffing round Jack as well.

'Fair enough,' said JoJo, 'but try and get back here for two. We've got ourselves a couple new prospects coming in. One just seventeen. An Irish lad. And his little brother too. Thirteen. The same age you were when you first showed your skinny arse round here.'

Thirteen. Christ, it seemed like a lifetime ago. Frankie's Old Man had sent him here to train with JoJo after he'd got mugged over in Islington one time. Had told JoJo to toughen him up. Have him beaten up, more like. At least that's how it had felt to Frankie those first few weeks until he'd found his feet. He'd come here nearly every day for three years after that, mind. Had loved it. And, by God, he was loving being back here again now since Jack had taken over.

'You should maybe even have a spar with the elder lad if you're feeling up to it?' JoJo said. 'Word is he's lightning fast.'

'Maybe I will,' said Frankie. 'Soon see what he's made of, eh?'

'Or he will you.' JoJo grinned.

'Aye, or that.' Frankie was way too savvy these days to think he could take someone just because he was bigger or older. Experience went a long way in a sport like this, but talent went further. First things first, though. 'You seen Jack around?' he said.

'He's not back from Brighton till the day after tomorrow.'

Brighton . . . Ah, yeah, that was it, why Frankie hadn't been able to get a hold of him on the blower. Jack had gone down the south coast on some residential management course. Basic small-business stuff. Not that Frankie could imagine him sticking any of that sort of bollocks for more than five minutes, no matter how much good it might do him and his prospects of turning his current job here into a genuine career.

'*He*'s in, though . . .' JoJo tilted his head up towards the glass-fronted office jutting out up on the mezzanine between the banks of seats.

He . . . Not once since Frankie had started training here again in January had he ever heard JoJo refer to Listerman the Lawyer by his name. Probably still resented him for having had the previous manager chucked headfirst through that window. Or *allegedly* chucked, at least. A punishment for till dipping, apparently. Though it was more likely Listerman had just fancied increasing his boss Tommy Riley's share of the business up to a nice round 100 per cent.

'Oh yeah, and he was asking after you,' JoJo said, a look of warning in his rheumy, bloodshot eyes. 'Said to send you up if you came in.'

'Did he now?' Frankie didn't like the sound of this.

Particularly the word 'send'. Like he was some kind of sodding parcel Listerman just got to dispatch whenever he
pleased.

'Hey, don't shoot the messenger,' JoJo told him.

'Fair enough.' Frankie started heading off.

'You're moving a bit lopsided there, kid,' JoJo said.
'Catch your shoulder on something, did you? Or some*one?*'

Nothing got past him. Never had. But when Frankie
looked back, he'd already turned his attention back to the
ring. 'Come on, Tiffany,' he barked. 'Look like you mean it.
Stop bloody pussyfooting around.'

Tiffany? Frankie grinned. He'd not noticed before, but
the girl in the ring in the blue headgear was none other than
Jack's new girlfriend. Or not exactly new now, eh? A whole
year they'd been going out. And as well as teaching yoga in
the new studios upstairs, here she was getting stuck in down
here. Frankie winced as, spurred on by JoJo's taunt, she piled
in with a whip-sharp combination which knocked her opponent's mouthguard clean out as she sent her stumbling back
onto the ropes.

Not the only useless piece of guard equipment around
here either, he saw as he reached the top of the stairs a couple
of minutes later. Listerman's usual grunt was standing sentry
outside the door to Jack's office. Well, Jack always called it
his office, but the truth was it was just another one of Listerman's in all but name. In much the same way that the James
Boys Gym itself didn't belong to either Frankie or Jack. The
black-and-white photos of their granddad and great uncle
in reception downstairs, who'd both been pro fighters back
in the day, were just there for added authenticity. For all

the Green Park lawyers, West End luvvies and NoHo new media kids who made up the membership, so they could all of them feel like proper little geezers as they trotted through their boxercise classes upstairs.

'You got an appointment?' asked the grunt.

You got a brain? Or any manners? Frankie was tempted to ask back. He must have told this dickhead his name a hundred times, but not once had he remembered it, the knob. But he kept his mouth shut, because what was the point? It would be like trying to teach a goldfish maths. And, besides, after Frankie's little trip to the Cobden Club yesterday, he'd had enough of argy-bargy with morons like this.

'Just tell him I'm here,' he said.

'Corporate Hospitality', a sign read above the door. Alphonse – for that was the dumb lunk's name – knocked four times, the same as always. Christ on a bike, it was hardly the cleverest of secret codes, was it? More Famous Five than MI5.

Frankie smiled, remembering what that old bird in the Paradise had said yesterday. She wasn't the only one now peddling conspiracy theories about Princess Di's demise, either. The waiter down at Bar Italia, where Frankie had grabbed a quick sarnie and double espresso on his way over, had told him he'd heard aliens had abducted Princess Di seconds before the crash in a flash of white light and switched her body for a double. Because, yeah, sure, of course, *that* made *so* much more sense than what had actually happened.

'Enter,' a voice shouted from the other side of the door.

'Who does he think he is, a porn star?' Frankie joked.

Alphonse didn't get it. 'No, mate, I don't think so,' he said, opening the door.

Frankie walked in.

'Ah, good,' Listerman said, 'I was hoping you'd turn up.' He peered through his glasses, looking Frankie's suit over the same way JoJo had. 'Going somewhere fancy?'

'Got a couple of meetings lined up with The Topster for later on.'

Frankie's main business partner in the Soho Open had got a couple of honchos from the Global Professional Snooker Association heading down to his sports agency's office on Haymarket later on to comb through their plans yet again, just to make sure everything was above board and conforming to their regs – something Frankie was thankful as hell he had Andy there to help him with.

'Good good,' Listerman said. 'The devil makes work for idle hands, as they say.'

'Told you that personally, did he?' Frankie said.

'Oh yes, most amusing. Now take a pew.' Listerman waved his bony hand at the little chair on the other side of his aircraft carrier of a desk.

Frankie sat down and looked around, as Listerman used a little stub of a bookie's pencil to scribble something down next to the long row of figures showing on the pad in front of him. The office had been done up a fair bit too since Frankie had last been summoned up here a few weeks back. Less health club, though, more pimp. A couple of red leatherette sofas. A glass-topped bar for booze and a matching table for coke. Along with a metal pole running floor-to-ceiling in the centre of the room for . . . well, not exactly what you might find in the head office at IBM, say, but no doubt striking just the right note for the kind of corporate hospitality on offer in here.

Listerman seemed to have had a bit of a facelift himself since Frankie had seen him last month. He still looked like a lizard in a suit, of course, but a slightly less wrinkly one than before. A lot less, actually. More like someone had ironed his forehead on full steam.

'So how was Florida?' Frankie asked.

'Yeah, good. Played a lot of golf.'

More like sat in a clinic with a bandage wrapped round his face, if the colour of his skin was anything to go by. Didn't look like he'd spent a second outside. The rest of him was vibrant enough, mind. He looked like a fruit shop, dressed in a maroon suit and purple shirt, with a plum-coloured tie knotted up nice and tight against his closely shaved, wattled neck. He pushed his little pad aside and flicked a dry roast peanut up into the air before catching it cleanly in his saggy ballbag of a mouth.

'Nut?' he asked, nodding at the packet of KP Dry Roasted on his desk. He flipped his pad over to a crisp white new page.

Only you . . . another thought Frankie kept to himself. Because, whatever this was about, he wanted to be out of here as soon as possible and with no bad vibes either. Listerman the Lawyer answered direct to Tommy Riley and no one else. Mess with him and Frankie was messing with Tommy too.

'No, thanks.'

'Right, well, let's get down to business, then. Why don't

you start by bringing me up to date on everything that's been happening tournament-wise, since I've been off on me hols.'

As Dougie Hamilton had so recently pointed out, the price of Jack getting his job here safe off the streets and under Riley's protection had been for Frankie to give up 20 per cent of the Soho Open. Meaning Listerman had been involved right from the launch down the Ambassador Club last year.

Frankie gave him a quick run-through of where they were at. How The Topster had finally locked in the sponsors and local TV and radio support he'd promised. How tickets had already sold out, both for the matches down the Ambassador Club and here at the gym, where Jack was going to be dismantling the rings and bringing in tables for some of the earlier rounds.

Listerman nodded, seemingly satisfied. 'And what about the presentation of the trophy itself?'

'Yeah, it's agreed,' Frankie said, 'Tommy's going to be the one to hand it over.' Not something that Andy Topper had been so keen on, truth be told. The sports agency he ran had half a dozen high-profile clients who'd have been much better at it than Tommy, and whose involvement would have got the tournament a lot more press attention too.

'Good,' said Listerman, 'because he's written his speech already *and* invited his mum.'

Well, whoopee doo. 'I'll make sure she gets the best seat in the house,' Frankie said.

Listerman scribbled that down. His 'Little Books of Fucking Promises', Jack had once referred to his notepads as. What got written down there never got forgotten. And woe betide anyone who promised Tommy something they later flaked out on.

'Tommy wants it to be him who hands over the Beamer's keys too,' Listerman said.

'Right . . .' And fair enough there, at least. Because Riley's involvement wasn't all bad. True to his word from last year, he'd stumped up that BMW 3 Series convertible he'd been owed, as an additional players' prize to encourage top-quality entrants.

'Oh, and on that,' Listerman went on, 'Tommy had a bit of creative input he wanted to give you too.'

'Oh, right?' Let me guess. A full orchestra playing Wagner's 'Ride of the Valkyries', while Tommy was lowered by helicopter onto the roof of the Ambassador Club? Something tasteful like that?

'A ribbon,' Listerman said.

'You what?'

'Tied around the motor.' Listerman crunched down on another peanut. 'Only, obviously not the actual motor itself, of course, not the one on the inside of the car. Because then no one would be able to see it, would they? What I mean is the ribbon needs to go around the chassis, the bit that people see, get it? Oh, and make sure it's a big ribbon too. Tied right tight round it like it's a great big box of chocs.'

'Chocs . . .'

'Oh, and he wants it in purple,' Listerman said.

'Purple?'

'Like my shirt.'

'A Prince fan, is he?'

Listerman frowned. Or at least Frankie reckoned he might have. It was hard to tell, what with his forehead no longer having the ability to move.

'Prince who?' he said. 'Charles? Is this something to do with Princess Di?'

'No, I meant the pop star.'

Another possible frown. Or not. 'I wouldn't know,' said Listerman. 'But let's try and stick to the point, eh, Frankie?'

Frankie gave up on the joke. 'And the point is . . . purple?'

'Exactly. Because of Tommy's fire.'

'His fire?'

'Yeah, his birth element. According to his Feng Shui . . . And don't smirk,' Listerman said, watching him. 'He's dead serious about it. Ever since he started shagging this new Chinese bird of his . . . Chenguang.'

Frankie hadn't yet had the privilege, but Jack had met her a couple of times and had told him her and Tommy were pretty tight. Tight enough that even Tommy's actual missus would give a serious shit if she saw them together, because Chenguang seemed to have him that much under her thumb. Best not take the piss about her Feng Shui, then, eh? Or he might find out just how much fire Tommy really had.

'She's told him purple's his lucky colour,' said Listerman. 'Or luckiest anyway. Closely followed by magenta, red and brown.' Listerman waved his hand demonstratively over his own clothes. 'Meaning our corporate colours should be the same.'

Again with the corporate. Was he joking? Apparently not. Then fine. Tommy Riley, Inc. this all now was. Putting the corpse into corporate. Maybe Frankie should offer that up as a possible tagline. Or then again, maybe not.

'Right,' said Frankie, 'then purple it shall be.'

Listerman scribbled that down on his pad. Frankie stood up. Seemed like their meeting was done.

'Oh yes, and before I forget,' Listerman said. 'What's your feeling about making new friends?'

'What?'

Listerman looked up sharply. 'Chums . . . pals . . . buddies . . .' His lips twisted as he said this last word, like it had left a nasty taste.

'My feelings?' Frankie said, suddenly wary – because Listerman wasn't exactly famous for his small talk, so what the hell was he on about now?

'Yes.' Listerman's eyes locked on Frankie's as he took a mauve – no, make that magenta – silk handkerchief from his jacket pocket and began slowly polishing his specs.

'Er, I don't really have any,' Frankie said.

'Yes, but all the same, I'm sure you'd agree that it's extremely important what kind of new friends one makes on one's journey through life?' Listerman's teeth smiled, but not his eyes.

'I suppose . . .'

'Only suppose?'

'Well, no, I mean I . . .'

'Agree?'

'Well, yeah . . .'

'Well, that's good,' Listerman said. 'Very good indeed. Because I always worry when people don't agree with me. And Tommy, he always worries the same.' Not even

Listerman's teeth were smiling now. 'And wouldn't you also agree that making new friends with people who your old friends are not friends with is a very bad idea? Particularly when these new friends are in fact your old friends' old enemies?'

Shit it. Frankie's throat turned dry. Because he meant Dougie Hamilton, didn't he? He'd been caught out, hadn't he? That's what all this was about. Bollocks. Someone must have seen him at the funeral.

'You're talking about Terence Hamilton's funeral, right?' Denying it would only make matters worse.

Listerman sat back in his chair and pressed his fingertips together in a spire. He said nothing, just watched.

'You're talking about me being there?'

'Ah, so my information *is* correct, then.' Listerman wrote that down. 'That is good to hear.'

'I can explain,' Frankie said.

But *could* he? Because what exactly was he meant to say? That Dougie Hamilton had personally asked him there? That Frankie had gone because he'd had no choice?

Because, no, he couldn't say any of that, could he? Because telling Listerman that would lead to him having to tell Listerman why, which would mean telling him all about the pistol with his prints on it. And telling Listerman that would be admitting that Dougie Hamilton now had him over a barrel. Leaving Frankie at best a risk, at worst an outright liability. And there was only one way that Tommy Riley ever dealt with them.

But what the hell was he meant to tell Listerman instead?

The first thing that came into his mind: 'The Old Man asked me to go.'

'Who, Bernie?' Listerman looked as surprised as a man with an entirely immobilized forehead could.

'Yeah.'

'And why exactly would he do that?'

'Er . . .' Frankie bluffed, ' . . . because they knew each other, didn't they? As kids. Him and Terence. And Tommy too.' A shit reason, but a reason nonetheless.

'I lost my virginity round the back of the bike sheds at school to a right little goer named Dorothy Kenton,' Listerman said.

'You what?'

'My point being that, even though I was once extremely fond of her, and in particular her firm little tits, she's not someone whose funeral I would feel in any way inclined or obliged to attend now. And I'd certainly not send along one of my nearest and dearest offspring in lieu of myself.' Listerman leant forward again, watching Frankie carefully, like a bank manager regarding someone who'd just reneged on a loan. 'Leaving me both surprised and perplexed as to why your father would have sent you. Because, you see, as far as I know, your father is a wise and sensible and, indeed, reliable man, who made his decision a long time ago to side with Tommy and not with those Hamilton cunts.'

Frankie swallowed. Far from quelling Listerman's suspicions, it looked like all he'd succeeded in doing was pushing them onto the Old Man.

'It's just something he asked me to do if I was passing,' Frankie said, floundering, 'you know, out of respect.'

'If you were *passing*? And did you just happen to be *passing* the Cobden Club *after* the funeral as well?'

Double shit. So Listerman knew about that too. Meaning he had someone on the inside? Christ, how much more might he know? Frankie had to stick as close as he could to the truth, without giving him an inkling of what him and Dougie had actually talked about. Unless, of course, his informant happened to be the twat with the bat who'd been the only other person in the room. In which case, Frankie was screwed.

'No, it was Dougie who asked me there . . . after he spotted me at the funeral.'

'Dougie himself?'

'Well, no. Through a third party.'

'A what?'

'A woman. Viollet something. A South African bird.'

Listerman wrote down her name.

'And why would he do that?' he then asked. 'Seeing as how you'd already paid your respects?'

'I don't know.'

'You don't know?'

'No.'

'And yet, regardless of young Dougie's known antipathy towards both yourself and your brother, you decided it was still a good idea to take him up on his kind invitation and trot along to see him at his club?'

'I felt it would have been rude not to.'

'Rude?'

'Disrespectful.'

'Disrespectful . . .' Listerman was still watching. Still not satisfied. Still wanting more.

'And . . . all right,' Frankie said, 'dangerous . . . I thought it would have been dangerous to tell him no . . . I thought that maybe by going there I might be able to somehow smoothe things over between us.'

'Smoothe . . .' Listerman scribbled that down too. 'Ah . . . now at least that makes a modicum of sense. Because of your brother, yes? Because of how you're still worried that Dougie Hamilton wants him dead?'

Frankie nodded.

'So what did he say?'

'Who?'

'Dougie, of course. When you spoke to him at the club. I'm assuming you did get to speak to him?'

'Er, yeah. He wanted to know why I'd been at the funeral . . . He was as surprised as you were that I was there. And so I, er, told him the same reason. That I was there because of my dad. And because I'd hoped to be able to talk to him about Jack too.'

'And what did he say to that?'

'That I wasn't welcome, even if his dad and mine had been at school.'

'And about Jack?'

The further Frankie could distance himself from Dougie right now, the better. Easy enough too, where Dougie's attitude to Jack was concerned. He just had to tell Listerman the truth.

'He said Jack was a coward and that Jack claiming he couldn't remember how he'd got covered in Susan Tilley's blood was never going to be good enough for him.' Frankie felt his cheeks burning even as he remembered Hamilton's words. 'He said that one day, once Jack wasn't so close under Tommy's protection, he was going to get a hold of him and get to the truth.'

'And that's a quote?' Listerman's pencil hovered over his pad.

'Yeah. Verbatim. That's what the wanker said.'

A smile played at the corner of Listerman's lips. 'Sounds like he fucked you off good and proper, eh?' he said.

Frankie could feel the sweat prickling on his brow. 'I was in there less than five minutes,' he said. 'Then he had his boys rough me up a bit and throw me out the back. They told me to get the fuck away from there while I still could.'

Listerman was watching him again, unblinking. First Frankie's face, then his clenched fists.

'Here, see for yourself.' Frankie unbuttoned his shirt and peeled it and his jacket back off his shoulder.

Listerman stared at the bruising for a couple of seconds, before finally nodding, satisfied. 'You should get some arnica on that.'

Fastening his shirt back up, Frankie watched the money man's bony shoulders relax. He plucked another peanut from the packet and flipped it up into his mouth.

'So you and little Dougie are still not exactly what we might call friends. And probably for the best, eh?' he said, crunching down. 'Because I know you still don't think you work for Tommy, officially, in spite of the . . . favours you've paid him back for these last two years.' He tipped the dust from the now empty packet into the palm of his hand and tossed it back into his mouth. 'But just because you don't work for him officially doesn't mean you get to work for anyone else . . . get it?'

'I got it,' Frankie said.

'Good, because, trust me, son, it's one of life's great truisms, that people who end up working for more than one master generally end up getting ripped a-fucking-part . . .'

4

Frankie didn't get a chance to catch up with Jack until he spotted him outside the Ambassador Club Wednesday morning at eleven, just before it was due to open up.

'What's all this then? Teatime on the *Titanic*?' he asked, grinning down at his kid brother, who was sunning himself on the pavement outside the club's front doors on a stripy deckchair, with Slim doing likewise beside him, while it looked like Spartak and Xandra were slobbed out on the pavement just a little further along, half hidden from Frankie's view with their backs to the brickwork.

'Less of the *Titanic*, bruv,' said Jack, peering up at him through his Ray-Bans. 'Ain't no icebergs round here. Just clear sailing as far as the eye can see. Or, rather, there would be if you'd just get your ugly mug out of my sun.'

'Morning, boss,' said Slim, 'and may I offer you the finest of felicitations on this delightful summer morn.'

'Indeed you may,' said Frankie.

'Mightily obliged.' Slim smiled, doffing his wide-brimmed leather hat, his long legs and scuffed cowboy boots sticking out of the bottom of his worn poncho, leaving him looking even more than usual today like the 'Outlaw Josie Fails', as

Xandra had taken to cheekily referring to him behind his back.

Xandra herself leant forward from where she was sitting cross-legged on Jack's right, in an Oasis T-shirt, torn-off jeans and bare, paint-spattered feet. She'd already started decorating the flat upstairs by the time Frankie had got back here from the James Boys Gym the day before yesterday. Some extra money for her, and a long-overdue change for him. He'd been tiptoeing round that flat like it wasn't really his for the last seven years, ever since the Old Man had been put away, acting every sodding day like he was coming back any minute – even though in reality Frankie still wasn't any nearer to getting the poor bastard out of Brixton bloody nick.

'You been hard at it then, have you?' Frankie said.

'Sweet Jesus, the work's not going to do itself,' she laughed, her Londonderry accent coming on strong now.

'You're an angel sent from heaven.'

'Even better, a lodger come up from downstairs, and one who grew up in a family building and decorating firm, you lucky get.'

True. And much luckier than she'd been herself, growing up in that same family with bullying and beatings and worse, until she'd run away to London – where Frankie had found her a couple of years back sleeping on the street just a way down here from the club.

'And just think,' she said, 'once we've got your little man crib not looking like such a boggin' shitpit, we'll soon have you back to courtin', eh? Oh aye, just think of all those lucky ladies, eh? Now hadn't they just better watch out?'

Lucky ladies. Chance would be a fine thing. And not just lucky ladies either. Any ladies would do. Because Frankie hadn't really had much of either of late, had he? The nearest he'd got to *courtin'* these last six months had been an answerphone message from Isabella a few weeks ago, saying she might be coming over to London some time soon. But, even then, when he'd tried calling her back at the restaurant in Mallorca where he'd met her last year, he'd been told she was back in Italy visiting her parents, and he hadn't heard a word from her since.

But probably just as well, though, eh? Because what with the tournament coming up, he'd hardly got time for himself, let alone anyone else. Added to which was Dougie Hamilton and whatever shitstorm he was currently stirring up.

Xandra flashed him a grin. 'So what do you think?' She leant back to give Frankie a full view of Spartak. 'Apparently, it's all the rage in the Crimea this time of year,' she chuckled.

The six-and-a-half-foot slab of Russian ex-military operative slumped beside her was wearing only a stained white singlet and matching underpants. His normally strictly vertical and lethally spiked bleached mohawk was flopping down listlessly over the right side of his otherwise shaved head.

'What the hell happened to him?' Frankie said.

Spartak didn't even look like he was awake, but somehow he still heard.

'Damned Georgians,' he growled.

'Georgians?'

'Cheating Georgians,' he growled even louder, still not opening his eyes.

Ah, so he'd been gambling again. A Georgian flat round the corner ran a notorious Tuesday night game. High stakes. Free drinks. A lethal combination.

'And, look, he's lost his pants,' Xandra said. 'Well, not his actual pants. Not in the British sense of the word. But as in his trousers, you know, like the Yanks would say.'

'Damned Yanks,' Spartak muttered.

Xandra put her arm round him, or as far round his wardrobe-sized torso as it would go, which wasn't really very far at all. 'There, there, diddums,' she soothed. 'Nothing's ever quite as bad as it seems. He's still drunk,' she told Frankie. 'What he really needs is his bed.'

'I'll go get the car round in a bit and give him a lift,' Frankie said. Yet another thing to add to his list.

'So where've you been, looking so dapper?' Jack asked.

Frankie was in a suit yet again, a slick of sweat down his back, itching to change into a pair of shorts and get himself a taste of the good life like these bastards here. But running this tournament was like trying to tame a wildfire. The second he got one bit under control, another flame sprang up. He'd had back-to-back meetings yesterday, and already today he'd been in with the council for yet another health and safety chat, and then in with his insurance broker too, to make sure everything was properly covered.

'Over on Beak Street seeing Dickie Bird,' he said.

'Christ, I hope you didn't get dressed up for him,' Jack said with a grin.

Frankie smiled too, because Dickie was hardly one for

smart dressing now, was he? He spent most of his life down in the basement studio of his sex shop round the corner, wearing little more than an SLR camera round his neck. He did a bit of non-blue work too, though, just to make ends meet, what with there being so much piracy these days in the throbbing world of porn, and he'd done Frankie a deal on design and distribution for pub flyers for the tournament.

Tickets had been selling well anyhow, through the various professional billiards and snooker associations who'd come on board to support, but Frankie was keen to get word of mouth out locally too. To give this tournament a proper London feel to it. To which, they'd deliberately held back 10 per cent of tickets, which they now of course needed to shift.

'Nah, I had a bunch of other stuff to do before that,' he told Jack. 'So how was Brighton? Hope you didn't bring back any crabs?'

'Haha. No. Just a stick of rock. I've left it on the bar inside.'

A car slid by, that Alanis Morissette song playing out the window.

'Ironic,' Frankie said.

Jack scrunched up his face. 'You what?'

'Never mind. How about that business course you went down there for? Any good?'

'Surprisingly, yeah. P&L? VAT, mate? I'm all over that shit from here on in.'

'Sounds like you've been paying attention.' Frankie smiled. Not what he'd been expecting at all.

'Yeah, well, maybe it's about time I started making up for all them classes I mitched off at school, eh?'

'Good on you,' Frankie said, meaning it.

'And what about you? You been keeping yourself busy?' Jack asked.

'Yeah, or this tournament has, at least.'

Jack nodded. 'And Xandra says you're doing up our flat.'

Our . . . Well, that was the first time Jack had called it that in a while. In fact, the last thing he'd said about it at all, as far as Frankie could remember, was on New Year's Eve on the back of half a bottle of Scotch they'd guzzled, when he'd refused to crash over, slurring on his way out the door, *No chance. I don't know how the hell you can stand it up there. It reminds me way too much of all that . . .* Meaning their parents' divorce . . . their mum's disappearance . . . the Old Man's arrest . . . all the greatest hits of their youth.

'Yeah,' Frankie said, 'I've decided it's about time I put my own mark on the place.' The avocado bathroom suite, the flock wallpaper . . . Christ, he couldn't wait for it all to be gone.

'Well, not too much, I hope. I mean, it is still the Old Man's for when he gets out . . . and it's my childhood too, right? I mean, I've still got a whole bunch of stuff up there . . . history . . .'

History? 'If you mean all your stinking old trainers and that bag of *Razzle* mags you've got stashed under the bunk bed, then you're welcome to them.'

Xandra snorted with laughter as Jack's cheeks burned red.

'JoJo said he called you upstairs,' Jack said, changing the subject.

He . . . Listerman . . .

'Yeah,' Frankie said, 'he wanted a little chat.'

'About what?'

'This and that.'

'Just shooting the breeze, then?'

'Pretty much.'

'Not checking up on me?' An edge to Jack's voice here. And with good reason. Both Riley and Listerman knew full well what an unreliable caner he'd been in the past. Meaning he was still very much on probation at the gym.

'Nope. He just wanted to talk through where we're up to on the Open. Your name didn't even come up, bruv.'

'Good . . .' But Jack sounded far from convinced.

'Other than to say that you were all set up for hosting the opening rounds over at yours,' Frankie added. 'Which you are, right?'

'Yeah, of course. I've got Taffy's boys coming down from NW10 to take down the rings on the eighth, and then Festive Al's driving the tables and seating over from Clerkenwell once it's clear.' Jack pulled out a Filofax from his pocket and flipped through it. 'Yeah, he's bringing them round on a flatbed at nine a.m. on Wednesday the tenth, so should be set up in plenty of time.'

Frankie whistled, impressed. 'Sounds like this little management course really has rubbed off on you.'

'Nah, just taking after his big brother. A natural, eh?' Xandra teased.

'Apparently we really missed out not seeing those two new kids, the Irish lads,' Jack said.

'Yeah?' Frankie regretted not staying around. But after

that meeting, well, it had felt like the walls of the whole building had been moving in on him. Like that scene in *Star Wars*, where all the good guys had nearly got crushed.

Jack nodded. 'JoJo reckons the seventeen-year-old's a real find.'

'Whereabouts in Ireland they from?' Xandra asked.

'Dublin.'

'Pah,' she grunted, flexing her muscles, her panther tattoo stretching out its claws on her bicep. 'Now what you really need is good County Antrim farming stock like me.'

'JoJo reckons he's got it. The elder lad,' Jack said.

'For real?' In all the time Frankie had known JoJo, he'd only said that about a few kids, Frankie being one of them.

'Says we should maybe get The Topster round to take a look.'

'Fair enough.' Andy Topper wasn't just a snooker agent. He specialized in the 'Holy Trinity', as he called them, them being snooker, boxing and darts. 'I'll get him to put in a call to JoJo and find out what's what. But it'll probably have to wait now until after the tourney's done.'

The phone started to ring inside.

'Not me,' said Slim.

'Ah, quit yer gurning, it's your turn,' said Xandra.

'Heads or tails?' Slim was already tossing a coin in the air.

'Heads,' said Xandra.

Slim caught it and slapped it down on the back of his hand. 'Tails.'

'Ah, bollocks, it's time I got earning my crust anyway. Look, here come the lads, right on time.' Rising, she nodded at Ash Crowther and Sea Breeze Strinati, who were walking down the pavement towards them, with their chess set and newspapers tucked under their arms, ready to take up their usual perch at the bar for the rest of the day. The other regulars wouldn't be far behind.

'Yup, I suppose we'd best get this show on the road.' Slim got up, stretched and yawned. 'So who's for breakfast? I picked up some nice ripe beef tomatoes and Welsh Cheddar from Berwick Street market on the way over. Toasties all round?'

Frankie and Jack both nodded. Frankie then turned to Jack and said, 'A quick question . . . you know, just on the back of Terence Hamilton having died.'

'What?'

'None of them have bothered you, have they? The Hamilton mob, I mean.'

'No.' A bit of a tremble in Jack's face, mind, as he said it.

'And I'm not saying they will, either, all right,' Frankie said, 'because you're still under Tommy's protection, but just if they do . . . you make sure you call me right a-bloody-way, OK?'

'Sure.'

Frankie nodded. 'Good. And, on another note, I'm heading over Brixton to see Dad later, if you fancy tagging along?' The first thing he'd done after getting back from seeing Listerman was to get on the blower to wangle himself a visiting slot at Brixton nick to see the Old Man today, so he could get their story straight, in case Listerman got someone on the inside to check up on what Frankie had said about why he'd gone to the funeral.

'Nah, you're all right,' said Jack, looking relieved not to be talking about the Hamiltons any more. 'I'm booked in to see him next week. I got to be getting back to the gym. I've got some membership drive ideas from that course I want to run by JoJo. Oh, but quick, before I go . . . Tiff asked me to get you to sign this.'

'What?'

'The entrance form for next year's London marathon.'

Frankie smiled. A little bet they'd had last week while out running together. Who'd have thought it? What a difference a year made. Frankie rested the form on the table and signed it with the Old Man's fountain pen that he'd taken to using in meetings.

'And don't forget,' Jack said, 'the loser pays for dinner at Quo Vadis.'

That posh place up on Dean Street. It would cost an arm and a leg.

'Yeah, well, no worries there, eh?' Frankie said. 'At least not for me . . .'

'Yeah, yeah, bruv, we'll see . . .'

A little twinkle of competition in Jack's eyes. Frankie liked that. Much better than the little red stoner roadmap that had patterned the whites of his eyes for the last few years until he'd got his act together.

'Oi, Frankie.' Xandra poked her head round the door. 'It's for you. Some girl. Sounded foreign. She wouldn't give her name.'

Jack wolf-whistled. 'Aye, aye. Anything you want to tell us, bruv?' he teased.

Frankie tried to smile it off and look casual. But already

his heart was beating faster. Because maybe it was Isabella? Yeah, it would be lovely to hear her voice. He followed Xandra inside, nodding at Ash Crowther and Sea Breeze Strinati, who'd already got their chessboard set up at the bar. A couple of other locals had crept in too while he'd been chatting to Jack. Stefano and Giuseppe, the waiters from Bar Italia, on table two continuing their never-ending series. The Man with No Name practising long shots on his own on table five. And Jewellery Sanj hunched over the fruit machine, alternating between punching buttons and cursing and sipping from his double vodka and Coke.

'Yeah, hi?' Frankie said, picking up the phone receiver at the bar.

'Frankie?'

Not Isabella. But he recognized the woman's South African accent straight away.

'Viollet Coetzee,' he said. 'And to what do I owe this dubious pleasure?'

'Dubious? Well, that's not very friendly,' she said. 'But perhaps I'm to blame, eh? Because maybe what I should really be doing is whistling . . .'

'You what?'

'To make you come. I don't mean sexually, you understand. I mean like a dog. Because that's what Dougie says he's done . . . trained you to heel.'

'How about you just get to the fucking point.'

'Tut tut.' This from Xandra. She was pointing to the jam jar next to the till that she'd Sellotaped a note to, saying, 'F-ing Frankie's F-ing Swear Box: All Proceeds To The F-ing Staff's F-ing Xmas Outing'.

'The fucking point,' Viollet's voice crackled down the line, 'is that you need to get your arse down to the Royal Academy to meet Mr Hamilton.'

'The where?' Had Frankie heard right?

'The Royal Academy.'

'As in the art place?'

'The very same. And now . . .'

'As in *now* now?'

'Oh, yes, as in exactly then. He's waiting for you there already. Oh, and Dougie said to wear something smart. I think his exact words were, *as if you had a real job.*'

What a bellend. Frankie put the phone down. Didn't bother with a goodbye. Just because her boss got to treat him like shit, it didn't mean she got to rub his nose in it too.

He tried to breathe deep, to push his heartbeat down.

'You OK?' Xandra asked.

'Yeah, yeah, sure.' But he wasn't, was he? Because why did Dougie want him there? What was he going to order him to do?

5

Frankie was sweating like a pig on a spit as he walked down Piccadilly in the blazing sunshine ten minutes later on his way to the Royal Academy. He probably looked about as happy as well. The skin on the backs of his hands was the colour of crackling. His whole body felt like it was burning up.

Still, at least he was feeling better than Spartak, who him and Jack had just wrestled into the Old Man's dressing gown, which had been the only thing big enough to fit him, before sticking him in a cab to go home and sleep it off.

Frankie passed Hatchards bookshop. Some paperback called *Into Thin Air* was stacked high in the window around a giant photo of a snow-covered mountain. Alongside was a poster advertising that new kids' book, *Harry Potter and the Philosopher's Stone*, which Xandra said was so good that even adults were reading it. Frankie sighed. He could have done with being magicked away from here himself. Or even a frozen mountaintop would be preferable to whatever it was Dougie Hamilton had in store.

He ducked into Fortnum's a couple of doors down. He was already running late, but screw it. A man had to eat and, thanks to Viollet's call, he was now missing out on Slim's gourmet cheese and tomato toasties, goddammit. He grabbed himself a pork pie at the deli counter. Well, a venison and cranberry pie, at least. Fortum's never did anything by half. He bagged himself a brace of their Scotch eggs to take away too. Slim's favourite. He'd once told Frankie they'd even been invented here.

Leaning up against the wall outside, he scoffed down one of the Scotch eggs. A poster on a billboard opposite caught his eye. Oasis's new album, *Be Here Now*. A Rolls sinking into a swimming pool. Another poster next to it was advertising some big new modern art show coming to the Royal Academy. *Sensation*, it was called. Underneath the word was a photo of what looked like a giant shark, of all bloody things, in a tank.

And just like that – *boom* – Dougie Hamilton was snapping away back in his head again . . . telling him to *sit*, telling him he had *sources*, cops on the inside who could still reopen an investigation into Frankie if Dougie just gave them the word. Shit the bloody bed, he had to somehow get that ruddy pistol back.

A mix of tourists and art students was already funnelling in and out through the arched stone entrance of Burlington House, the RA's main building. A bunch of lorries were parked up on the pavement outside with covered crates of all shapes and sizes being unloaded and carried in by teams of workers. Two cop vans were parked alongside, with several coppers watching on. A proper show of force. Whatever was inside those cases must be worth a mint.

Frankie kept his head down as he walked past. God only

knew what Dougie Hamilton had dragged him here for, but he doubted it was anything as above board as cultural enlightenment. And plenty of cops round here already knew his face, from what had happened to both his brother and his dad.

Frankie clocked Viollet straight away in the inner courtyard. She was sunning herself on one of the benches, all shiny black hair and shades, like Uma Thurman on her date night with Travolta in *Pulp Fiction*.

'You're late,' she told him, as he sat down beside her, not even turning to look at him.

'I stopped to get some food.' He offered her the Fortum's bag. A friendly gesture. The last thing she'd be expecting, right? Might even crack that cool, calm exterior of hers, and maybe even reveal a weakness or two. 'Scotch egg?' he asked, shooting her his warmest smile.

'I'm vegan.'

'And there was me thinking you were from Mars . . .'

Another flash of mutual recognition in her eyes? No way to tell with those shades. 'You should work on your one-liners,' she said.

'And you on your smile.'

Still nothing. He could have been talking to a shop dummy.

'Hmm,' he said, biting into one of the Scotch eggs. 'This one's made with black pudding. That's congealed pig blood, in case you were interested.'

There . . . stick that in your vegan pipe and smoke it. But again . . . nothing. Squinting up at the sun, he loosened his white shirt collar beneath his black suit.

'You're sweating,' she said. 'Not nervous, are you?' Ah. So it was her turn now to try and press his buttons, was it?

'Just hot.'

'This isn't hot.'

'No?'

'You should try Joburg this time of year.'

'That an offer?'

'Just some friendly travel advice.' She sounded annoyed. Why? Because she'd let their conversation slip into chat?

'I didn't know you did friendly,' he said. 'Although . . .'

'Although what?'

Time to give that cage of hers another rattle and see what fell out. 'Just that I couldn't help noticing you with Dougie . . . in the back of that car outside the Paradise. You two seemed . . . how shall I put this? Snug.'

'You talk too much.'

A trace of irritation in her voice But why? Because what he'd spotted between them was secret? Or something more complex than that?

'You're not the first person to tell me that,' he said. 'They used to call me motor mouth as a kid. But don't worry. You'll get used to it.'

No reply. But that in itself was enough. Because she hadn't contradicted him, had she? Meaning he was right about what he'd already guessed – that the two of them would be spending a lot more time together, like it or not, before whatever this deal with Dougie was done.

'This way,' she said, standing up. In her heels, she was taller than him. And in her black skirt and jacket every inch as smart as their sophisticated surroundings.

Frankie followed her as she set off for the entrance.

'So are you going to tell me what this is about?' he asked.

'All good things come to those who wait.'

Good things? Fat chance. Frankie could already tell from the glint in her eyes, as they entered the cool of the building and she took off her shades, that whatever was about to go down here was bad. And not as in Michael Jackson bad either. Not as in cool. But as in real bad. Rotten to the core. And more than likely highly detrimental to his health.

*

'What time do you call this then?' demanded a posh City boy voice.

Dougie Hamilton was sitting on an ornate stone bench in the oddly poky entrance of the Royal Academy, beneath an ancient, threadbare tapestry and in between two decapitated Roman marble busts. The place was already buzzing with a hum of voices. A steady flow of tourists and students filing back and forth between the various galleries and staircases beyond. Dougie was sporting pale suede loafers, a white suit and a panama hat with a black band. Who did he think he was? The man from bleedin' Del Monte?

'Eleven forty-five,' he answered instead.

'Forty-seven,' said Dougie, glancing up through his big black sunglasses at a great big grandfather clock near the bottom of the stairs. 'Next time someone telephones you on my behalf, you need to think of it as a dog whistle that's been blown, do you understand?'

Frankie was half tempted to tell him to fuck off. Because

the twat with the bat wasn't here now, was he? But maybe that was the point. With that Browning Hi-Power pistol in his possession, Dougie didn't need thugs any more to make Frankie do what he said.

'I'll take your retarded silence as a yes,' Dougie said, adjusting the brow of his panama. Leaving his empty take-away coffee cup down on the bench, he got up. 'Right then, Fido, time to take you for a little walk.'

On all fours? But, no, it seemed like for now at least Dougie was content for Frankie to remain vertical, as he set off without looking back. Which was just as well, because, pistol or no pistol, Frankie wasn't sure how much more of this he could handle, and the only canine action he felt like performing right now was cocking his leg all over this smug little bastard's sockless ankles.

'No, not you,' Dougie said, as Viollet fell into step beside them. 'You go and enjoy the sunshine. I'll come find you when we're done.'

Turning on her heels, she headed for the exit. Interesting. So it seemed like Frankie wasn't the only one Dougie had at the end of a leash.

'Excuse me, sir. I think you've forgotten something?' A security guard had just stepped in front of him and Dougie, blocking their path.

'Who, me?' Dougie glared at the guard as though he must have mistaken him for somebody else.

'Yes, sir,' he said. 'Over there. On the bench.'

Dougie glanced back at his drained coffee cup and the remnants of his Pret A Manger sandwich like he'd never seen them before, then turned his head to face the security guard again.

'No,' he said, 'you're mistaken.'

Dougie made to walk on, but the guard just blocked him again. He was late-sixties, tough-looking, with a long, curved half-moon scar on his neck. An *impasse*. Dougie's cheeks flushed with annoyance. But Frankie just smiled. Go on. Do it. Make him pick it up.

'I said you're mistaken,' Dougie repeated, taking off his shades.

Only this time, instead of blocking him again, the guard just moved aside, his cheeks reddening. What the hell?

'In that case, please accept my apologies then, sir,' he said, staring down at his shoes.

Dougie walked on. 'My father always told me to stand my ground,' he said, 'no matter what, and to get your way, even if that means telling someone that black is white. Because most people, they'll back down, because most people, no matter how hard they think they are . . .' He glanced sidelong right into Frankie's eyes. '. . . they don't really want to fight.'

Yeah, most people, you arrogant bastard, but not me. Just you wait until I get my mitts on that gun. Then we'll see who backs down.

Dougie reached a doorway marked 'Tibor Gallery'. The entrance was roped off with a sign saying that cleaning was in progress, but Dougie just unclipped the rope and let it fall. 'Don't worry,' he told Frankie, 'I'm friends with Crispin Entwistle. He's the Director of Artistic Development here.'

Huh. So that was probably more likely why the security

guard had let him off, because maybe he'd seen Dougie here before with this Entwistle geezer. Frankie followed Dougie into the gallery. Polished wooden floors. Classical sculptures. What looked like seriously old oil paintings covering the walls. And no one in here but them.

'As part of my initial investigation into you,' Dougie said, walking on, 'I learned that you'd been in the middle of an art A-level when your father got arrested.'

Frankie nodded. He'd even used to come here on school trips, before dropping out after the Old Man had been nicked.

'And?'

'And I'm guessing that, as part of that course, you would have studied art history?'

'Yeah.'

'Including classical artists like those currently being exhibited here?'

'Maybe.'

'As well as more modern artists too?' he said as they walked on.

'I suppose.'

'Like who?'

Frankie thought back. That whole part of his life – school, art, the person he'd been, the life he'd hoped to have – it felt now as though it had belonged to somebody else.

'Dalí,' he said. 'Picasso, Lichtenstein, Warhol . . .'

'As recent as pop art then,' Dougie said. 'And what about the market? Did you learn anything about how the modern art market works?'

'No, it was more just stuff about the artists themselves and the techniques they used.'

'All well and good,' Dougie said, 'but it's the contemporary art market I want to talk to you about today. I take it you do know what contemporary means?'

'Recent,' Frankie said.

'Yes, but how recent?'

'I don't know. Last year. Last month?'

'Go on.'

'Yesterday . . .'

Dougie nodded at him to continue.

'Even today?'

'Correct. And even tomorrow too. And that's kind of why we're here, Frankie. Not just because of where the contemporary art market's at right now, but because of where we want it to be.'

We . . . Frankie slowly shook his head. There *was* no *we*. Dougie Hamilton had always been, was now and always would be a *them*. Frankie felt the sweat start to prickle on his skin. What *was* this all about? Where was the sting?

'You see, Frankie, putting a current market price on an old piece of art, like this Van Eyck here, it's comparatively easy, because we know what someone paid for it the last time it was put up for sale and what it's insured for.'

'Right.'

'But deciding the price of a truly contemporary piece of art, by which I mean something so brand new that it's never even been seen in public before, that's not so easy. So what do you think an art dealer does there? How do you think they decide on what price should be set?'

Frankie shrugged. 'I don't know. Just chuck out a number and see if anyone's mug enough to pay it?'

Dougie smiled. 'Not quite. Because whatever number they do decide on, it needs to be realistic, by which I mean a number that somebody actually might pay. Or else the sale will be considered a failure and the artwork in question a dud. So how do you think they decide that? What do you think that would depend on?'

'I suppose how good it was . . .'

'Spot on. But who decides if something is good or not? Or how good it is?'

'I dunno. Critics?'

'Yes, but not just them. Getting the right art dealer to handle the sale can make or break a young artist's reputation too. Being collected by the right collector can do the same. It's all about perception, you see. All about getting so-called experts to endorse something. And then there's who'll show your work . . . which galleries, and museums and venerable artistic historical institutions, like this.'

Dougie led Frankie out of the gallery and across another hallway to a further roped-off doorway with uniformed security guards either side. He presented a laminated ID card and the elder of the two guards inspected it, before unclipping the rope and waving them through. Meaning Dougie really was connected here then. They passed a large sign saying that photography was strictly prohibited.

'Welcome to the beating heart of the contemporary art scene,' Dougie said.

Frankie gawped. Hard not to. Because, what the hell? It

was like he'd just stepped into some kind of mad, messed-up dream. Or nightmare.

'They're calling it *Sensation*,' Dougie said, with a dramatic wave of his arm.

'No kidding,' Frankie said, because, yeah, he could see where they – whoever *they* were – were coming from on that, all right. Because his own senses were reeling. *Blam*. A massive head on a wall with its top missing. *Blam*. A bunch of naked shop dummies glued together wearing trainers. *Blam. Blam. Blam*. Even what looked like an unmade bed in a corner. All by artists he'd never heard of. Rachel Whiteread, Damien Hirst, Richard Patterson, Jake and Dinos Chapman, Chris Ofili.

'This place is mental,' Frankie said, but he was smiling too. Because it wasn't just crazy, all this stuff, some of it was pretty funny too. And pretty beautiful in its own way. And pretty cool.

'You like it?' Dougie said.

'Some of it. Some of it I . . . just don't bloody get at all. Oh, shit, look.' He pointed over at where a couple of blokes in white overalls had just finished pulling a massive dust sheet off a giant perspex box. 'It's that bloody shark.'

'You know Hirst's work?' A look of mild surprise and pleasure crossed Dougie's face.

'Who? What, no, it's just that I've see a picture of it before.' On the billboard outside.

'*The Physical Impossibility of Death in the Mind of Someone Living*,' Dougie said, standing beside him.

'You what?'

'That's what it's called.'

75

'Say that again.'

Dougie did. And, yeah, Frankie got it. Because it kind of made sense, didn't it? Because it didn't look dead. Not really. Sure, not alive, but not dead either. Too . . . somehow *alert*, like at any second now it might flick back into life and suddenly smash free. Frankie walked around it, his heartbeat racing as he stared into the creature's pitiless eyes. But it wasn't just the shark's eyes he felt on him. It was Dougie's too. Boring into him from his half-reflection in the perspex. Every bit as predatory and cold.

'Everything in here is owned by a man called Charles Saatchi,' Dougie said.

'What? The advertising bloke?'

'Yes.'

Saatchi & Saatchi. Yeah, Frankie had heard of them. Brothers. Just like him and Jack. Oh, apart from the fact they were stinking rich and successful, of course.

'He's one of those important collectors we were discussing . . . the kind who can make or break an artist just by buying their work. The rest of the art world takes note of what he does. What Saatchi endorses, other collectors want to buy as well.'

'And he endorses all this, does he?'

'Every piece. They're his. It's him who's organized this exhibition here. And that, of course, means that the Royal Academy is endorsing every piece in here too.'

'Meaning all of these might soon be worth a fortune . . .'

'Precisely.'

'No wonder they've got all those coppers stationed

outside. That's what they're unloading from those lorries, right? All this?'

'Quite so.'

Dougie was still staring at him. But whatever that play-fulness had just been in his eyes, it was now gone.

'There's one more animal I want you to see,' he said.

'What?'

He led Frankie over the back of the room and stopped in front of a plinth. Frankie smirked and then sniggered. The artwork – if you could call it that, which yeah, if it was in here being exhibited, then he guessed you could – consisted of what looked like a cute little Jack Russell dog. Standing up on its hind legs, it was holding up a protest placard with the letters 'R.I.P.' written on it.

'Bloody hell, is it real?' Frankie said. 'Is it stuffed?'

'Well, it doesn't look too happy to me.'

A joke. Frankie turned to Dougie to check, but there was no smile there.

'And let me guess,' Frankie said. 'I'm somehow meant to relate to this specifically, am I? Because of what you told me on Sunday, about who's in charge and what I am?' Frankie couldn't bring himself to say the actual words . . . *your dog.*

'No.'

'No?' Frankie was surprised.

'It's by an artist called Savid Digley,' Dougie said.

'It's actually pretty funny, isn't it?' Frankie said. 'When you think about it.' A kind of silent protest, against . . . well, how fucked up we're all going to end up . . . and how nobody really cares. Or that's certainly what it was saying to Frankie right now.

'Even better, it's portable,' Dougie said.

'Portable?'

'As in carry-able.'

'Yeah, I do know what that means. And why's that such a good thing?' Frankie asked. But even before Dougie answered, he suddenly, hideously, already knew.

'Because you, my faithful hound, are going to steal it for me,' Dougie said.

6

Frankie stood in the courtyard of the Royal Academy with the sun burning down on him as Dougie Hamilton walked away. *Because you, my faithful hound, are going to steal it for me.* That bastard. That total loony bastard.

He turned to Viollet. 'And what about you? You not going with him?' Like the lapdog you are. Not that he was any better. Christ, more like worse.

'I've still got work to do here,' she said, waggling a silver camera at him, no bigger than the palm of her hand. 'Neat, huh? It's digital. So small you'd hardly even know it was there.'

Meaning none of the security guards inside would know it was there either, or what she was photographing, let alone why.

'You already knew about it then? Why he bought me here? His big idea?'

'Who said it was his idea?'

'What, you're telling me it was yours?'

'I'm not telling you anything you don't need to know. Or haven't you worked that out by now?'

Frankie shrugged. What difference did it make whose idea it was? He was screwed either way.

'You should get going,' she said. 'Haven't you got a tournament to run?'

He really hated her then. 'And so that's it, is it?'

'What?'

'He just gets to drop that bomb on me . . . about what he wants me to do . . . about his insane idea . . .' *To steal half that bloody stuff in there.* Frankie nearly said it out loud. Because, oh no, it wasn't just that little doggy Dougie had his beady eyes on. It was half a dozen other pieces. He'd got a whole goddamn shopping list he wanted Frankie to deliver. 'And then he just expects me to sit back and wait for further instructions?'

For the first time today, Viollet raised her shades. He saw it again in her eyes, that flash of recognition, that look. Without warning, she reached out and gripped his jaw in her hand.

'For such a handsome fellow, you really do sometimes look so terribly sad.'

'Handsome?' he said, thrown.

'In a crappy boy band kind of way.' She trailed her manicured nails down the lapel of his jacket, before running them back through her hair. Then *snap*, down came the shades, and she was walking away, back through the main entrance into the Royal Academy and out of sight.

'So who was *that* then?' another female voice whispered in his ear.

Frankie flinched. 'What the –'

But then he saw who it was. Sharon Granger. *Detective*

Granger. If she even *was* still a copper. Christ, it was two years since he'd last seen her. Her green eyes glinted in the pale morning sun, the same eyes he'd been trying to avoid getting caught gazing into ever since him and her had first ended up sitting in the same history class together back at school.

'Well?' she asked, smiling.

'Er . . .' *Nobody,* he nearly said. Stopped himself. Because if Sharon had clocked Viollet walking away from him, she'd probably seen her gripping his jaw as well. 'Just, er . . . someone I bumped into . . . an old mate . . .'

'Mate?'

God, he sometimes hated the English language. 'Friend . . .' he clarified. '. . . who, er, sometimes used to call in at the club.'

'A female snooker player?' Sharon's eyebrows bobbed. 'I never knew they were so glamorous.'

'No, it was always, er, more the cigarette machine she was interested in. She worked down the road in a . . . shop . . . a store . . . an establishment . . .'

'An *establishment?*'

Christ, now he was making her sound like a stripper.

'But not any more,' he said. 'No, I think she quit . . . or moved on . . .'

Great, so now she was a retired stripper. Just shut up, Frankie. Stop talking. The more bullshit like this he made up about Viollet, the more she'd stick in Sharon's mind.

Too late. Sharon was already sweeping her hand back over her short black wedge haircut, as she looked around, a glint of suspicion in her eyes. He glanced quickly round too, wondering which direction she'd come from. How good a look at Viollet had she got? And, Christ, what if she'd seen him with Dougie as well? Because she'd know exactly who he was, all right, from when she'd worked the Susan Tilley case. Plus, if she was still a cop, she'd also know he'd taken over his dead father's firm.

'So, you're back then,' he said, quickly changing the subject.

She looked her long-trousered charcoal-grey suit and polished black boots up and down. 'So it would appear.'

'From Hong Kong,' he specified.

Where she'd gone to be with him. *Nathaniel*. Her boyfriend.

She blushed slightly. 'It didn't work out.'

It. As in the job she'd been promised with the Hong Kong police force in the run-up to the handover to China? Or *it*, as in her and Nathan's relationship? Frankie couldn't bring himself to ask. Didn't want to look too much like he still cared.

He spotted it then, her cop radio, there, poking out of her jacket.

'And what about Snaresby? You now back working for him?'

Her smile hardened. 'That's right.'

'And how is the great Detective Inspector? Still trying to bang up innocent people like my brother?' No, not the time or place, but he couldn't help himself, could he?

'Do we really have to go through all this again? He was just doing his job, Frankie. We all were.'

'No. Not him.'

Because, for Snaresby, it had been personal. Frankie bloody knew it. Snaresby had *wanted* Jack put away. Had made no bones about it. But why? He still didn't know. Because he really had believed Jack had killed that girl? Or because he'd been working for Terence Hamilton and that's what Terence had told him? Leaving him as one of Dougie's sources now?

'Can I ask you something?' he said. Because, yeah, why not? Maybe bumping into Sharon like this was just Fate finally giving him a helping hand.

'About what?'

'Jack's case.'

'But why? It's closed.'

'Because I know that at the time you thought that I was somehow –'

'Getting yourself involved? Trying to help out your brother? And getting yourself black and blue with bruises for your efforts?' Her eyes had hardened too now. 'Yeah, I just didn't know how.'

'And what about the other cops working the case? Were there any other lines of –'

'Enquiry? Into you? Or anyone else?'

'Yeah.'

'No . . . or I'd have carried on looking into them . . .' She didn't blink as she said it. ' . . . *and* you . . . and kept on until I got to the truth . . .'

He believed her. Meaning Dougie was bluffing, the lying lawyer bastard. Whatever sources he had couldn't do shit about opening any old investigations into Frankie, because there hadn't been any. Meaning all Frankie had to do was get hold of that pistol and Dougie wouldn't have anything on him at all.

All he had to do . . . Hah, if only it was going to be that simple, eh?

'Why?' Sharon asked.

'Why what?'

'Why are you asking me this? Why now?'

A good question. And one he suddenly had a mad urge to answer too. To just tell her what that crazy bastard Dougie was up to . . . and about how he was forcing Frankie to help him . . . to tell her about that pistol with his prints on it too . . . but to tell her why they were on it . . . and that, yeah, the cops might have nailed the right person for the murder of Susan Tilley, but there'd been someone else behind it too, someone who'd got off scot-free.

But what if she didn't believe him? Or what if she did, but no one else did? What if Dougie slipped that pistol to the cops and Frankie ended up going down for life for something he'd never done? It was too big a risk to take.

'I don't know, it's just . . . a long story,' he said, 'something for another time.'

She pursed her lips, annoyed he was holding back. 'So what are you –'

'Doing here?' Frankie said. 'Oh, you know . . . it's just one of those places I like coming to . . .'

'No change from school there, then, eh? Still the wannabe artist at heart?'

'More like never gonna be,' he said, relieved to be moving the conversation on. Relieved too that she hadn't seen him with Dougie, or she'd definitely have mentioned it by now. 'How about you?' he asked. 'You here on duty? I noticed the other lads out front.'

'Yeah, we're putting on a bit of a show of force for this new exhibition they're putting on . . . they're worried there might be trouble.'

'Trouble?' Frankie's ears pricked up.

'One of the exhibits . . . it's a giant image of Myra Hindley, would you believe it, made up out of smaller images of a kid's hand?'

'Hindley as in the Moors murderer?'

'I know, I mean, it's hardly surprising it's upsetting people, is it? Or I don't think so, anyway. But the organizers won't hear of leaving it out. It's almost like they're willing to court the controversy it will bring. No publicity's bad publicity, isn't that what they say?'

But before Frankie could answer, another voice butted in: 'And look who it isn't. *Mister* Frankie James, no less, no more.'

Frankie didn't need to turn round to discover who this one belonged to. He already knew. Snaresby. Detective Inspector Snaresby. Sharon's boss and the on–off bane of Frankie's life. Only very much on now, of course. Because there was absolutely no sodding way he'd forget Frankie having been here today, and once the news of the heist went public, he'd link him right to it.

'DI Snaresby,' Frankie said. 'Funny, isn't it, how every time you turn up, I'm about to leave?'

'Indeed it is.' All six foot six of Snaresby glared down at him through unblinking grey eyes. 'It's almost as though you had an aversion to me.' Snaresby's chapped lips peeled back over his Cheddar yellow teeth. 'Which I'm certain, of course, isn't true. Because on top of my obvious natural charms – something I'm sure our mutual acquaintance Sharon here can vouch for?'

'Er, absolutely, guv,' she said, eyes glued to her shoes, looking like she wanted to be anywhere but here.

'Yes, on top of those, it wouldn't be remotely in your interest now, would it, to be getting on the wrong side of me?'

'Oh, I don't know. I kind of thought that's where you liked me most.'

Snaresby ignored the comment. 'Particularly with your tournament coming up so soon.'

Frankie remembered the visit he'd got from Snaresby last year outside the Ambassador. The Detective Inspector had raised the subject of the Soho Open back then too and had warned Frankie *to keep in with the right people*. His exact words. But meaning who? The council? Or Tommy Riley? Frankie had guessed the latter, seeing as he'd not heard a peep out of Snaresby on the subject since Tommy and Listerman had taken their stake in the business. But even if Snaresby was working for Riley on some level, did that mean he couldn't be working for Dougie Hamilton too? As one of his *sources*? And if he was, did he already know why Frankie was really here today?

Snaresby extended a lanky arm from his creased suit jacket and checked his watch – a Breitling, the exact same model that Frankie had noticed a number of Tommy Riley's associates sporting, the kind of posh ticker people got as rewards for long service.

'Sharon, would you do me a favour?' Snaresby said. 'My car . . . I do believe I forgot to put my permit on the dash as I left the house this morning.' He handed her a set of keys and a pound coin. 'Would you mind checking and, if it's not there, top up the meter, there's a dear.'

The patronizing prick. Sharon didn't exactly look well chuffed at being given this task either. Hardly the kind of cutting-edge detective work she'd signed up for. Rolling her eyes, she walked away.

'I'll see you around then, Frankie,' she said.

Frankie nodded. He wanted to watch her, had to tear his eyes off her. Snaresby might be a prick, but he was an observant one too. Frankie didn't want him getting into his head. Snaresby looked him up and down. Retrieving a grubby handkerchief from the pocket of his baggy trousers, he wiped the sweat from his balding head.

'Left your toupee at home too, did you?' Frankie asked.

'Oh, very droll.' Snaresby's tongue darted out over his lips. 'And how *is* the imaginatively titled Soho Open progressing?' he asked.

'Fine.'

'I am pleased.'

Frankie didn't like the wolfish smile that came with this. 'You are?'

'Well, of course. I mean, on top of naturally wanting to encourage honest entrepreneurship and all forms of community cohesion within my manor, I have secured myself a ticket. Or indeed a pair of them. For myself and my good lady wife.' Snaresby pulled out his polished Zippo from his jacket pocket and sparked up a cigarette. 'She's quite a fan of the baize, you know, is Mrs Snaresby. Snooker loopy, she is. Loves that Jimmy White, she does. We're both looking forward to it very much.'

Frankie stepped back to avoid the plume of smoke Snaresby was now blowing his way.

'Switched to menthol, have you?' he said.

'Oh, you do have a good memory,' Snaresby grinned.

'It's more the stink of the Juicy Fruit gum you're normally chewing that I remember,' Frankie said. 'This comes as a pleasant relief.'

'Oh, no, I've not given that up.' Snaresby hooked his little finger inside his mouth and fished out a spitty grey wad of gum on the end of his grubby fingernail. 'It's just this one's been in there so long I'd forgotten it was there at all. But thanks for reminding me. A medical friend did warn me that smoking and chewing simultaneously can be hazardous to one's health.'

Frankie winced as Snaresby wrapped the gum up in the same handkerchief he'd wiped his forehead on and tucked it back into his pocket.

'What?' Snaresby asked, catching him staring. 'Waste not, want not. I thought your generation were all over that kind of recycling lark.'

Frankie just glared. The Juicy Fruit wasn't the only thing about Snaresby he'd not forgotten. While reading the Old Man's case files last year, he'd discovered that Snaresby had been one of the chief investigating officers who'd put the Old Man away. Or fixed the evidence against him, more like, was how Frankie saw it . . . the Old Man's prints that had ended up all over the cases the looted safety boxes had been emptied into . . . the confession of the gang's leader, who'd then hanged himself in prison before the case had even gone to trial.

'So how do you feel about people dying twice then, Inspector?' Frankie said. A question he'd been itching to ask him to his face since he'd last seen him, just to see how he'd react.

Snaresby took another long pull on his smoke. 'Ah, yes. You're referring to my former colleague, James Nicholls, I infer?'

'The one you told me was dead.'

James Nicholls and Craig Fenwick had been the other two officers who'd worked with Snaresby on the Old Man's case. Fenwick had since moved to Australia, but last year Snaresby had told Frankie that Nicholls was dead. Only he hadn't been, had he? Because Frankie had then discovered he was living in Kew. Only the same day Frankie had gone there to visit him and quiz him over whether he'd helped stitch up the Old Man, Nicholls had topped himself. Just a coincidence? Fat bloody chance.

'Well, I suppose that's because in a way he was to me,' said Snaresby. 'Metaphorically speaking. What with him having turned his back on our noble profession and taken the cloth.'

Nicholls had become a vicar, of all bloody things. 'Maybe because he felt guilty,' Frankie said. 'Because of everything you and him and Craig Fenwick did. Because of how cor-rupt you all were.' He'd said this last bit loud enough for a couple of people next to them to have turned.

'You'd better watch your mouth, young man,' said

Snaresby, stepping in. 'Because that's slanderous, that is. And something I could nick you for right here.'

But instead of backing off, Frankie grinned so hard it nearly split his face. Because there – right there in the centre of Snaresby's eyes, he could see it – that flicker of doubt, of fear. The first time he'd ever seen him rattled. But because of *what*? Well, that could only be one thing. Because he knew Frankie was on to him and because he *did* have something to hide.

Frankie shouldered past him. Hard.

'Don't you . . . you come back here,' Snaresby growled after him.

But Frankie just kept on walking. Because he wasn't the one who'd done anything wrong. Not like he now knew in his guts that bastard had.

7

Corrupt. That was the word that had done it, that had triggered Snaresby. That and linking the three of them together.
Him, Fenwick and Nicholls. The old gang.

Only they weren't history, were they? Not for Frankie.
And that's what had really got to Snaresby, wasn't it? The
fact that Frankie still cared, still saw them as linked together,
even now after Nicholls was dead. Yeah, Frankie might
already be a dog in some people's books, but he was one in
Snaresby's now too. Only not just any old dog and certainly
not a lapdog. More like a terrier. One that would never stop
digging. One that would never let go.

He was still smiling at Snaresby's reaction – at that
knowledge, written there in his bulging eyes, that there *was*
still something buried in his past that Frankie could expose
– when he picked up his jet-black Capri from the multi-
storey just down the road from the Ambassador Club.

Heading south of the river over Vauxhall Bridge and
down through Lambeth, he let the V8 engine rip, remembering that first day the Old Man had let him drive it,
just after he'd turned seventeen and had passed his test.
They'd headed up into Essex that afternoon and had caned

it through the country lanes and out onto the M25, when the Old Man had told him to really put his foot down and see what she could do.

Exhilarating. That's how it had felt then and how it felt now too, as Frankie finished the stop/start run of traffic lights through Stockwell and Brixton Hill. And *exhilarating* . . . yeah, that's how it still felt too, thinking about Detective Inspector Snaresby's purpling face . . . like a naughty little boy who'd just been caught out.

He parked the Capri in the maze of side streets round the back of HM Prison Brixton, having the same nightmare of finding a spot as he always did whenever he visited the Old Man. Staring at the empty seat beside him for a moment, all the triumph he'd been feeling dropped away. Seven years already, the Old Man had been inside, with still another eight years of his sentence left to run – unless Frankie could somehow find proof that he shouldn't be in there at all.

He went through the usual rigmarole of security, before grabbing a table in the already crowded Visitors' Room to wait. A stink of floor polish and Cup-a-Soups. Mumbled conversations all around. He'd got changed before heading over here . . . into casuals, his old Levis, Nikes, and a plain white T . . . the kind of gear he always wore whenever he visited . . . because the one time he'd come here in the usual suit he wore whenever he was bossing the club, he'd hated it, seeing the Old Man's eyes looking him up and down, missing all the pukka clothes he'd used to like wearing himself when he'd still been on the outside.

'All right, son,' the Old Man said, walking over towards

him now in his badly fitting grey jogging bottoms and sweatshirt. 'Not like you to be in on a Wednesday.'

His voice was all big and boomy. All *fuck off* and hard. Not for Frankie's benefit, mind. More for all the other inmates chattering in the background. Didn't matter how long the Old Man had been in here, Frankie never got used to it, the lack of proper privacy. The fact that *everything* here was all about show. That you could never properly relax.

'Yeah, sorry about the short notice, Dad.'

'Slim sick, is he?'

Wednesday was normally Slim's day to visit. Him and the Old Man went back, way back, like as far as the Stone Age. Slim had already been working the bar down the Ambassador Club when the Old Man had first leased it in '84 and the two of them had been firm friends ever since.

'Nah . . .' Frankie said.

The Old Man pulled up a chair and sparked up a fag, all in one fluid motion. He leant back in his chair, looking Frankie over.

'So how come you've switched with him and come in today?' he asked.

Nothing got past him. Or at least where Frankie was concerned. Never had. No point in bullshitting him either. He knew Frankie too well, even more so, in a weird way, since he'd been inside. Had more time to focus on him when they were together these days. Wasn't so distracted by running the club and trying to make ends meet.

'Just wanted to give you the heads-up on something,' Frankie said, keeping his voice nice and low. God only knew how many of the other forty or so lads in the room had connections with either the Riley or the Hamilton gangs.

'On?'

'I had to go down Terence Hamilton's funeral and Lister-man got wind of it. The only thing I could think of to tell him was that I'd gone there because you and Terence had been at school together. You know, to kind of pay your respects.'

'My fucking what? To that prick. I wouldn't have pissed on Terence Hamilton if he'd been on fire, alive or dead.'

Bernie James smiled a jagged-toothed smile, as if picturing the scenario for real. In spite of a few spare pounds of paunch pressing up against his sweatshirt, he was still in pretty good shape, broad-shouldered and toned from working out down the prison gym. Yeah, Frankie reckoned he could have still taken Terence Hamilton, all right. Even before he'd got sick.

'I know, I'm sorry. It's all I could think of,' Frankie said.

'And what did Listerman say?'

'He looked . . . well, a bit surprised . . . a bit like you do now . . . Look, Dad, it won't get you in any trouble, will it? Because if it does –'

'No, forget it. If anyone asks, I'll tell them it's true. Tell them I was stoned, or something, when I asked you . . . tell them I made a stupid mistake . . .'

'Thanks.'

The Old Man stared at him evenly. Hard eyes. Something of the shine of a black ball about them. Eyes that had used to be gentle sometimes. Something that had been lost. 'And is that what you've made?' he asked. 'Some kind of stupid mistake too?'

And there it was again. Nothing getting past him. Frankie nodded, feeling sick to his guts having to admit it in front of him like this, like he'd failed his GCSE bleedin' French all over again, like he'd failed his bleedin' life.

'Cos I can't see any other reason, you being there at that funeral, unless you'd somehow got yourself in hock to him or his kid.'

Frankie sighed, feeling his shoulders slump. Even if it had been safe to talk about it in here, where would he start? The pistol Dougie Hamilton currently had in his possession was the same one the Old Man had made sure Frankie got a hold of two years ago for protection when all that nightmare had been going down with Jack. And not only did it now have Frankie's prints all over it, but driving over here just now he'd started wondering what if it had the Old Man's prints on it too. Meaning that if Dougie Hamilton ever did come good on his threat to hand it over to the cops, they might end up getting two sets of James men's prints on a murder weapon for the price of one. And then there was whatever that pistol might have been used for before. God only knew where the Old Man had got it and whether its ballistics might match up to anything else.

'I know you can't talk about it now . . . here . . . but if I can offer a word of advice, son,' the Old Man said.

'What?'

'Don't put your life – or your liberty – in the hands of either of them, not bloody Dougie Hamilton, but not Lister-man and Tommy Riley either.'

Well, it was too late for that, and the Old Man must have seen it too in his eyes.

'But if you do have to choose between them,' he went on, 'then you choose based on who you think you can trust the most, and who you think can get you the furthest, and whatever decision you make, you make sure you make it for yourself, and with an eye to the future, your future, not theirs . . . an eye to winning, son.'

The way he said it, the look that went with it, it was obvious he wasn't just talking about his own loyalties to Tommy here. No, he was talking about something bigger than that. About Frankie somehow using them instead of them using him, of somehow putting himself completely out of their reach, of somehow coming out on top.

'But you do still know I don't want this, Dad,' he said. *This.* He meant this life. His own life being tangled up with theirs. Because he still wanted to build a future for himself off the bloody streets and away from bastards like the Hamiltons and Rileys of this world and everything they stood for and did.

'Beggars can't be choosers,' said the Old Man. 'Sometimes that's just how it is.'

He could have been talking about himself, about how he'd ended up in here.

'What about that detective?' the Old Man asked.

He meant Matt Dyer, the private investigator Frankie had hired at the end of last year to look into his case – and, specifically, into the people who might have been instrumental in framing him. Dyer was a retired copper himself, but one who'd specialized in investigating bent cops back in the eighties for the Police Complaints Authority. Even better, he was a Jock with no London connections, so had no compunction whatsoever about having a good nosey round in the Met.

'Still nothing,' Frankie said.

A weekly question. The same answer. But that had been part of the deal with Dyer. He only took on cases he thought he could make a difference to, he only got paid on results, and he'd only be in touch if he found something.

The Old Man nodded and sparked up a fag.

'I did bump into Snaresby, though,' Frankie said.

'What? Where? I told you to keep away from him. If he even suspected –' The Old Man had dropped his voice down to a whisper again, but Frankie held up his hand anyway. He knew what he was going to say. That Snaresby might try to stitch Frankie up himself if he ever got wind of the fact that Matt Dyer was looking into him too.

'I didn't mention Dyer at all. I did ask him about Nicholls, though,' Frankie said.

The Old Man looked away, annoyed.

'I couldn't help myself. I asked him why he'd lied to me about him already being dead.'

'And what did he say?'

'It's not what he said, it's how he looked. He's fucking guilty, Dad. I know it. It's because of him you're inside.'

'And what about . . . the third little piggy,' the Old Man asked.

He meant Fenwick, the other cop who'd put him away and who'd since moved to Australia.

'Still no news on him either. But Dyer said he's looking into it. We're just going to have to be patient and wait.'

'And Kerr?'

Yet another little piece of the puzzle they had Matt Dyer working on. Frankie had shown the Old Man the photograph he'd stolen from Nicholls's flat after he'd hanged himself. It had shown Fenwick, alongside Nicholls and Snaresby, but there'd been a fourth man there too. And one the Old Man had recognized as well. A Soho face. Danny Kerr. An accountant. A bent one, who'd died in a car crash a few years back. But Dyer had said he was going to look into the circumstances surrounding that too.

'Again, nothing . . .'

'Fine.' The Old Man nodded, resigned to the fact. He smiled. 'Let's talk football then,' he said. 'So what do you reckon to Ian Wright's chances of getting over two hundred club goals by the end of the season?'

But even as they sat there chatting through all things Arsenal, Frankie couldn't help thinking about what the Old Man had just said. About him maybe having a choice to make between Hamilton and Riley. And about whether it was already too late, because Hamilton already had him onside. And about what Riley would do if he ever found out Frankie was working for the other side. He'd fuck him, he would. And not just Frankie. Because his reach went way, way deeper than that. Into Jack's life. Here into Brixton Prison too.

Yeah, get caught crossing Tommy Riley and it wasn't just Frankie who'd end up getting royally screwed. His whole sodding family would too.

8

The next dog whistle to summon Frankie James from his otherwise already frantic existence blew shrilly in his ears two days later on the afternoon of Friday 5th September, just as he'd finished running through the latest tournament paperwork with the Old Man's cousin, Kind Regards.

'Who was that?' asked Xandra, clearly spotting the fact that the corners of Frankie's mouth were doing their best to hang down around his ankles in despair.

'No one. Wrong number.'

What the caller had actually said, in her by now horribly familiar South African tones, was, 'There's a black cab waiting for you outside the Raymond Revuebar. The driver knows where to take you. Now hurry up. The meter's running and you know he doesn't like to be kept waiting.'

Kind Regards looked up at him over his half-moon specs, from where he was still going through the fine print of the contracts he'd got laid out on the bar.

'All looking good,' he said, 'I just need your signature here . . . here . . . and here.'

Frankie took out the Old Man's pen and signed where Kind Regards had indicated.

Kind Regards snapped his case shut and tapped its lid. 'I'll get them their copies back. All looking good, though. The boy done good.'

'Thanks again.' Frankie meant it. Kind Regards had been bossing all the legal work for the tournament right from the get-go. And all at cost.

Frankie said his goodbyes and headed out, telling Xandra he was off to check round the local pubs to see that Dickie Bird had indeed distributed and flyposted the flyers as per his instructions. He was dressed well down, in shorts and a T-shirt, but, sod it, would Dougie even care?

He got to the rendezvous Viollet had given him in under five minutes. The cab was there waiting as promised, outside the strip club, or gentlemen's club, as its owner Paul Raymond preferred.

It turned out the meter running line was just a metaphor. There was no meter. No cab driver either. Just the massive bulk of The Saint wedged into the driver's seat. He was picking at the ginger stubble on his head, glowering at Frankie in the rearview.

'I wouldn't let Dougie catch you moonlighting like this,' Frankie said, yanking the door shut.

'Good to see you keeping your sense of humour up,' said The Saint. 'That's what they did in the war, according to my old mum. Even when they knew they were doomed.'

The Saint pulled away.

'So what's with the cab then?' Frankie asked.

'One of Dougie's initiatives. He says we're much less likely to ever get stopped by the filth in one of these, when we're out and about on firm business.'

'But don't people just, I don't know, flag you down all the time and try and get in?'

'With a face like mine, scrote? That happens a lot less than you think.' The Saint sneezed. 'Fucking hay fever,' he growled, reaching for the stereo. 'Streisand,' he said, shoving a cassette tape in. 'I saw her live once, you know. Out in Vegas four years ago. I flew over specially, like. Absolute magic, she was. Not a dry eye in the house.'

The sound of Babs singing 'Don't Rain on My Parade' washed over Frankie as The Saint drove on and the Soho streets flowed by.

'Cheer up, son. It might never happen,' said The Saint, flashing him a brown-stained grin. 'Oh dear, it already has.'

The cab started slowing down around twenty minutes later. Limehouse. Narrow Street, to be precise. What used to be the heartland of London's docks, but these days was just full of old warehouses being converted into offices and flats.

They passed The Grapes on their left. One of London's oldest and bestest boozers, with its own little riverside terrace. Everyone from Pepys to Dickens to Arthur Conan Doyle had got hammered in there over the years. Including Frankie James on his nineteenth birthday. He could still remember throwing up in the Thames.

The Saint pulled over a hundred yards on. An old brick building, three storeys high. Frankie gazed up at the windows glinting in the sun. No way to tell if anyone was home.

'Out,' said The Saint. 'Punch the buzzer on the door.'

'Where are we?'

'Are you deaf, scrote? I said *out*.'

The Saint turned up the volume and stared straight

ahead as Streisand continued to blare out 'Memory'. It looked like something was glistening at the corner of his eye. But nah, it couldn't really have been a tear, could it? Must just have been a trick of the light.

Frankie walked up to the building's front door. Just the one buzzer. Meaning what? This whopping, sodding place was privately owned? But owned by who?

He pressed the buzzer, half expecting to hear footsteps approaching and then see a butler appear. Instead all he got was a click as the door swung open, with no one to be seen inside at all. So maybe it was haunted then? Or Dracula's pad? Who knew?

Frankie shivered as he stepped inside. He didn't trust Dougie further than he could spit. Inside it was gloomy and stank of petrol. What windows Frankie could see, as the door creaked shut behind him, were high up and so choked with cobwebs and ivy that hardly any light could get through. Enough, though, to see that this was in fact a garage. And there, plumb centre in the middle of the room, were three of the most beautiful cars Frankie had ever seen.

A Corvette Stingray and a Ferrari Dino. And last, but not least, an Aston Martin DB5. The exact same one as from that James Bond film, *Goldfinger*, if he wasn't mistaken. Hell's tits. The nearest Frankie had ever got to getting close to something like this was the toy one he'd had as a kid.

He couldn't help himself. He walked over and trailed his fingers along its sleek, shiny flank. Then jumped back almost a foot.

'Boo!' a super-deep voice boomed out, followed by a horrible, strangulated whine of static.

'What the hell –?' Frankie clamped his hands to his ears and looked around. But he couldn't see a sodding soul.

'Whoah! Too loud, right?' the voice screeched. Another whine. More crackling. 'Better?'

'Er, yeah,' Frankie called out. 'A bit.'

'Coo-li-o.'

Coolio? As in that American rapper who'd had a hit a couple of years back? 'Gangsta's Paradise', or something like that? Yeah, maybe this being his pad made a bit more sense than Dracula, eh?

'OK, so you'll find the elevator over there to your left.'

Frankie turned to look.

'No, your other left, dude.'

What, so whoever this was could see him? Frankie clocked it then. A CCTV camera bolted to one of the ceiling beams. He spotted the lift doors too, set into the far wall, and set off towards them.

'Tah-dah! Or bingo, or yahtzee, or whatever the fuck you Britishers say.'

Britishers? This guy's accent . . . what was he? A Southern Yank? Alabama, or some such shit, it sounded like.

'So yep, yep, come on down . . .'

Come on down? What the hell?

'I mean, that Bruce Forsyth, he's hilarious, yeah?' the voice continued. 'I mean, I totally love that shit. *The Price is Right?* And *The Generation Game* too? The man's a genius. Totally insane.'

'Er, right,' Frankie said. Now this was just getting surreal.

'No, seriously, I *am* a massive fan of those shows. We receive them all back in Amsterdam where we've been hanging . . . and what's that catchphrase of his again? *Nice to see you, to see you . . .'*

'Nice,' Frankie said.

'Damn. That's right. *Didn't he do well?'*

'Er, who is this talking, by the way?'

'Levi. Like the jeans. But you can call me Rivet. Everyone else does.' Frankie glanced across to see the camera still tracking him.

'Well, OK. And, um, in case you're wondering why I'm here, I've just been dropped off here by The Saint,' Frankie said, the sentence suddenly sounding utterly ridiculous beside these cars.

'Yep, and I'm totally looking forward to seeing you and working with you too, Frankie boy. Now hit that button, and let's make this face to face.'

The lift was old school, like it had been hauled right off a movie set. Frankie pressed its flickering, illuminated button and its gears hummed into life. Peering in through the zigzag of its metal concertina doors, he looked up, wondering how high its shaft went, but it ceilinged out just a few feet above his head here at ground level. Weird. Meaning whoever it was he'd just spoken to, they had to have been talking to him from down . . . *there*. Wherever the hell *that* was.

He rode the lift down and stepped out into what looked like a living room. A well posh one at that. A sleek white dining table ran down the middle of a black tiled floor, long enough to seat maybe as many as thirty guests. A pear-shaped crystal chandelier hung centre stage from a high vaulted ceiling. But it wasn't all pretty-pretty. Plenty of industrial touches too. Exposed brickwork. Cast-iron girders. Whoever owned this place wasn't trying to hide it from its past.

Frankie could smell fresh coffee. Good coffee too, and God only knew he could never get enough of that. He followed his nose on past the dining table and into a kitchen.

Finally, people. A man and a woman were sat around a square metal table. Her, slim and athletic-looking, with gothy black hair, and enough studs and jewellery hanging off her face to start a shop. Him, skinny and wrinkly and looking 110, with long grey hair. Neither looked up, both focused on what was laid out on the table before them. A bunch of what looked like architectural drawings. Photos too. Loads of them. A kind of mosaic. And, yeah, Frankie recognized some of them too. Like the Digley piece. That funny little dog. Dougie Hamilton's contemporary art shopping list, no less.

A third person was already walking towards him from the other side of the room, a wiry little bloke in a white T-shirt and jeans with trendy little reading glasses perched on the end of his nose. He couldn't have been more than five feet tall, with a broad white-capped smile and a massive mop of white blonde hair that would have put Billy Idol to shame.

'Guys, this is Frankie James,' mini-Billy said.

So his was the deep voice Frankie had heard upstairs.

'Great to meet you, Frankie, an honour.' His thin-wristed grip was as strong as a vice. 'And Frankie, these are the guys.'

'Er, hi,' Frankie said.

'On the left we have Luuk.'

'Luke,' Frankie said.

'No, *Luuk*.'

'Yeah, that's what I just said.'

'Nuh-uh, it's not.'

The grey-haired *Luuk*, now with one of those jeweller's loupes clamped to one wrinkly eye socket, again didn't look up. While the goth girl just shook her head at Rivet, like he was making matters much more complex than they needed to be.

'And sitting next to him,' Rivet continued, 'rolling her eyes at me like I've developed a mild retardation, is Lola. As in the Kinks song, only she really is all woman. No hidden dicks inside her pants.'

Lola just flipped him the finger, her bright-brown eyes twinkling. Turning to Frankie, she said, 'Hey.'

'Hey, indeed.' Rivet steered Frankie on towards another doorway. 'There'll be plenty of time for idle chitchat later, but for now, Frankie old bean, you'd better head through there, because the others are waiting.'

The *others*? Meaning Dougie? And who the hell else? Frankie felt that nasty little shiver running down his spine again. What was that phrase? Into the lion's den? And no one even knew he was here.

Just get on with it. He still needs you. Right? He walked on through the doorway, and around another corner, then sucked in his breath and squinted as the bright light hit him. Instead of another room of whatever basement complex he'd assumed he was in, dead ahead of him now was what looked like a giant greenhouse, or conservatory, or *arborium*? Was

106

that even the right word for something as crazily grand as this?

It stretched up high, way high, as in whole storeys high. There were whole bloody trees inside it. Palms, creepers, all kinds of tropical-looking shit. Bees buzzed. Butterflies flitted. The air smelt of honeysuckle, eucalyptus, lavender, rose.

He walked on, weaving his way in between the sculptures that were dotted all around. Even a sodding fountain. And, yeah, now he got it, what this place was – one of those old warehouses alongside the Thames, only its back half had been knocked down to make room for this gorgeous green slice of paradise.

He stepped out into the garden beyond and there, past the garden wall, a whole fifty feet away, he could see the oily river itself stretching all the way across to the Oxo building, and the Tate, and the spire of Southwark Cathedral . . . the whole South Bank of the Thames lined up like cardboard cut-outs.

He turned and looked up at the building he'd just walked out of. Six storeys, he counted, including these three demolished ones where the garden now was down here below street level. Yeah, beautiful, it was. Wicked. Like a Bond villain's hideaway.

Now all he needed to do was find bloody Blofeld himself.

Then, right on cue, he heard voices. Over there.

9

Three figures sat beneath a pagoda beside the red-brick wall that formed the garden's riverside perimeter. Dougie and Viollet were two. The third person had their barn door of a back to Frankie and a no-fuss crew cut. Another two men stood ten yards further back, both of them suited, idly watching.

'Ah, and, finally, our guest has arrived,' Dougie said.

He smiled flatly at Frankie. In spite of the sun, he was again wearing tweed, an open-neck white shirt and red cravat. He didn't get up to shake Frankie's hand or anything as friendly or even businesslike as that. Kept both hands on his lap, his golden signet ring glinting in the sun almost like an invitation, like a part of him was expecting Frankie to kneel and kiss it. Only then Frankie saw it wasn't a signet ring at all. Just a simple gold band on his wedding finger. But why? For his dead fiancée? How bloody crazy was that? The two of them had never even got hitched.

'Viollet, of course, you know already,' Dougie said.

She was another study in kick-arse black today. Black shoes. Black skirt. Black shirt. Black shades. The only concession was her lips – bright red – which slowly curled now into a smile.

'Well, hello again,' she said.

'And last but not least . . .' Dougie swivelled in his wicker chair to face the third figure. 'Allow me to introduce you to Bram.'

Bram? What kind of a bloody name was that meant to be? Even weirder than *Luuk*. The only Bram Frankie had ever heard of was the one in *Bram Stoker's Dracula*, that Gary Oldman film that had come out a few years back. What was that line him and Jack had used to say to each other all the time when they got pissed? Oh yeah. *Listen to them, the children of the night. What music they make!* Hey, maybe he should try it now. This massive bastard looked like he could do with a laugh.

Bram stood, and kept standing up, extending like a friggin' fireman's ladder, before finally turning to look down on Frankie. Christ, Frankie stepped back. Didn't seem smart to stay any closer than he had to to this. This guy made even The Saint look like Danny DeVito. So who the hell was he? Jaws to Dougie's Blofeld?

He waited for the guy to speak, but he didn't. A hard face, with what was either a burn or a stork mark on his forehead, leaving him looking like Gorbachev on steroids. Frankie had always thought of old Gorby as one of the nicer Russian dictators, but this lad, ten years Frankie's senior, had clearly not got the message on that. Scowling, though. Oh, yeah. He was a world bloody expert at that, if the way he was looking at Frankie now was anything to go by.

'Frankie,' Frankie said. 'Frankie James.' Hey, hey. When in James Bond land . . .

Nothing.

'Bram's dumb,' Dougie said.

'You what?' Bloody hell. Talk about rude. Brave too, mind, with the size of this fucker.

'I mean he can't speak.'

'Oh, right.' Frankie turned back to Bram and smiled awkwardly, before giving him an even more awkward thumbs up. Like a dick. 'Sorry, mate,' he said. 'I didn't know.'

Big boy didn't look like he gave a shit either.

'You're going to be working with Bram from here on in,' Dougie said.

Here on into *what*? 'Yeah?' Oh, great. And what jolly pals they'd surely one day be.

'Or more *for* him, really,' Dougie said. 'Now *sit*.'

Another nasty touch of the Barbara Woodhouses, then. Frankie was getting well sick of this. But what other choice did he have? He walked round the cast-iron table they were sitting at and perched himself on the last available chair. A silver coffee pot on the table. Antique china cups and sugar bowl. All very *Lovejoy*. Or at least it would be, if only somebody would smile.

'Coffee?' Dougie said.

'Sure. Thanks.' Well, it was better than being offered Pedigree Chum. Frankie helped himself and took a genteel sip. Good stuff too. Freshly ground. The best thing that had happened to him all day.

'Nice place you've got here,' he said.

'It used to belong to David Lean,' Dougie said. 'The

director of *Lawrence of Arabia*, *Dr Zhivago* and *A Passage to India*.'

'And *Bridge on the River Kwai*,' Frankie said. Because, oh yeah, he could be a dab hand at Trivial Pursuit too. And arts and lit was his special subject. Bring on the fucking brown cheese.

'He designed it all,' said Dougie, 'the garden, the bedrooms, the home cinema, the lot. He hardly ever left the place the last few years of his life. Just held court here, visited by the likes of Steven Spielberg, as well as just about every "A" list actor under the sun. You climb over that wall and there's even a private beach.'

Frankie wasn't sure if this was an invitation. Or, if the tide was rising, a threat. Either way, he didn't move.

'Lord Owen's a neighbour,' Dougie continued. 'And did you know right there was where Sir Walter Raleigh set sail for the New World?'

'No.'

'Makes you think, doesn't it?'

'Yeah.' But about what? How nice it would be to be on that ship with old Walty boy right now. Probably not what Dougie had in mind.

'I feel a close affinity with people like that,' Dougie said. 'Explorers. Adventurers. People who really leave their mark on the world.'

Delusions of grandeur? Nothing psychopathic about that.

'My dear departed dad,' said Dougie, 'he always believed in living modestly, so as not to draw attention to himself, particularly where the police were concerned. Which is why he set my mother up with the nice but far from spectacular house she lives in in Dagenham. But I've adopted a rather more modern outlook and see property as more of an invest-ment . . .' He waved his hand expansively. '. . . and it's my firm belief that this lovely little part of London here is about to take off like a space shuttle. David Lean spent six million doing this place up, but I just got it for three. And you know what?'

'What?' Frankie said.

'Five years' time and you can bet your bottom dollar I'll be selling it for nine.'

Or hopefully catching a horrible cold, like Frankie's dad had done back in the late eighties, after he'd invested his money in a couple of flats just before the whole market had gone tits up.

'Do you remember our little chat the other day?' Dougie said. 'About the contemporary art scene?'

So, finally, they were cutting to the chase. Frankie noticed Bram watching closely now. He noticed too the lanyard round his neck, with a thin pen in a loop attached. Probably for talking to people like Frankie who didn't know how to sign.

'Sure,' he said.

'And about how prices get set based on how an artist's reputation is endorsed by various collectors, dealers, galler-ies and museums where their works appear, so that even pieces made out of elephant dung – I mean literally shit – can become worth a fortune.'

'You mean the Chris Ofili?' – a piece called *The Holy Virgin Mary*, made partly out of elephant dung. Frankie had

read about it in the exhibition notes he'd picked up yesterday from the RA while out on a run.

'Quite so.' Dougie took a custard cream from the plate
on the table and prised the top half off, before scraping the
creamy middle off with his teeth and frisbeeing the rest over
the wall. 'Well, there's an even better way to help bolster an
artist's reputation in tandem with all that.'

'And what's that?'

'Notoriety . . . infamy . . . that's the best kind of publicity
there is, the fastest way of all to grow a reputation . . . I'm
assured by my contacts in the business.' The way he said it
– *contacts* – he made them sound like something much more
collaborative than that. '. . . and a perfect match too for the
kind of art that will be appearing in the *Sensation* exhibition, wouldn't you say? Shocking publicity to match the
shocking art?'

'Like the Myra Hindley piece.' Was that what he was
talking about? The controversy Sharon had said it was
pretty much guaranteed?

'A bit like that, but better.'

Frankie didn't understand what any of this had to do
with him. 'I would've thought this show already had the
perfect man to stir something like that up.'

'You mean Saatchi? Well, yes, but I'm talking about
something even bigger, even more shocking than even someone like him could cook up. I'm talking about something so
outrageous that it will really put this exhibition on the map.
Globally. And permanently. So the prices for all the artists
involved will shoot up and keep on shooting up, making a
fortune for everyone involved.'

And, yeah, suddenly Frankie could see it, how all that might work. What was it Sharon had said? No such thing as bad publicity?

'And so, you see,' said Dougie, 'it's not just important that the robbery takes place, but *how* it takes place.'

'Huh?'

'It needs to be as shocking and headline-grabbing as possible. We want it to be a mystery for the press to ponder over, for years, almost a work of art in itself, leaving everybody wondering how on earth we got all those pieces out of there without being seen. I've even got a headline for it to feed a friendly journalist pal of mine after the event, to get things started. "The Houdini Heist". What do you think?'

Frankie thought he was fucking nuts. Because, surely, pulling off a bloody art heist was going to be hard enough in itself, without having to make it eye-catching and clever and wacky as well? He glanced across at Viollet. Was she hearing this? Did she agree? But, shit, she wasn't even listening, was she? Just staring out across the Thames.

'And that's where Bram here comes in,' Dougie said. 'And why I brought you here to meet him and his associates today. Because he's something of an expert in this field, not only in robbery, but in creating the time and space within a robbery to accomplish what you need, as you'll come to learn.'

Bram's face remained blank. Meaning what the fuck, he was a member of the magic circle, sworn to give nothing away? If this was meant to be the Houdini behind the heist, then Frankie was far from convinced. For God's sake, he didn't even have a cape.

'But do you know what the best part is, Frankie?' Dougie said, a smile now twitching at the corner of his mouth.

'What?'

'All those lovely little pieces we saw being set up in the Royal Academy the other day, they're not the only pieces by those artists that will go up in value once we've pulled this off. *Everything* they've ever done will skyrocket in value.'

Now Frankie saw it. What was really in it for Dougie. Charles Saatchi might own everything in there, everything that was being exhibited, but not everything those artists had done.

'You've invested then? In them? In those artists? In their other works?'

'Maybe me. Maybe some friends of mine.' OK, right. His *contacts*. 'It doesn't really matter. All that's important is that our little robbery leaves the whole art world scratching its head and digging into its collective wallet to invest in the artists concerned.'

'And after the robbery?' Frankie said. Because, really, that was all that mattered, wasn't it? What happened then. What happened to *him*. How far in the clear he could put himself from this whole friggin' caper. And how fast.

'What do you mean?'

'What are we going to do with them? All the exhibits we're nicking? Ditch them? Destroy them?'

'Now why on earth would we do that?'

'You mean you're planning on keeping them?' Was he having a giraffe?

'You sound surprised.'

'But I thought you just said that the whole point of this

robbery was publicity? To drive up the prices for all the other pieces you've invested in.'

'The main point –'

'Then why keep these other few bits that can implicate you in the crime?' Implicate *us*. Implicate *me*.

'Ah, yes. Well, that's the other clever bit, you see. We're going to sell them.'

'*Sell* them?' Proof, then, that he really was batshit crazy. 'And who the hell is going to buy them? They're going to be hotter than the surface of the sun.'

'Oh, I don't mean now. I mean perhaps in five years from now, or ten, or even fifteen, because why not? After all, their value's only going to keep on going up. But don't you worry, Frankie, there'll always be buyers for this kind of thing. Maybe not the kind of buyer that will ever loan the piece to a museum, or even show it in daylight ever again. But buyers, all right, buyers with so much money they don't care how much they spend, buyers who just want to possess something that no one else can.' He grinned, fully this time, as wet and wide as a wound. 'And besides,' he then added, 'who said *I'm* going to be keeping them at all?'

Frankie didn't like the sound of this. Not one bloody bit. Christ, was there any way, any way at all, he still might be able to somehow wriggle out of this? Or, even better, get himself thrown out? He turned quickly to Bram and looked pointedly at him.

'You do know that I have absolutely no experience in this kind of work, don't you?' he said. Might as well just throw that out there. Who knew? Maybe old Gorbachev here might have some kind of veto he could play. 'As in not a bloody clue,' Frankie hurried on. 'In fact, the last thing I stole was a handful of Black Jacks from the cornershop when I was nine years old.' Meaning if old Dougie boy here has in any way led you to believe otherwise, then now's your chance to give me the flick.

No such luck. Old Gorby said nothing. Didn't even shrug.

Frankie sighed. All he could do not to hold his head in his hands. Because he was screwed, wasn't he? Totally and utterly screwed. 'Fine,' he said, feeling his whole body slump, 'so take me through it. What's the sodding plan?'

'Oh, no, Frankie,' Dougie said. 'One step at a time. This is just an introductory meeting. All that, the planning, Bram here will be contacting you separately about that.'

Well, that was going to be an interesting meeting for sure, what with Frankie not being able to sign and Bram not being able to talk. Oh yeah, this little heist they'd got going on had success written all over it, right?

*

'Viollet said you were talking to a cop,' Dougie said, a few minutes later after Bram had gone back inside. 'Two cops, actually. A woman and a man.'

Frankie glanced across at Dougie's informer and shot her his best *well, thanks a fucking bunch* look. For what it was worth, which wasn't much. Viollet still had her shades on and was giving nothing away. But, hell, she probably had photos of him with Sharon and Snaresby on that natty little camera of hers, didn't she? So not much point in him denying they'd met.

'They were involved in Jack's case,' he said.

'Susan's case,' Dougie hissed, his cheeks suddenly mottling.

'Er, yeah. Sorry. Right.'

'Snaresby and Granger,' Dougie said. 'Viollet said you and the Granger woman looked like you were friends.'

'Snug, Dougie,' Viollet said. 'The word I used was "snug".'

Snug. The same word Frankie had used to describe Viollet in the back of Dougie's car. Frankie rolled his eyes. Couldn't help himself. So that's what this was about, her shopping him like this? Some kind of petty revenge?

'Something you'd like to say?' Dougie asked.

'Nah. Nothing. Just something in my eye.'

'And the two cops?'

'We went to school together.'

'What? You and the Detective Inspector?' Dougie deadpanned. 'I always thought he was older than you.'

A shit joke. But the smartarse bastard had given something away with it too, hadn't he? *Always.* So this wasn't the first time Snaresby had popped up on his radar then. The two of them had history. Doing what? Just Susan Tilley's case, or something else?

'I meant Sharon,' Frankie said, realizing his mistake as soon as he'd said it.

'Oh, so you're on first name terms, are you?' said Dougie. 'That is properly snug.'

'It was nothing,' Frankie said. 'She just saw me there, said hello, end of.'

Dougie watched him the same way he'd watched him back at the Cobden Club, when he'd been grilling him about what he knew about Jack's involvement in Susan Tilley's death.

'Yeah, well do yourself a favour, Frankie, and choose your friends a little more wisely in future. We wouldn't want to think that you were getting too close to the other side.'

The *other side*? Christ, like Frankie was now on Dougie's team for good. He pictured Listerman. Felt bile rising up in his throat. Because of what he'd said. About it being one of life's great truisms that people who ended up working for more than one master generally ended up getting ripped apart.

'Sure,' Frankie said, 'I'll keep that in mind.'

Dougie beckoned Viollet over with a wave of his manicured hand. She leant down beside him and he whispered something in her ear.

'Viollet will drive you home,' he then said.

'It's fine, I can get a cab,' Frankie told him. Right now, even the thought of that woman made his skin crawl.

'No, I insist. I want you to realize that even dogs get to taste some of the finer things in life, so long as they're well behaved.'

Frankie was just opening his mouth to ask him what the hell he was talking about, but Dougie held up his hand.

'But first,' he said, 'before you go, there's something else I'd like you to see. Or, rather, someone.'

Viollet grimaced, as though the point Dougie was making was somehow moot.

'This way,' she said, setting off across the grassy lawn, back towards the building.

Frankie followed her. But where? Back inside to meet more of Bram's people? No. She kept to the right of the huge conservatory, skirting around it to the building's back wall, to where a flight of worn brick steps led down. Neither of them spoke. Frankie was still smarting about her having shopped him to Dougie like that about talking to Sharon. And, yeah, well fine, if she wanted to keep this strictly business then he'd make sure to skip the small talk too.

At the bottom of the steps was a solid-looking, black wooden door. She knocked on it loudly three times.

'Who's there?' a muffled voice called out a few seconds later.

'Me. Viollet.'

A key turned in the lock. The door opened. A short, thickset man in his mid-fifties peered out of the shadows inside, sweat glistening on his forehead.

'Who's he?' he grunted, looking Frankie suspiciously up and down.

'The boss told me to bring him here.'

'For keeps?' The man grinned as he said it.

Viollet didn't answer. The man pulled the door wider. He was naked from the waist up, with what looked horribly like dried blood smeared and spattered all over his chest-hair and arms. Frankie's heart skipped a beat. What the hell was this? He didn't like the look of this at all. He turned to look back over his shoulder. Because, yeah, maybe he should just get the hell out of here now. But there were already two blokes standing up there at the top of the steps, the same slick, suited geezers who'd been stood over by the garden wall before. Up close, he recognized one of them from the Paradise. Mob muscle, then. Must have been told to follow him and Viollet here. No way was he going to be able to slip past them.

'Well, then, don't be shy, come on in,' said the short man, bowing theatrically, as he waved Viollet and Frankie through.

Frankie felt the hairs on the back of his neck bristle as he walked past. What was this place? What did Dougie want him to see? A dank corridor led them deeper into the building. Cobwebbed brick walls. Yellow light bulbs flickering every couple of yards. A damp stink in the air. No, something worse than damp. More animal. More like old sweat and piss. Footsteps behind. Looking back, Frankie saw the bare-chested man was following. A white grin of uneven teeth in the gloom. He'd shut the door behind them leading out. Then voices up ahead. Chatter. A debate. A crackle of static. A radio show, then. Had to be.

Frankie stepped out into a vast, arched brick storage room. Then stopped dead in his tracks. His heartbeat stuttered, then hammered. Spit filled his mouth. He had to bite down on his tongue just to stop himself from throwing up.

There, right ahead of him, with two spotlights shining down, was a man manacled in a crucifix position on the wall. Or what was left of a man. If it even was a man. Whoever it was had been so beaten and battered and torn it was impossible to tell. He was literally drenched in blood.

'Pretty, i'nt he?' grinned the bare-chested man, resting a hand on Frankie's shoulder.

'Get the fuck off me,' Frankie snapped, pushing him away.

'Touchy, touchy. No need to be so rude,' the man laughed.

A groan. Bloody hell. Was it the man on the wall? The radio? Frankie couldn't tell. The bare-chested man walked over to a table set up against the wall. It had bats on it, crowbars, knives, even a sodding blood-stained electric iron. He picked up an apple sitting next to it and took a noisy bite.

'The fucking echo in here,' he complained, 'it's doing me head in. I'll be glad to see the back of this fucker, I tell you. When is it they're moving him out?'

'Just as soon as we're done,' Viollet said, pressing up against Frankie.

He was trembling now. From fear. She must be able to feel it too.

'Dougie wanted you to see what happens to people who let him down,' she whispered softly in his ear. 'And what will happen to you if, for whatever reason, you decide that pistol isn't enough to keep you doing what he tells you, and you decide to go squealing to your cop friends instead.'

Frankie slowly turned to face her. But to say what? That they weren't his friends? That he had already considered it, but had already chickened out? Because what was the point of telling her anything? Because she wasn't even a real person anyway, was she? Just another face of Dougie's. Another set of limbs doing whatever he said. Just exactly like Frankie was himself. But the coldness in her face then flickered, just for a second.

'Please, Frankie,' she whispered, pressing her finger to his lips, 'just do us all a favour and don't end up in here like him.'

10

The Aston Martin DB5 pulled out of the warehouse garage and onto Narrow Street with a roar so loud that people walking by stopped and stared. But up front, in the driver and passenger seats, Viollet and Frankie said nothing. He just stared straight ahead, trying not to close his eyes. Because whenever he did, he saw him again – whoever he was – those manacles . . . that blood . . . his pulpy mess of a face . . .

Was it him who'd groaned? Could he really have still been alive? Was there any way he could help him? But how? They'd already been moving him out – his body . . . It was already too late.

Frankie just wanted this journey done, just wanted out of here, and back into his own life. Problem was, instead Viollet was taking them the scenic route, nice and slow, like they were on a friggin' jolly, out along the river and then round Parliament, before finally gunning the Aston Martin up the Haymarket and on through Piccadilly Circus.

'Do us a favour,' Frankie said, the first time he'd spoken since he'd entered that basement, 'and drop us off somewhere I might not actually get seen by the whole bleedin' world.'

His world, he meant. Or Tommy Riley's, at least. Because that's where they were now. Right in the middle of Tommy's turf. And the last person Frankie needed to be seen with right now was Dougie Hamilton's right-hand man . . . or woman, Alsatian, whatever. Because that was the other thing, what he'd seen in that basement, he knew Tommy could match it. Tommy could and would hurt him just as bad.

He stared out the window, trying to swallow down the panic building up inside of him. But fuck. Fuck. Fuck. What the hell was he going to do? How the hell was he going to stop Dougie or Tommy ending by cutting him up?

'I said not here. Did you hear me?' he snapped.

She still didn't answer, but she didn't turn down Poland Street either. She carried on instead to the same multi-storey where Frankie kept his Capri. Drove right up to the top floor and – wouldn't you know it? – parked up in the bay right alongside it. Shit a brick. Was there anything this bloody woman and her even bloodier boss didn't know?

'Well, aren't you going to say thanks?' she said, still firmly in her shades-down mode.

'For what? Showing me your handiwork down in that basement?'

'Who said it was mine?'

'Who said it wasn't?'

She didn't answer. Meaning what? She'd had a part in it? In whatever had been done to that poor bastard? Or not?

'Who was he?'

She shrugged. 'Someone Dougie didn't like.'

'And you? Did you . . . did you do any of that to him?'

125

'Would you believe me if I said I didn't?'

He didn't know.

'So maybe let's just not talk about it at all. Anything else on your mind?'

'Well, yeah, as a matter of fact, there is.'

'So shoot,' she said.

'Like thanks for grassing me up,' he said, 'to your boss about me talking to those two cops.' Because, Christ, that was making him shiver now too. And could have landed him right there in that basement as well, if Dougie had got it into his head even for a second that Frankie was some kind of snitch.

'*Our* boss,' Viollet said, getting out. 'And don't take it so personally, Frankie. I work for Dougie. Keeping him in the picture's just part of my job.'

'And where do you think you're going?' he asked, getting out too.

She pipped the car's alarm and walked towards the lift. 'Oh, didn't I say? You're taking me back to your place.'

'No, you bloody didn't. And, no, I'm bloody not.'

'It's not a question, Frankie.' She hit the lift button. 'It's not even my idea.'

'Dougie wants you to come back to my place?' Frankie didn't understand. *I want you to realize that even dogs get to taste some of the finer things in life, so long as they're well behaved.* What the hell? So that hadn't just been about the car ride? But about Dougie putting Viollet on the menu? No way. He couldn't believe that was true. No way could he see her taking an order like that. Even from him.

She took out her camera, the same one she'd had at the

Royal Academy, the one that had no doubt provided all those photos Frankie had seen the rest of Bram's crew poring over inside David Lean's old pad just now.

'He wants me to check how much storage space you've got,' she said. 'Along with a few other things.'

Storage space? Oh, shit. What else was it Dougie had said? *And besides, who said I'm going to be keeping them at all?* The alarm bell that had started ringing in Frankie's head back then started up a right old clattering now.

'That wanker's planning on keeping all his nicked gear round at mine?'

Viollet nodded.

'But . . . but that's not even just my business, that's my bloody home.' The lift doors opened. 'I mean, you are joking, right?'

'Nope. You see, Dougie's got a very healthy attitude towards risks.' She stepped into the lift.

'Yeah?' He followed her inside. 'How bleedin' so?'

'He doesn't take any. He gets other people to take them for him.'

'Like him not coming with us on his little dog-stealing expedition?' Something changed in her expression as he said it. 'Oh, and let me guess, you're not coming either, right?'

'I just do what I'm told.'

'But all this shit he wants me and Bram and whatever to nick –'

'Art, Frankie. Remember, it's art,' she told him, as the lift doors closed.

'What-fucking-ever. Even if we do somehow get what-ever pieces he wants out of there, why can't he just keep them somewhere else?' *Anywhere else. Anywhere nowhere near bloody me.*

She finally lowered her shades and looked him briefly in the eyes. 'Oh, come, come now, Frankie. Let's not pretend that either of us has got a choice.'

More silence. But what did she mean? Did Dougie have something on her too?

'So who is he, then? This Bram?' Frankie said, as they stepped out onto the street and headed for the club. 'Just what is it that makes him such a . . . expert in this field?'

'I believe the phrase you *rooineks* use is *he's got form.*'

'*Rooineks?*'

'It's how we back home refer to you rednecks who always get so badly burned in the sun.'

Frankie thought back to the Hamilton boys in the Paradise, and yeah, fair enough, she wasn't far wrong.

'And how would a *yarpie* like you know what form someone like Bram has got?'

'*Yarpie?*' Her eyebrows arched in amusement. 'Touché. Though for your information *yarpie* generally tends to refer to someone who's worked on a farm – which I can assure you I have not.'

'No, I already know where you've worked. Ex-police, right?'

'Who told you that?'

'I've got my sources . . .' He'd wanted it to sound mysterious, as well as knowing, to try and get one up on her, but instead she just smiled.

'The Saint? Yeah. He's got an appropriately big mouth for a guy his size.'

'And is that how you know Bram's form, from back when you were a cop?'

'No, I moved to Europe after that. The Netherlands, if you must know. Private sector. Security.'

'A broad church that . . . and Bram was a colleague of yours there, was he?'

'More the other side of the fence . . .'

A crim then. Someone she'd caught? Or had maybe worked with? Because she must have crossed over to the wrong side of the fence herself at some point, or she wouldn't be working for Dougie now.

'But you trust him, right?'

'Trust is a very broad word.'

'I don't mean with your wallet. I mean with this gig, this heist.'

'I wouldn't have brought him in if I didn't.'

'Then I guess I'm just going to have to trust him too.' Frankie slowly shook his head, because, come, come, of course, he didn't have a choice. 'After you,' he said, opening the Ambassador Club's door.

'Hey, thar, boss,' Slim said, as Frankie led Viollet up to the bar.

'Hey yourself. Everything OK?' Frankie looked round. Ten or so punters in here. A few locals having a drink. But what did she make of it? Viollet. Hard to tell with those shades of hers on. And why should he care anyway? This was just business to her. Just like he was too. So what if she had incredible blue eyes? The sooner he got her out of here, the better.

'And can I get either of you a nice cold beverage to tickle your tastebuds on this far from inclement day?' Slim asked.

'Sorry, he's a bit of a walking dictionary,' Frankie told Viollet. 'No, we're good thanks, Slim. Vio – I mean Miss Coetzee here, she's with the, er . . .' Christ, what was she with? The Hamiltons? Murder Inc. ' . . . er, council,' he said. 'And we just need to run through a few quick fire regulation issues before she can sign off on the certificate for the tournament.'

Slim looked Viollet up and down, from her Gucci shades to her Jimmy Choos.

'The council, eh?'

'Yeah.' Frankie felt his skin prickle. He'd never been much of a liar, especially where friends were concerned.

'No clipboard?' Slim asked Viollet.

'Everything I need, I keep it up here,' she said.

'I'll bet you do.'

'Just chuck us the keys, will you?' Frankie said.

'Whatever you say, boss.' Slim blew a thin plume of smoke towards Viollet, before turning to the till.

'So, er . . . where do you want to start?' Frankie asked.

'The basement.'

Slim tossed Frankie the keys and he caught them clean and led Viollet through to the back of the club and unlocked the basement door.

'It's kind of creepy and spidery down here,' he warned, resisting the urge to add, *So you should fit in just fine.*

He hit the light switch and led her down into the windowless room. It was still pretty empty in here from when him and Xandra had cleared the worst of the crap out the year before last.

Viollet walked slowly around, gently drumming her knuckles on the bare brickwork every couple of feet. Even with the single bare light bulb on, it was still gloomy enough for Viollet to have had to take off her shades, so he could now see those eyes of hers again. So, yeah, maybe not such a terrible environment, after all.

'Good and solid, and plenty of room for what we've got in mind,' she said. 'Dry too. Of course, you're going to need to put in a dehumidifier, just to be on the safe side. And make sure the filter's changed on a daily basis. By you. Not Hopalong Cassidy up there or anyone else. Oh, and get the locks changed too. We don't want anyone else down here but you.' She glanced back up the stairs. 'And the door. We're going to need something much more secure.'

'Anything else?' Sarcasm. Boom.

She ignored it. 'Uh-huh, these old pipes . . .' She meant the ones running across the ceiling and was tall enough to press her fingers up against them. 'They're cold. Are they even connected to anything?'

'What do I look like, a plumber?'

She looked him up and down. 'I thought I already told you I thought you were more boy band.'

'Crappy boy band,' he corrected her.

'Like there's another kind?'

'Fair enough. But no, I'm not exactly the practical kind.'

She tapped the pipes again. 'OK, so find out what these are doing here. Then get them either stripped out or re-routed. And have the ceiling checked too. It looks solid enough, but we need to be sure.' She was already walking back up the stairs. 'Oh, and cost isn't an issue. Just get the best. Dougie and his associates will be picking up the bill.'

Huh, well that was something, at least. Frankie grimaced. *Idiot.* Because he was falling, wasn't he? Right into Dougie's trap. Into doing what he was told, when he was told. *And* into then feeling grateful too for whatever pathetic scraps he was thrown.

'Oh, and Frankie?'

'What?' Those blue eyes of hers were staring right into his.

'I really can't impress on you how important it is that you don't talk to anyone else about what you're going to be keeping here.'

She didn't need to say any more. Frankie could still see him, that man . . . or what was left of him. Had he had kids? A wife? Did anyone even know he was gone?

He followed Viollet back up the stairs.

'What's through there?' she asked, pointing at the door at the end of the corridor.

'Xandra's place.'

'Who's she?'

'I'm she,' said Xandra, coming up behind them, walking through from the bar with a stack of empty beer crates in her arms. 'Full-time lodger. Part-time manager, caretaker. At your service.' She put down the crates and stood arms folded, that black panther of hers flexing. 'And who might you be?' she asked.

'Miss Coetzee? From the council. Fire regs,' Frankie said.

Xandra stared Viollet dead in the eyes, clearly thinking

she didn't exactly look like your regular council type. 'You will forgive me if I don't drop down on one knee,' she said.

'Oh, curtsy, I get it,' Viollet dead-toned. 'What a very original sense of humour you have.'

Xandra smiled at her flatly. 'So what's fire regs got to do with the basement?' she asked.

'Er . . .' A good point. Frankie's mind went blank. He looked to Viollet.

'Wine,' she said. 'He's applied for a licence to keep wine down here. With proper heating and humidity controls.'

Wine. Of course. In a cellar. A wine cellar. The perfect cover.

'But you don't even like wine,' Xandra said to Frankie.

'No.'

'You don't even drink.'

Viollet raised an eyebrow at this.

'It's not for me,' Frankie said.

'Then who? The club? What's wrong with the storeroom round the back of the bar that we already use?'

'This wine's, er, different,' said Frankie. 'Expensive. An investment. It has to, er, be kept in the right conditions, or else it will . . .'

'Degrade,' Viollet said.

'And that seriously needs a council licence?' Xandra said, still not fully buying it. But the last thing Frankie needed was her or anyone else sticking their nose in. Do that and they'd only end up in danger too.

'Yeah,' he said, 'because of the temperature control equipment, right?'

'Correct,' Viollet said, turning her back on Xandra.

133

'There's also a back alley here running along the buildings that your fire escape leads out onto,' she said to Frankie. Another statement, not a question.

'Dog Shit Alley's its official nomenclature,' Xandra said. 'Sorry, another one of Slim's,' she added. 'It must be catching.'

Viollet ignored her. 'Show me,' she told Frankie.

He unlocked the back door and stepped outside with her into the sun. For a second, he felt the months and years hurtling backwards, and remembered shoving Jack out here on the morning he'd turned up covered in blood, with Snaresby's thug cops already smashing down the club's front door.

Viollet looked up and down the alley which ran along the backs of the buildings, then her eyes seemed to settle on something just past the bins at the south end. She walked towards it. What the hell was she up to now?

'What is it?' he said, following her. 'Oh, and by the way, if you wouldn't mind not actually ordering me around in front of the people I work with, then that might, just might, make them think that you haven't actually got me doing all this shit for you under duress.'

She ignored him and kept walking, finally stopping next to a single-storey red-brick building at the end of the alley. Well, building was being generous. Because, whatever this was, it was strictly utilitarian. No windows. Just the one door, made out of metal, and painted green. Plastered across its centre was a fluorescent sticker, with the words 'Thames Water' printed beneath a running tap symbol. Frankie had never even noticed it before, even though he must have snuck down here for hundreds of crafty cigarettes as a teen-ager over the years.

'Don't tell me,' he said, as he watched her reading it. 'You're planning on getting a real job? An honest day's wage for an honest day's work? Giving something back to the community for a change?'

'Is that meant to be funny?'

'Ah, well, the test for that is if it makes you do this.' Frankie smiled.

'It doesn't.'

She walked back down the alley to the back of the club and stared up the fire escape leading onto the roof.

'What's up there?'

'The sky.'

'I mean lower than that.'

'My flat.'

'There next.'

He opened his mouth to protest. But why bother? She'd already made the unilateral decision to use his basement as a lock-up for stolen art. What on earth would make her think that she couldn't do whatever the hell she wanted in his home as well?

He led her back out through the front of the club and in at the flat's street entrance, rather than going up from the club. Both Slim and Xandra were already busy behind the bar and dealing with customers, thank God, because he didn't want either of them seeing him taking her upstairs, not with their suspicions already aroused as it was. What he had to avoid at all costs was them getting even a sniff of the truth. It was one thing his life potentially being ruined over this, but no bloody way was he going to be taking either of them down with him. The less they knew, the better. The only way to keep them safe.

Frankie's mum stared disapprovingly down at Viollet from her vantage point on the hallway wall.

'Who's she?'

'My mum.'

'Are you sure?'

'Eh?'

'She just seems too pretty to be related to you.'

'Ha bloody ha.'

'She live here with you?'

'No, she's . . .' He didn't want to get into this. Not with her. ' . . . no longer around.'

'Nice feel to the place,' Viollet said, walking ahead of him down the corridor, trailing her fingertips across the flock wallpaper.

'I'm getting it done up.'

'Yeah?'

'Yeah.' Though why the hell was he telling her that? Who gave a shit what she thought?

She walked through into the lounge. Xandra had already finished redecorating the bathroom and kitchen and had now started prepping in here. Groundsheets covered the furniture and floor. The walls and ceilings had all been sugar-soaped and fillered.

'I thought you said you weren't the practical kind?' Viollet said, as Frankie joined her.

'I'm not. This is Xandra's work. The girl you met down-stairs.'

'And she's . . . ?'

'Not my girlfriend. I'm not her type.' Viollet waited for him to say more, but he didn't. Xandra's private life was none of Viollet Coetzee's friggin' business. 'Listen,' he said. 'I really don't know why we need to be here.' Because what was she planning now? Christ, he dreaded to think.

She stuck her head round the bathroom and spare-room doors, then walked through to the kitchen. 'You live here on your own, then.' Another statement.

'What makes you say that?' And more to the point, what bloody business of yours is it, anyway?

'One plate in the sink. One knife. One fork. Football clutter all over the walls.'

'Oi, that's not clutter, those are collector's items that –'

'One PlayStation control on the living-room sofa . . . one *Mission: Impossible* DVD case on the table . . . one dirty running kit and one wet towel on the bathroom floor . . .' She pressed 'Play' on the little midi sound system on top of the microwave. AC/DC's 'Thunderstruck' started pumping out. She just raised one eyebrow as though that settled the argument.

'That's not proof of anything. I know plenty of girls who like AC/DC, actually,' Frankie said, but she was already walking back down the corridor.

'And through here?' she said.

'My bedroom.'

She walked in ahead of him.

'It's not exactly very homely, is it?'

She had a point. The Old Man had never been one for clutter when this had been his, and in spite of Frankie's decision to try and make the place feel a bit more his, all he'd actually done was move his Arsenal scarf – another *collector's* item, thank you very much – in from where it had been hanging off his top bunk in the spare room and pinned it up here on the wall above the window. But who the hell was she to be criticizing his choice in interior decor anyway? Surely not even Dougie thought his current control of Frankie ran to that?

'Oh, and let me guess,' he said, 'your bedroom, wherever the fuck that is, is no doubt jam-packed with loving little domestic flourishes . . . crystal perfume bottles on the windowsills, fluffy toy bunnies on the crocheted pillow cases?' More like a razor-sharp bloody samurai sword on the wall and a sawn-off shotgun under the bed.

She smiled at him tolerantly, the same way he always did himself whenever one of the locals got pissed and on a political rant down at the bar.

'If you even have a home,' he said. 'I mean, of your own. Not wherever it is that Dougie's got you shacked up.'

Her cocksure smile slipped at that. A sore point. Because it was true? Because he was right and something serious *was* going on between them?

'Just to be clear,' he said, 'I'm not saying that just because you're a bird.'

'Bird?' That raised right eyebrow again.

'Girl.'

And again.

'All right, woman. Whatever. No, I'm saying it because I saw you in the back of that limo with him outside the Paradise on the day of his dad's funeral and –'

'Yeah, a point you've already raised.'

'Only I didn't just see you getting into it and sitting beside him . . .' Frankie watched her carefully. '. . . I saw you kissing him too.'

'And you're telling me this because . . . ?'

What a question. But why *was* he telling her this? Because he was annoyed at her? For marching him round his own club and now his own bloody flat too? Because her whole bleedin' holier-than-thou attitude was making him feel even bloody worse about himself than he already was? Or just because he wanted to knock her down a peg or two and remind her that she was every bit as much a pawn in Dougie's games as he was himself?

She answered her own question with another: 'Because you'd rather it was you in the back of that car instead of him?'

Frankie's cheeks prickled. 'If you mean would I rather it was me calling the shots . . .' *And not being shat upon.* '. . . then, yeah, I would.'

She looked him dead in the eyes. 'You know that's not what I meant.'

That prickle turned to a burn. 'Look, I don't know what kind of power play this is –'

She ignored him. 'Mind if I take a seat?'

'Or whether there is an actual reason why we're up here.'

But she was still ignoring him. She sat down on the edge of the mattress and used the toe of her left shoe to prise off the heel of her right.

'As in a real reason,' he said, 'like to do with our business, this whole fucking scheme that you and Dougie have cooked up . . .' Frankie was trying his best not to look down at her legs. Trying, and almost succeeding too. '. . . and if there is, I think that maybe you should just, you know, cut to the fucking chase, OK?'

'OK then. Strip.'

'What?'

'Oh, come on, it's not like one of your friend Slim's long words. Not like inclement,' she said, removing her shades and unleashing those blue eyes again. 'I'm sure you know what it means.'

'Huh?' Had Frankie just heard right?

'Just take your clothes off.'

OK, so he had.

'Seriously. I want to see what you look like. Under that.'

Frankie tugged at his shirt. 'This?'

'Yeah. But not just that. Those too.'

She was staring at his shorts.

'And this is to do with Dougie's crazy scheme how exactly?' Was she serious? What, was she checking him for a wire? Christ, he'd seen that in enough crime shows, but did she really think he –

'Oh no, this has got nothing to do with Dougie at all.'

'No?'

'This isn't him asking. It's me.'

What was it she'd said before? 'And you're telling me this because . . . ?'

Again with that arched right eyebrow. Her left shoe went next. She propped up two pillows against the bedhead and leant back against them.

'Whenever you're ready,' she said.

Should he just tell her to piss off? To get out? To . . . stop slowly unbuttoning her shirt . . . the way she was doing now? Yeah, of course. The last thing he needed was to get tangled up with this one any more than he already was. For one thing, she was a killer. Or at least according to The Saint. And if even that big lump of steak was scared of her, then Frankie sure as hell should be too. And who knows what part she'd had in that poor fucker's fate in the basement? And, for another, she worked for Dougie. And, for a third, she was with him that way too. Or, at least, she hadn't denied it, meaning something was certainly going on.

So, yeah. Definitely a no. Only . . . only he couldn't quite get the word out, could he? Especially not now she was easing off her skirt, still watching him with that raised eyebrow and that twinkle in her eyes.

'Well?' she said.

Sod it. He pulled his T-shirt off over his head.

'Not bad,' she said.

Her eyes settled on his shorts again.

'I should warn you,' he said. 'I've got nothing on under these.'

'Good,' she said, smiling. 'That should speed things up considerably. Now enough prevaricating.' Done in the same tone she'd said *inclement*. 'Just get them *off.*'

*

It was dark by the time they'd finished. Frankie's phone must have rung five or six times in the intervening time and his doorbell twice too. Probably Slim or Xandra wondering where the hell he was. For once, he didn't care. Whatever it was, they could handle it. He was done in. In a good way. Something he'd not felt in a long while.

Viollet was lying with her head on his chest, smoking a cigarette. Oddly, he'd not even been tempted to cadge one off her. There was nothing he really felt he needed right now.

'So, do you think you would have come here if he hadn't told you to?' he asked, running his hand through her hair. He still couldn't quite believe it. That she was here. That they'd just done what they had.

'Into the building, or your bed?'

'To me . . .'

'Oh, I think so. Even if I hadn't had to come here to check out the cellar, I think I might have found a way. Why? Do you think you'd have invited me yourself?'

'Well, that would have been a . . . bold move, wouldn't you say?'

'What, am I that intimidating?'

He groaned. Happily. She still had him gripped in her hand.

'No, I don't mean it like that,' he said.

'Then what?'

'I mean because of him.'

'Dougie?'

'The boss's girl is generally considered to be off limits. Hazardous to the health.'

'I'm nobody's girl.'

'No, I can believe that. But you are still with him, aren't you?'

'It's complicated.'

'Too complicated to get into now? With me?'

She reached over and stubbed out her cigarette on the ashtray he'd put out for her on the bedside table. Her skin looked golden in the glow of the street lamps filtering in through the blinds.

'Well?' he asked, as she lay back down and slid her arm around him.

'You really want to get into this? Now? Why I'm with him?'

He stared down at her naked body. 'Now does seem like an appropriate time.'

'OK, er . . . because he's got an enormous cock?' she said.

'I'm serious.'

'Fine.' She rolled her eyes. He was still getting used to seeing them all the time. 'Because he's got a great sense of humour?' She smiled, something he still couldn't get used to seeing at all. '*And* an enormous cock.'

'Because he *is* an enormous cock, more like,' Frankie said.

'He's not so bad, when you get to know him.'

'We'll see . . .' Frankie had always tried to look on the bright side. That's what his mum had always taught him. No matter what. But, Christ, whenever he thought of Dougie, all he saw was dark. Because, forget all his posh clothes and posh words – he was just as nasty a wanker as his dad had ever been. Maybe even worse.

'So what about us?' he asked. Hadn't meant to. But here it was. Out there. And right away, he could see it was the wrong thing to have said.

'There is no us,' she told him, no longer smiling.

'No?'

'No.'

'So what's this?' he tried, trailing his fingers down her arm that was hooked around his neck.

'My arm.'

'And this?' He kissed her softly on the shoulder.

'My shoulder.'

'And this?' He started to move his head down lower, but she pushed him away.

'This . . . *all* of this,' she said, 'this was a one-off. Past tense.' She rolled away from him and sat on the edge of the bed. 'Call it curiosity,' she said.

'Curiosity?'

'Curiosity satisfied.' She stood up and picked up her knickers from the floor.

'And now?'

'Now I go back to my boss. Our boss,' she said, continuing to dress.

'And it's that easy for you, is it? To compartmentalize like that. Pleasure in this box. Business in that.'

'It's what works best. For everyone,' she said.

And maybe she was right. Because this couldn't work, could it? It would only lead to trouble for them both. And yet . . . there was something about her, even now, standing with her back to him, pulling on her shoes, about to walk back out of his life. What *would* happen if he asked her to stay? If he told her he wanted to see her again? But when she turned he saw that the moment had already gone. *This*, what had happened here, had gone. It was over. That steeliness was back in her eyes. No more pleasure. Just business now.

'Maybe you've got a point,' he said, standing up.

Her eyes dropped from his face to his waist. 'And maybe you do too . . .'

A trace of a smile there, and he couldn't help smiling back. 'Yeah, well you seem to have this effect on me. Had,' he said, pulling on his shorts. 'Because that's what this is now, right? Past tense?'

'Yes. And probably best not to mention this to anyone either. As in ever. For both of our sakes.'

She didn't have to say it, but he knew she was thinking it too. That warehouse basement. Get caught messing with Dougie, and that's where they'd both end up.

'Aye,' he said. 'Amen to that.'

11

With the tournament's opening night now less than a week away, Frankie spent the next five days running around London like a blue-arsed fly. From having felt well organized for the last few months, all his careful, careful planning and preparation for the tournament now seemed suddenly horribly half-baked.

At least he'd already written the speech he was going to give before the opening matches, thanking all the sponsors and the powers that be. He'd been practising it in his free time so much that already he was now practically saying it in his sleep. He'd also written so many lists and left them lying around the place – the bar, the tables, the stairs, the ruddy bog – that Xandra had even written 'Write more lists!' on one of them.

Thank God, though, that he at least had help from people like her. That's what he kept telling himself as the week wore on: he wasn't alone. Andy Topper and Kind Regards were dealing with the bulk of the business side of things, leaving Frankie to concentrate on the logistics. And he'd at least done a good job delegating what he could here.

Jack had got the James Boys Gym nicely primed, with its

rings temporarily shipped out, in time for Festive Al delivering the four competition tables round there on Wednesday afternoon. Meanwhile, back at the Ambassador, as well as helping Slim and Frankie get it as near to looking like a top-flight sporting venue as it was ever going to, Xandra was bossing the conversion of her downstairs flat into a Green Room for the players to hang out in between frames, and had temporarily moved in upstairs into the spare room bunk beds with her girlfriend, Maxine, who thought this was the funniest thing in the world.

But throughout all this was the heist itself, hanging over Frankie like the Sword of bleedin' Damocles, threatening at any second to drop down and spear him right through his noggin like a ruddy kebab.

He still didn't even know when the actual robbery was taking place, though the *Sensation* exhibition itself opened in just over a week, so it would have to be some time before then, right?

He'd done what he could to prepare. The basement, in other words. He'd outsourced the work, and the builders had arrived Monday to get stuck in, much to the annoyance of Xandra, who was still labouring under the illusion that the only thing going to be stored down there was plonk. But with Dougie picking up the tab, cost wasn't an issue and speed was. Frankie had needed the whole job done before the tournament kicked off, so he'd paid through the nose for it. By Thursday afternoon, it had all been fitted up to the specs Viollet had stipulated. A good job too. Who knew, if Dougie ever did decide to shift these art pieces on, then

Frankie might even get into wine investment and storage for real.

Come Thursday, eight o'clock, and he'd just checked on the dehumidifiers and temperature down there, before locking the basement's new and practically bombproof door. He'd had a hell of a day. Apart from cajoling the builders into getting done on time, he'd been overseeing the removal of the club's tatty tables, the delivery of the competition tables, and the erection of the blocks of tiered seating for the audience. Oh, and he'd squeezed in an interview that The Topster had set up with the *Evening Standard*, to boot.

Well knackered, he was, and planning on an early one and a takeaway pizza, Hawaiian, with extra pineapple on top. Only then the bar phone rang, and it was Viollet, with another set of instructions on where to meet The Saint for his latest ride. Without so much as a bleedin' *hello* either, like last Friday night had never happened at all.

The ride in the back of The Saint's cab passed in a blur. The big man up front tried making conversation, but Frankie wasn't in the mood. The Saint gave up after a while, and banged on more Streisand. Somewhere in the middle of her singing 'You Don't Bring Me Flowers', Frankie fell asleep, and when he woke up they weren't even in London at all. The countryside. He shivered, watching the dark silhouettes of the trees flow by. He hated it out here. Away from the sirens, the car alarms and the smog. Quiet, it was. Too quiet. This was how horror films always started, with journeys like this.

Another twenty minutes of winding lanes and piss all else and The Saint pulled up into a pub car park. 'The Bat &

Ball', the sign said. Well, thank heavens for small mercies. At least it wasn't The Slaughtered Lamb.

'Welcome to Berkshire. You look right knackered,' said The Saint, getting out. 'Well pasty. You should get yourself a holiday sorted. And soon too. Seriously, yeah?' He stared hard at Frankie for a second or two. 'Somewhere nice and far away?'

'Er, right.'

Frankie followed The Saint up to the pub door. No music, no laughter coming from inside. But look on the bright side, at least there was little chance of bumping into Tommy Riley or any of his squad this far out of W1.

'Oh no, not you, Wee Willie Winkie,' said The Saint, looking back at Frankie as he reached the front door. 'This is where I'm going to have myself a few nice warm pints of Good Old Boy and quietly frighten the locals, before I head back into town.'

Frankie wondered what his chances were of getting a real cab around here. Somewhere between zero and none.

The Saint pointed a fat finger into the dark fields at the back of the pub. 'You go thataway.'

'But . . .'

'Thataway, scrote.' Growling a phlegmy laugh, The Saint stooped and squeezed his bulk in through the pub door and heaved it shut behind him.

Thataway. Whichaway? Frankie walked cautiously in the direction he'd been pointed. But there was nothing. Not even a sodding farm track. Just black hedges and a starlit sky. Something cried out in the bushes. Some kind of sodding bird. Or at least he hoped. But then he noticed a gap in the hedge. A gate.

Heading for it, he spotted some dim lights shining at the back of the field beyond. He made towards them, readying himself to scarper at any second. Because you could run into anything in a field like this, couldn't you? A pig. A horse. Even a bull.

A caravan. That's what the lights were, he saw as he got close. Nice too. All silver and shiny. What you might call a bit of luxury kit. Four little windows all giving off a nice warm yellow light. Meaning somebody had to be at home. He took a deep breath before he knocked on the door. The Saint had mentioned driving himself back into town, but hadn't said shit about Frankie, had he? Meaning what? Maybe Frankie wasn't going back at all? He heard music as he got closer. That Foo Fighters shit that Xandra was into. Felt kind of out of place out here.

He rapped his knuckles hard on the caravan door. Whatever this was, time to just get it done with, and then get home.

No reply.

'Knock, knock,' he called out.

'Who's there?'

'Frankie.'

'Frankie who?'

Frankie recognized the voice right away. Rivet. Well, thank God for that. Far better him than that evil bare-chested fucker from the warehouse basement, that was for sure.

'Frankie goes to fucking Hollywood. Who do you bloody think?' he said, pushing the door open and stepping inside.

'So, how's it hanging, bro?' Rivet asked, grinning up at him from the little bench he'd been lounging on.

'Yeah, good, man. Good.' Frankie looked around. Lots of wood and hippy curtains and cushions. Well spacious too. 'A nice little place you've got here,' he said. 'For a minute there, I thought you'd set up a burger van.'

'Good one.' Mini-Billy Idol hit him with a high five, which Frankie promptly missed making full contact with.

'Sorry, mate,' he said, shaking his hands instead, 'I'm bollocks at that shit.'

'You hungry?' Rivet asked.

'Now you mention it.' Frankie's nostrils twitched. He could smell cooking: chilli. Right on cue, Lola stuck her head round the corner from what he guessed must be the galley, with a ladle in her hand, and flashed him an awkward little smile. 'Smells good,' he said. 'Count me in.'

'Rivet made it,' she said, 'but I'm just spicing it up.'

Rivet fixed Frankie a Diet Coke and then Bram came through from one of the rooms out back. He acknowledged Frankie's existence with a nod, before slumping down at the table at the end of the living area. Rivet and Lola then served up food and the four of them chowed down. Frankie couldn't help noticing, on the window ledge behind them, piles of what looked like the photos and architectural plans he'd seen them studying when he'd first met them down in David Lean's old pad.

'So, if you don't mind me asking,' Frankie said, 'why the hell are we meeting out here in the sticks?'

'The what?' said Lola.

'The middle of butt fuck nowhere,' Frankie explained.

'Oh, because this is where we're staying.'

'For real?'

'Hell, yeah, for real. Why not?' Rivet asked.

'Because it's . . . I don't know,' Frankie said. ' . . . While I get it, yeah, that it's nicely, er, salubrious, it's not exactly convenient for where we're going to be operating, is it?'

'Salubrious. Cool word. Hey, Bram,' Rivet said, 'you got any idea how to sign it?'

Bram signed something quickly back, which Rivet copied. 'Neat,' he said.

Then Bram signed something more complicated.

'He says that's the whole point. To be as far away from the city and all its distractions while we're planning. To purify our clarity of thought.'

How very zen. 'Fair enough,' Frankie said, not wanting to rock the boat – or caravan, anyhow. Aside from needing this lot to be right on the top of their game, if this heist was to go off as planned, he quite liked them. As individuals, that was. Not in the wider sense, in that they were working for Dougie. But, all that aside, they were OK. Even Bram seemed all right today.

'So where's Luke?' he asked.

'Huh?'

'*Luuk*,' he said. He meant the guy with the jeweller's eyepiece, who'd been studying the plans in the basement of that warehouse on Narrow Street.

'Oh, right . . . er, well, that's kind of another reason we've moved out here,' Rivet said. 'We ran into a little trouble back in town.'

'Or he did,' Lola added.

'With the authorities,' Rivet said.

'You mean we've been compromised?' Frankie felt his blood run cold.

'Well, hey, I don't know about you, Frankie, but I was *compromised*' – he used his fingers to put this last word in quotes – 'way back when I was a teenager.'

'I don't mean that. I mean *this*.' Frankie nodded at the photos and plans.

'Luuk . . . he drinks,' Lola said.

Bram signed.

'Way too much,' Lola translated.

'And the long and the short?' Rivet sighed. 'He got himself arrested fighting in some bar. And that's when the authorities discovered he didn't have a, well, valid passport.'

'*And* had broken his parole,' Lola said.

'In the Netherlands.'

Frankie gawped, but then something hit him. 'But, in that case, we can't go on, can we?' he said, jumping at the chance. 'With any of this. We'll have to cancel it. Because now that *he*'s been arrested, this whole robbery's bloody scuppered, isn't it? Because what if he talks?'

'He won't.'

'You don't know that!'

Bram held up a meaty middle finger to his lips.

'Yeah, Bram's right,' said Lola. 'You really should keep your voice down, in case anyone hears.'

'Like who?' said Frankie. 'We're in the middle of a field.'

'Hey, I don't know. Maybe there's foragers,' Rivet said.

'Foragers?'

'OK, then. Badger baiters . . . owl spotters . . . poachers.'

'Poachers? We're in Royal bloody Berkshire, 1997. Not Mills and bloody Boon, 1897.'

'Mills and what?' asked Lola.

'The point being, Frankie, just keep the goddamned volume down,' Rivet said.

An order. Not a request. Rivet's whole pally demeanour had just been switched off like a light. Because, yeah, here it was. Frankie wasn't boss of bloody anything, was he? Just here to do as he was told.

'OK, OK, but I mean it,' he said, 'he still might talk. If he's in real shit over this parole, he still might just decide to –'

'He's Bram's brother.'

'Brother?'

'Baby brother.'

'But he looks about a hundred and ten,' Frankie said, picturing that wrinkled bastard down there in that converted warehouse again.

'Yeah, well a fifteen-year horse addiction will do that to a guy,' Rivet said behind his hand. 'Not something Bram likes us to talk about, though, OK?' He cleared his throat. 'So how about we all now just get down to business?' he said.

With Frankie still fuming, Rivet and Lola cleared away the plates, while Bram spread out the photographs and the plans on the table.

'So let's start with you, Frankie,' Rivet said, as him and Lola sat back down. 'Why do you think you're here?'

'To help you rob that place.'

'Yeah . . . but why you?'

'I don't bloody know.' What was this? Twenty questions? 'Because Dougie can make me. Because I can handle myself. Because he knows I might come in useful in certain circumstances.' Violent circumstances, he meant. But he didn't want to get into that now. 'And, yeah,' he added, thinking back to his chat with Dougie at the Royal Academy, 'because I know a bit about art.'

'Yeah, right,' Rivet laughed, glancing at the others, who were smiling too. 'Dougie Hamilton chose you, because you nearly once got an Art B-level –'

'A-level.'

'Whatever, and because you know so much about Chris Ofili and modern art, yeah?' Another smile.

'So that *isn't* the reason?'

'Hell, no,' Rivet said. 'You're just one of, like, ten schmucks Dougie's got dangling over various things that he could have used for this. It just so happened that when Big Brains here . . .' He meant Bram. ' . . . got to thinking about how to crack this nut, it turned out you were the best person, geographically speaking, to help us out with this shit.'

'Geographically?'

'Uh-huh.'

More signing from Bram. Another snigger from Rivet. Lola too this time.

'Exactly right . . . the shit led us straight to you.'

155

'What shit?'

'The sewers. The ones that stop right outside your door.'

Frankie just stared, because what the hell was Rivet talking about now?

Bram jabbed a finger at one of the pieces of paper on the table.

'That there's a sewer map,' Rivet said. 'I mean, I think there's a more technical term for it, actually. Like a schematic, or some such. But, yeah, a map. One that leads from right here, at the access point in the courtyard at the Royal Academy . . .'

Bram traced his finger along a zigzagging route across the map.

' . . . to here,' Rivet said, 'just outside your club's back door. Or less than a hop, skip and a jump away, anyways.'

Frankie leant in to get a closer look. A black circle on the schematic, with '17 C' written alongside it.

'What *is* that?'

'A sewer maintenance point. With an entrance up on ground level. You've probably walked past it a thousand times before without even noticing it was there.' And, oh yeah, now Frankie saw it. That little red-brick building at the end of the alley at the back of the club. The one Viollet had inspected when she'd come round. The one she must have already known was there.

'You're planning on bringing all the artwork out through the sewers?' Frankie could hardly believe it, but he could see from their faces it was true.

Bram signed something fast at Lola, who cracked up laughing.

'What?' Frankie said.

'He said, "In London, it'll probably be quicker than going by taxi."'

Lola smiled. 'And *that's* why Dougie chose you for this . . .'

Frankie stared down at the map again. 'Because I live near "17 C" . . .'

'Right.'

'*And* because you owe him,' Rivet said. 'Because you've got no choice.'

Owe him? More like he'd been mugged.

'Bringing all the pieces out this way and into your club means there's zero chance of us getting seen.'

A quick flurry of signs from Bram.

'Abracadabra, indeed,' Rivet said. 'It'll be like all those pieces just vanished in a puff of smoke . . . leaving the cops, and anyone else who tries working out what the hell happened, scratching their heads and at a complete and utter loss. The perfect Houdini move,' he said, smiling at Bram, who grinned gummily back. 'Exactly what Mr Hamilton wants.'

Mr Hamilton? It didn't quite ring right to Frankie's ear. Sith Lord, or *Führer*, now that would have been more apt.

'But . . .'

'But what?' Rivet said.

'Once they realize they've been robbed, what'll stop them sending . . . I don't know, dogs, whatever, down into the sewers after us? And what if they then track us as far as round the back of the club . . . *my* club?' Christ, and what if they then found that CCTV footage of Frankie there at

157

the RA less than two weeks before with Dougie friggin' Hamilton? What then?

But far from looking panicked, Rivet was smiling. 'Don't worry, we're going to misdirect them.'

'Huh?'

'Make it look like we took all those goodies out by another route,' Lola said.

'An almost impossible route,' Rivet said. 'To keep that element of magic that's going to make this such a goddamn attractive proposition for the press.'

Something to – what was it Dougie had said? – *really put this exhibition on the map. Globally. And permanently.*

'Such as?' Frankie said. Because, OK, so he might not have looked round the whole building exactly last time he'd been there, but there was no getting away from the fact it was slap bang in the centre of London, surrounded by other buildings and roads jammed with potential witnesses to any dodgy-looking shenanigans that went down.

'Don't worry, that's Bram's department,' said Lola.

Bram signed and Rivet translated: 'And a good magician never reveals his –'

'Secrets,' said Frankie. 'So, basically, what you're telling me is you don't trust me,' he said.

Bram signed something.

Rivet nodded. 'Nope, it's just we do everything on a need-to-know basis is all. And that whole side of things, it's just not something you're going to be involved with on the night.'

'All that stuff's down to me,' Lola said.

'So which bit of the plan *do* I need to know?' said

Frankie. 'And when *is* the night? Or don't I get trusted with that information yet either?'

The three of them exchanged glances. Bram nodded his great big crew-cut bucket of a head.

'Monday night.'

'Which Monday? This Monday coming?' Frankie felt a rush of adrenaline.

'Yeah, that's right. The fifteenth.'

Bloody hell. The day after the tournament finished. Oh well, that was just dandy, wasn't it? Because, yeah, oh sure, he'd be nicely rested up, with plenty of energy for the heist. Not.

Lola shuffled the papers around and pulled out a set of floor plans with an arrowed route marked on it. Her long shirt sleeve rode up as she stretched. Track marks on her arms. A junkie, then? She looked way too healthy. Ex, then. Way back. Meaning maybe her and Luuk had been – Frankie realized she'd seen him staring . . . . They all were. It hit him harder than ever, then. Pally as they might be, these guys were a team and he was just the new kid on the block. Someone they'd been landed with. Someone, he now saw, they'd cut loose the second anything went wrong.

'Once we're inside, and leave the how of all that to us too,' Lola said, 'you're going to be going this way with Rivet and Bram . . .'

Frankie followed the route she traced on the plans. It led from the sewer access they'd pinpointed inside the Royal Academy grounds and on into the depths of the main building complex, to what looked like, yeah, he reckoned it was, the same gallery Dougie had taken him into, where the exhibition pieces were being unpacked.

'You're going to need to memorize this,' Lola said, 'as well as the exhibits we're going to be asking you to extract.'

She pushed one of the piles of photographs across to him, all of them portable works by the various artists Dougie and his pals must have invested in.

Frankie looked from Lola to Rivet to Bram. 'And the alarms?' he said. 'I mean, I take it there *are* alarms. And state-of-the-art ones too, right?'

Another series of looks between the three of them. Another nod from Bram.

'OK, so that's where our fifth columnist comes into play.'

'You've got a guy on the inside?'

'Another poor schmuck Dougie's got on his books,' Rivet said. 'This poor prick's kid owes gambling money. Helping us is his way of paying it off.'

'What? And he's going to just what? Kill the alarm while we're in there?' Could it really be that simple? Frankie doubted it or people would just be blackmailing museum employees all the time. 'What about everyone else who's working there? Won't they guess something is up?'

Bram nodded.

'Exactly,' said Rivet. 'Plus, then our guy would be the first person the cops would be looking at. Which is why we need to be smarter. *He's* not going to switch it off. He's going to get his *boss* to decide to switch it off.'

'But how?' More looks between them. This time no nod. 'Something else I don't need to know, right?'

'Don't sweat the details, Frankie,' Rivet said. 'Bram says it's going to work . . . and that's all you need to know.'

Frankie stared at the big guy for a couple of seconds. Bram stared unblinking back. Clearly not exactly the worrying kind. Well, OK, fine. Have a little faith. And maybe even pray. A lot.

'And this sewer,' he asked, 'it is big enough, right? To manage this. For us to carry these pieces back through?'

'I'm not saying it's going to be easy,' Rivet said.

Bram pinched his nose between his massive forefinger and thumb. A half a smile to go with it.

'Or pleasant,' Rivet said. 'But, yeah, with the right equipment, and a bit of luck, we should be OK.'

Luck. Great. And Frankie had had such a good run of it of late.

'OK,' Frankie said. 'So run me through it again. From start to finish. If I'm going to do this shit, then I want to do it right.'

Bram reached for the little pad hanging from the lanyard that he wore around his neck. He slid a thin pen from the loop on its side and flipped the pad open and started to write. He then turned the pad round so that it was facing Frankie.

'The right choice,' the message said.

Yeah, right. Like Frankie had any choice at all.

12

Friday the 12th finally arrived, but it might as well have been Friday 13th for all the joy it brought with it. Another new day, another new summons. Only this time, at least, it wouldn't be the cheery old Saint who'd be picking Frankie up. Small comfort, though. Because the call had come from Tam Jackson, chief arm breaker to Tommy Riley himself.

Frankie took the call just after he'd got out of the shower at 8 a.m., and was already sweating like he'd just got back from a run by the time he got dressed. It was another blazing-hot day outside, but that wasn't what had got him so worked up. It was the thought that Tommy might somehow have once again found out that he'd had contact with Hamilton's mob. Plain and simple guilt then. Guilt and fear.

Plus, another meeting like this was the last thing he needed today. He hadn't got back from his little pow-wow in the country with Bram and his crew until well late, when he'd finally got a cab to pick him up, and he was bloody knackered. Not only that, he had a shedload of things to get sorted before the first paying punters arrived for the opening matches of the inaugural Soho Open tournament, which kicked off at 1 p.m. today.

Xandra was in the kitchen with Maxine, tucking into a couple of bowls of Crunchy Nut, by the time Frankie got there. He ran her though the million and one things that needed doing as he slugged down a scalding hot coffee and scoffed a slice of Mother's Pride with marge. He lied about where he was going. Said he'd got to go sign some contracts round at Kind Regards' office over in Shepherd Market.

She told him she'd be fine holding the fort until he got back. She was normally totally unflappable, but even she had a little look of apprehension about her today. Because this was it, wasn't it? The day they'd been aiming at for over a year. The first day of the rest of his life.

She had one bit of good news, though. The *Evening Standard* was already out and there Frankie was, two pages in from the back, smiling like a good 'un too. Not nearly as bad as he'd reckoned. The headline read, 'London Open Right On Cue'. Not bad either. Not bad at all. Who knew, maybe this augured well for the rest of the tournie? Here was bloody hoping anyway, because surely some luck had to come his way soon?

He put a smile on Xandra and Maxine's faces in return. Told them he was booking them into a hotel for the night at that new refurbed place up on Charlotte Street, complete with dinner and a bottle of champagne in their room. His treat. To say thanks, like, for all Xandra's help. However it all went from here on in, he told her, he couldn't have got it all this far without her.

But hard not to feel the guilt too, as she hugged him. Because even though he'd been planning on giving her some treat like this anyhow, he'd made it this Monday, because that way there'd be nobody here when he got back with those artworks from the heist.

*

'Well, well, well. If it isn't my erstwhile travelling companion, Mr Frankie James. What a pleasant surprise.'

Frankie turned to face the polished red Jag that had just pulled up outside the club, where he'd been waiting for five minutes already. Mackenzie Grew flashed him an ivory smile through the open driver's window. Some things never changed. He still had his trad mod haircut, like that singer from Blur had made all popular again, but that Grew had been sporting since his first Jam concert back in '79. Only his face looked a little older from when Frankie had gone out with him to fetch Tommy Riley's goddaughter back from Ibiza last year. He'd clearly been having himself way too much sunshine and good times since.

'Yeah, you must be proper gobsmacked,' Frankie said, 'just happening to bump into me right outside my club . . . exactly when Tam told me to be here.'

'Well, if you got yourself a nice little mobile telephone like everyone else is getting . . .' Grew waggled a palm-sized black phone at Frankie. '. . . then I wouldn't need to stalk you like a member of our much maligned paparazzi, would I, love?'

'I take it you're not here to try and get a free frame.' Grew was a pretty good player. Or had been. Frankie remembered how him and a bunch of Riley's other lads had used to hang out in the Ambassador after hours with Frankie's dad back in the day. Only then there'd been some trouble. Some kind of fight. The Old Man had never said what.

'No, but I am looking forward to your tournament,' Grew said. 'A nice little initiative. Good on you. Make a name for yourself. That's the way to get on.'

Frankie remembered what the Old Man had said when he'd last visited. Something similar. Weird, though, to think that Grew too thought he might have it in him to make a real go of things.

'I'll put you down on the door list,' he said. 'Any trouble, just ask for Spartak. He's gonna be bossing security tonight.'

'Good lad. Even I wouldn't want to have to force my way past him. He makes that saying *size of a house* more like a statement of fact, right?'

'Right.'

'Right, now in you pop.' The central locking clicked. 'I know you've got a lot on today, so I'll try and get you there and back as fast as I can.'

Frankie's stomach twisted as he got in. More guilt, right? Over him having consorted with the enemy. Wasn't that what they'd called it in the war? Punishable by what? Firing squad. And, no, he might not work for Tommy officially, but he still liked some of Tommy's people who he'd worked with. And being Grew's enemy . . . well, that wasn't just dangerous, it made him feel bad too.

Grew held out his hand in greeting, the sleeves of his white Paul Smith suit and black shirt sliding back to reveal a glittering hunk of Breitling watch wrapped round his sinewy wrist. Another Breitling like Snaresby's. Another little coincidence that left Frankie wondering which side the Detective Inspector was batting for.

'Clunk, click, every trip,' Mackenzie said, sparking up a Marlboro Red with his little silver German Lugar pistol-shaped lighter. He gave Frankie a friendly squeeze on the bicep as Frankie fastened his seat belt and they pulled smoothly away from the kerb. 'Impressive, bro,' he whistled. 'You been hitting that gym again, or what?'

'Yeah, well, it's free now, ain't it?'

'True, true.'

'You any idea what Tommy wants?' Frankie watched Grew closely, trying to gauge whether Tommy might somehow have got wind of anything.

'Nah.' Grew smiled, nicely enough. But that didn't mean shit. Frankie could still remember the last time he'd seen him, back on that beach in Ibiza, grinning and holding a pistol to that bastard Duke's head, not giving two shits about his begging . . . or his burned hair and charred skin.

'Here, I'm serious about the phone,' Grew said. 'Check this puppy out.' He tossed his phone to Frankie, who caught it clean. 'A Nokia. It's got a calculator and a calendar and a clock on it and everything. Even Snake. Remember Snake? That game off of the old Atari back in the eighties?'

'Yeah, I remember.' Back in the old arcades too. Though Double Dragon, that two-player street-fighting game where you got to batter the hell out of all sorts of gangsters with knives and baseball bats, that had always been more Frankie and Jack's thing.

'I've got a mate who's just set up a shop over on Tottenham Court Road,' Grew went on. 'Says they're flying out the door. But I can get him to stick one aside for you, if you want?'

Frankie handed it back. 'I already get enough sodding phone calls as it is.' For all the bloody good most of them had done him of late.

'You sure? It's even got a pager function on it . . .'

'Positive.' And, anyhow, Frankie had always hated those wankers with pagers clipped to their belts. *Star Trek* wannabes, the lot of them. Always looking like they were waiting to be beamed up.

'And of course what with it being portable, it's brilliant for scoring gear too.' Grew raised a teasing eyebrow. 'Though I heard you were back on the straight and narrow, after your little lapse in Ibiza. Or should I say *large*?'

'So where are you taking me?' Frankie said, ignoring the dig. He still felt bad about it, how wasted he'd got, how it had then taken him months to sort himself back out again.

'Ah,' said Grew, turning on a Small Faces compilation and turning 'Itchycoo Park' up, 'well, wouldn't you know it, just like the fucking country, we're going to the fucking dogs.'

*

Even though Walthamstow Stadium wasn't open to the public today until six, Frankie still couldn't help feeling there was something in the air, something electric, something exciting, something raw, as he followed Grew down the side of the track towards the kennels.

Frankie coming here with the Old Man when he was a little kid probably had something to do with it. The Old

Man and Frankie's granddad, whose shoulders had been so wide they'd always had to open the gate round the side of the turnstiles to let him through. Well, that's what Granddad had always told Frankie anyway, but looking back at the way the crowd had always seemed to step back magically to give them all space whenever they came here on race day, Frankie now reckoned it probably had more to do with his granddad having been one of the Richardson gang's chief enforcers back in the day.

Yeah, and he'd have felt right at home here today, an' all. Frankie spotted a bunch of wide boys in suits over at the trackside bar. Of course, that shouldn't have been open yet either, but from the volume these jackals were talking at, they'd already had a few. A couple of them were even lying back in the grass working on their tans, with their chilled amber lagers glinting in the sun, but the dark-brown tan of the one whose eyes locked with Frankie's first didn't need any work on it at all. Jesús. The third musketeer from Frankie's Balearic adventure. On loan to Tommy from the gang he was now affiliated to out there.

'Amigo, it ees dammit fukeen good to see you.'

'And 'o-bloody-la to you too, Jesús,' Frankie said, as Jesús came over and first hugged him, then kissed him on both cheeks, before shaking him firmly by the hand.

'So how ees life?' Jesús asked him, smoothing down the lapels of his perfectly pressed pastel-blue suit. '*Todo bien?*'

'Yeah, *todo*, mate, *todo*,' Frankie said, even though in truth *todo* might actually already be pretty fucked up, as far as his relationship with Tommy was concerned.

The rest of Tommy's lads had clocked Frankie by now. A

couple of the more friendly ones shot him a nod or a smile. Others didn't. Like the concrete-browed Tam Jackson, who shot him an evil black *I wanna kill ya* look instead. Followed by a *fuck you, dickhead* stare, topped off with a *you're dead meat* sneer. But not much point in reading too much into any of that, eh? The two of them had never exactly seen eye to eye, with Frankie never having kowtowed to the grisly, shaven-headed thug like practically everyone else who ever came into contact with him always did.

Frankie saw Whitney before he did Tommy. Tommy's ten-stone Doberman was howling like a banshee and looked like she'd just done a massive, T-Rex-sized crap on Tommy's nephew Darren's shoe, much to everyone else's amusement.

'Will someone shut her up?' a voice snapped. No mistaking its *or else* dulcet tones.

'Shut it, bitch,' Darren yelled at his charge, jerking Whitney hard by the lead.

But if he'd been expecting a pat on his back from Tommy for his efforts, he was mistaken. The crowd of lads quickly parted, as Tommy came barging through, dressed in brand-new bright-white Nike trainers and a purple Nike tracksuit instead of his usual bespoke black suit, and marched over and punched Darren hard on the arm.

'Not like that, you moronic tub of lard,' Tommy snapped, smoothing down his close-cropped, thinning hair. 'Look what you've bloody done now.' He glared down at the dog who was whimpering on the ground. 'You've really hurt her feelings. I meant you to shut her up with love.'

'With love?' Darren said, wobbling nervously now like a blow-up Michelin man in his two-sizes-too-small suit.

He might have been twice Tommy's weight and half his age, but even just looking at the two of them here side by side, you'd only ever have backed one of them in a ruck. Tommy still had it, all right. The muscle, the tone, the command.

'Of course, with love. Like this. There, there, who's Daddy's lovely little girl, then?' he soothed, crouching down next to Whitney and gently tickling her behind the ear. 'And don't fake it either,' he warned Darren, getting back up. 'Dogs can tell if you're being insincere. It's hard-wired into their genes. Just like women.'

'There there, now, who's a pretty –' Darren tried.

'What the fuck was that?' Tommy snarled.

'But you said to –'

'She's not a bleedin' parrot. Just talk to her in a normal sort of voice. Keep it real. Like you would with a girlfriend.'

Half-smiles crossed the faces of Grew and the other lads. Only half, mind. They'd all seen this game play out before. You didn't want to catch Tommy's eye when he was in the middle of losing his rag, or before you knew what was going on, it would be you being laughed at by the others, as Tommy bawled you out.

Only Jesús actually had the bollocks to say anything. 'I do not lick doggies,' he told Frankie. 'I do not lick their sheets.'

Frankie sniggered. Couldn't help himself.

'Something funny?' Tommy asked, looking up sharply.

'Er, no,' Frankie said.

'Good.' Tommy sniffed, still annoyed, his dark eyes quickly scanning the faces of the others, in case anyone else felt like taking the piss.

No one did.

A whirring sound. Over on the track the gates snapped open and a white greyhound shot out in pursuit of the mechanical hare already racing ahead of it round the track.

'Well, make some fucking noise then,' Tommy yelled. 'Make like a fucking crowd.'

The boys did as they were told, running over and shouting and hooting and waving their arms in the air like a pack of baboons as the dog hurtled past.

'See, the whole point of us being here,' Tommy told Frankie, 'is to give that little beauty there, my lovely little Lucky Nine, all the practice he needs to win. Hence the beers. And the shouts. Just like a real meet, eh?'

Well, whatever it was, it looked like it was working. Lucky Nine was already streaking round the bend like greased lightning out of sight. Tommy stared after him with a look of genuine pride on his face.

'Ah, *sí*. OK, so *ahora comprendo*.' Jesús was grinning. '*Pensado* . . . I had thought that leetle men would be on it too.'

Frankie stared at him open-mouthed. Was he saying what he thought he was? 'What, you mean, like jockeys?'

'*Que?*'

Frankie mimicked holding a horse's reins, bobbing his shoulders like he was just coming into the home straight at the National.

'*Sí*. A . . . hockey . . .' Jesús didn't quite manage to say the word.

'Hockey? You what?' Tommy had turned back to face

them. 'No, Jesús. Christ alive. Hockey is something you do with sticks . . . understand? Like football, but with sticks.'

Jesús looked even more confused than before, but before this delightful and educational conversation could continue any further, Whitney set up barking again and Tommy growled and stomped off, muttering under his breath.

Jesús reached into his pocket and offered up a little plastic bag. 'Gummi Bear?' he asked.

'No thanks, *hombre*,' said Grew, heavy on the 'h'. He lit a smoke instead.

'Yeah, all right,' said Frankie.

'But not the –'

'Yellow ones,' Frankie said, smiling. 'Because, yeah, I remember, they're yours.' He took a black one instead.

Jesús smiled back, genuinely pleased by Frankie having remembered, and took a yellow one out for himself and popped it into his mouth.

'Right,' Tommy said, joining them again. 'Let's take a little walk, shall we, gents?'

Tam Jackson was with him, still eyeing Frankie like he was really hoping that he'd done something wrong – something that only he, on Tommy's orders, could make right. And preferably with a bat.

'You too, Darren,' Tommy barked back at his nephew, who was still whispering sweet nothings into Whitney's ear, while simultaneously trying to wipe the dog shit off his shoe on the grass. 'Because Christ knows he could do with the exercise,' Tommy muttered under his breath.

Darren hurried after them.

'It's my doctor, see?' Tommy said, setting off around the

172

track at a swift old pace. 'Said I needed to take up regular and vigorous exercise. And cut down on me cholesterol and eat less carbs. He's diagnosed palpitations, see . . . with an . . . oh, bollocks, what's the proper name for it?'

'Ectopic beat,' said Tam.

'Yeah, that's it. Sounds like a nightclub in Chelmsford, though, eh? But it's not. It's something that needs monitoring, or it could get out of hand. And I tell you what, Frankie, you can't be too careful at my age, as I'm sure your own father would tell you, because none of us are getting any younger, and the universe can be a cruel, cruel mistress . . . I mean, just look at that cunt Terence Hamilton.'

At just the sound of the Hamilton name, even one of an altogether older and deader generation than the one Frankie was currently dealing with, Frankie felt the spit drying up in his mouth, as he forced his Gummi Bear down.

' . . . carking it from cancer like that . . .' Tommy continued, 'but, of course, you'd know that already, wouldn't you? What with you having been to his funeral . . . at his shitty bastard prick of a son's personal request.' He threw Frankie a sideways look that made him feel sick.

'I wouldn't exactly say it was like that –' Frankie started to defend himself.

'No, no, I know. Valerie made that perfectly clear.'

'Valerie? Who's Valerie?' Frankie asked.

'Valerie Listerman, of course,' Tommy said. 'Who'd you bloody think?'

'Er, no one,' Frankie said.

Grew was already pulling a warning finger across his throat at Frankie, telling him not to laugh. But he needn't have bothered. Not even discovering Tommy's *consigliere*'s first name could have brought a smile to Frankie's lips right now. Because, again, that poor bastard in the warehouse basement was flashing into his head, only this time, instead of it being that bare-chested wanker there scoffing that apple beside him, it was Tam. And it wasn't that faceless screwed bloke manacled up on the wall, it was Frankie.

'But no, no, don't you worry your head about that,' Tommy said. 'We're here to talk about something else.'

'And what's that?'

Straight away, he wished he hadn't asked, because Tommy stopped dead in his tracks and just stared at him. Tam Jackson closed in, a sly little smile playing at the corner of his mouth. Uh-oh. This did not look good. This did not look good at all.

'Sometimes,' Tommy said, 'even when you're training a dog like Lucky Nine there . . .' He pointed over to where he was now being led back to the kennels. ' . . . a dog who you reckon is shit hot and set to win and so therefore well worth banging a few bob on . . . sometimes, even then, you need to take a few precautions just to make sure it is them who's going to be crossing that finishing line first.'

Frankie nodded. 'Training, right? And all that cheering?' But what had any of this got to do with him?

'Only sometimes, in certain circumstances, it makes more sense to take a few precautions with the opposition too,' Tommy said.

Tam's grin widened. But *opposition* . . . what did he mean? The Hamiltons?

'Race fixing,' Tommy said.

'Oh, yeah, right,' Frankie said, relief washing over him. Shit, was that all they were talking about. Well, thank fuck for that. And it didn't exactly come as the biggest surprise that Tommy might have a finger in that particular pie. But still Frankie couldn't see why Tommy was telling him this.

'Understand?' Tommy asked.

'Er, yeah, sure,' Frankie said.

'Good.' Tommy smiled, but there was nothing warm about it, nothing at all. 'Then you'll understand an' all that sometimes you need to take similar precautions in other sporting events too.'

Frankie's whole world seemed to slow. Because shit . . . this was a bloody metaphor of sorts, because Tommy wasn't really talking about fixing dog races at all, was he? It was another sport entirely that he had in mind.

'Please, Tommy. No,' Frankie said.

'It's just business, son.'

'No, not this . . . please, I've worked so –'

'Hard? *Hard?* Is that what you were about to say?' A tightening curl to Tommy's lip. Tam Jackson leant in over Tommy's shoulder, watching Frankie, and loving every second.

'Yes, Tommy,' Frankie said.

'And don't you think *I* work hard too?' Tommy demanded. 'And that *this* . . .' He tapped his Rolex. '. . . and *that* . . .' He was pointing at his limousine, over there in the car park. '. . . and even *her* . . .' He was waving now at a dark-haired Chinese woman dressed in flowing purple silk who was smiling at him from her seat just over in the stands. '. . . are things that I deserve, rights that I have earned? And that all

175

this . . .' His arms were up now and stretching wider and wider, encompassing . . . *what*? Here, the stadium? East 17? London? The whole world? ' . . . shouldn't be mine? Or that you have a right to any of it more than me?'

'No, Tommy, but –'

'But, fucking nothing,' Tommy snapped. 'I don't deal in buts, only dos and don'ts, and you're going to fucking well do as you're told, because, trust me, son, you're not going to like the consequences if you don't.'

Frankie gritted his teeth. But it was no good. He had to say something. Wouldn't be able to live with himself if he didn't even try. 'But you're going to make money out of the tournament, anyway, Tommy. I promise you. It'll be a success. And it'll grow . . . and you're a partner . . . and every year it does, you're going to make more and more money.'

'Didn't I just say no *buts*?' said Tommy. 'And not only is that a fucking *but*, it's a friggin' *if* as well. Because you don't *know* if this tournament will bloody well work or not, or if it does, then if it will grow, and if it does grow, then if it will carry on growing and making me money.' He held out his arms to the stadium. 'It's like this place here. It all looks so solid . . . so permanent . . . so . . .'

'Investible,' Tam said, his nasty little piggy eyes shining with delight, like he'd just spotted a new trough to stick his snout in.

'Yeah, Tam, that's the word, investible,' Tommy said, 'because look at it, it all works on the surface just fine, doesn't it? Doesn't it?' He practically snarled these last two words.

'Yeah,' Frankie said.

'Yes,' Riley hissed, 'until it don't. Because that's what happens to most businesses, Frankie. Over time. Most of them wither up. Then die. Like Hackney fucking dogs, right? Part of the fucking furniture, wasn't it? Until it weren't.'

Hackney was another track Frankie had used to come to with his grandpa. It had gone bust just a few months ago, back in April. Some swindler with his hands in the till, according to that *Cook Report* programme Frankie had watched on the box.

'And then, you see, suddenly, they ain't so fucking investible at all,' Tommy said. 'And I should bloody know, because I had money in it, didn't I, in Hackney, only now it's all gone.'

'But, please,' Frankie said again, hating Tommy now, and hating begging even more. He could feel his hands curling into fists, but he could still see Tam Jackson glaring at him. But it wasn't just Tam, it was Jesús too, and Grew watching him real close, and slowly, ever so slowly, shaking his head, telling him, *Don't be a mug, kid. Or there'll be nothing I can do.*

'I guess what it all boils down to is this, Frankie,' Riley said. 'I don't like being out of pocket, which is why I'm afraid, old son, that while I'm happy to have invested in your little sporting enterprise, not yet knowing whether it will be a success or not, I'll be buggered if I'm going to not make some decent wedge out of it now while I know I still definitely can.'

Was this what it really came down to then? Tommy losing that money in Hackney meant he was now going to take it out of Frankie's tournament instead?

'That's right, Frankie, you see I've changed my . . . my . . . Tam?'

'Investment strategy,' Tam said, still standing just behind Tommy, so the boss couldn't see how much of a kick all this was giving him.

'Yeah. From here on in, see, no matter what I myself and the firm get involved in, we're gonna be looking at not just long-term gains, but short-term too.'

Frankie just stared. He could feel himself sagging, like he'd just had the stuffing knocked out of him. Every involvement he'd had with Tommy before had had a fairness to it. A favour given, a favour repaid. First with Riley helping Frankie clear Jack's name two years ago, and then with Frankie helping Riley get his goddaughter back from that prick in Ibiza last year. A quid pro quo. Wasn't that the phrase? But this . . . this was different. This had nothing to do with equality or mutual respect. And everything to do with Frankie being told.

13

On the ride back into Soho, Tam Jackson sat in the back of Grew's Jag and explained to Frankie the way the scam was going to work. Pat O'Hanagan, the Northern Ireland bookie and player-manager who Tommy had introduced Frankie to back at last year's launch, controlled two of the top four seeds already entered in the tournament, one in each half of the draw. The plan was to guide them both through to the final, where the one Tommy had backed right from the start was going to win, frame per frame at the point differentials O'Hanagan and Tommy had already agreed.

So far so simple, but the smart bit was this: while O'Hanagan reckoned his boys were maybe good enough to get through to the final on their own merits, there was still the possibility they might not. That's where Frankie came in. His job was to keep Tommy in touch, via Tam Jackson, about how each of the two bent seeds' matches were progressing. Any sign of them losing and it would then be up to Frankie to arrange access to the players' Green Room during one of the breaks, so that Tam Jackson and a couple of Tommy's other thugs could pop in and have a little word with whoever the seed was up against, to deter whoever it was from wanting to win.

The only comfort Frankie had was hoping that this might not ever actually happen, in that Pat O'Hanagan's two seeds might make it through to the final on merit, without anyone needing to have a little word with anyone in the Green Room. Because once that happened, well, Frankie wasn't stupid . . . no matter how sneakily or terrifyingly Tommy's thugs went about their business, it would only be a matter of time before the rumours started. Maybe just amongst the players at first. But then the agents . . . the federations . . . the fans. Until the Soho Open and everything Frankie had ever hoped it would turn into would instead be turned into mud.

*

But, of course, it wasn't just the tournament's reputation Frankie had to worry about, was it? But the very real prospect of the law getting wind of what he was up to as well. The prospect hit him in full three-dimensional horror vision as he stood outside the front doors of the Ambassador at one o'clock that afternoon, with a pleasantly clean-cut and sober Spartak Sidarov at his side, welcoming the punters in.

Snaresby was one of the first to arrive. Frankie spotted him near the front of the queue that had been steadily building over the last half-hour, before Spartak had opened the doors. He felt the same old burn of adrenaline he always felt whenever he clapped eyes on him. Fight or flight. But when

Snaresby reached him, instead of his usual sneer, he actually smiled.

'May I introduce my wife?' he asked Frankie, as Xandra checked his tickets.

'Er, sure,' Frankie said, a little thrown.

Mrs Snaresby looked surprisingly normal, not remotely gangly or greasy-looking at all. Oddly pretty too. Or for someone who'd ended up with a human arachnid like him.

'Congratulations on getting this off the ground,' she said. 'I've been looking forward to it so much.' The way she said it, like she'd been following the whole story of how the tournament had come about and was progressing, right from day one. 'I'm such a big fan of Stephen Maxwell.'

Maxwell. One of the two bent seeds. Snaresby's face gave nothing away. Did he know? And if he didn't, what would he do if he found out? Throw the bloody book at Frankie, no matter how much he might be smiling now. Unless he really was on Riley's books.

'Me too,' Frankie lied. 'We're dead lucky he's here.' Or dead, anyway, at least.

'Well, we mustn't hold you up,' Mrs Snaresby said, taking her husband by the hand.

'We got here nice and early,' Snaresby said, 'to give us the best possible view. I wouldn't want to miss a thing.'

Something threatening about the way he said it? Something else for Frankie to worry about? Like he didn't already have enough. Or maybe he was just being paranoid? Christ, he hated this. He'd been looking forward to this afternoon for months, but now he just wanted it done. All because of that bastard Riley. Yeah, all because of him.

Stephen Maxwell was already back there in the Green Room and would be the first player up on table one. Frankie was already feeling sick at the prospect of what might happen if he started to lose.

And right on cue, Tommy Riley and his boys were the next faces to turn up. Grew and Jesús too. Eight in all, including the same Chinese woman who Frankie had seen at the track. But none of that queuing malarkey for them, thank you very much. Bosh. Straight to the front, with Tam Jackson leading like a bull in search of a china shop. Nobody else who'd been waiting in line dared say diddly squat.

'Looking good and busy, then,' Tommy observed, peering past Frankie and Spartak into the club beyond.

'Yeah, it's a sell-out.' Hah, and in more ways than one.

'Hello, Frankie. I'm Chenguang,' said the Chinese woman. Tommy's new girlfriend then, way too beautiful and young for him, of course. An American, from her accent. He'd not been expecting that.

Mrs Riley not joining us this evening? Yeah, if only Frankie had the balls to ask. Imagine Tommy's face. Seeing that might even make up for some of the damage that he'd done.

'Welcome to the Ambassador Club,' he heard himself saying to Chenguang instead.

'Thanks.' Chenguang was dressed, just like at the track, in head-to-toe purple silk, matching Tommy's tie. Sponsored by Ribena again, then, eh? He remembered what Listerman had said. For luck. She took out a small purple corsage from her Hermès handbag, as if reading his mind, and reached up and pinned it onto the lapel of his black suit.

'Thanks,' Frankie said, meaning it, because bloody hell, he couldn't have enough luck tonight, 'and now, if you'll follow me, I'll take you through to your seats.'

He led her, Tommy and the rest of them through to the reserved VIP section on table one, where the first of today's first-round matches would be starting in just under half an hour. A bit of banter with Grew and Jesús and he called one of the hired-in waiters over and left them to it.

The six competition tables were divided by high walls covered with the various sponsors' logos, with the seating around each already filling up. A nice buzz of excited conversation was building too. The bar was good and busy, with Slim on top of everything and extra staff drafted in. Andy 'The Topster' Topper was over on table two, chatting to the match officials the snooker federation had sent round. He was bossing all that, so there was nothing for Frankie to do there. In fact, everything looked good, but it wasn't what was out here on show that was the problem, was it? Christ, his heart was hammering hard.

'Are you feeling all right?' Kind Regards asked, seeing Frankie leaning back against the bar.

'Eh? Er, yeah. Of course.'

'You sure? Only you're looking rather pale.' Kind Regards looked far from convinced. He waved across at his wife, Mary, who was sitting right down the front of the seating overlooking table one, next to Jack and Tiffany and JoJo. Even better seats than he'd given Tommy, with a nice lateral view from where they'd be able to catch all of the action.

'We're both so proud of you,' Kind Regards said. 'And your mum would be too. And of course the Old Man.'

Frankie was gutted he couldn't be here. Her too, wherever she was. He could feel his heart hammering even more. Sweat was breaking out across his brow.

'You nervous about your speech, is that it?' said Kind Regards, still frowning. 'Just remember what I told you before the launch last year.'

And, oh yeah, Frankie remembered it all right. How could he forget? *You've got to own it. Make it yours*, was how Kind Regards had put it. *Or one day someone else will take it away*. Only it hadn't made any difference, had it? Because that's exactly what Tommy Riley had just done. Taken what Frankie had built. Taken it and broken it and ground it under his boot.

'I'm just going to go upstairs and have myself a couple of minutes,' Frankie said. 'I need a glass of water, a breather for a sec.'

'Yeah, good idea, you do that.' Kind Regards patted him on the back.

Frankie weaved his way back through the crowd to the door and out into the street. Better. Not so hot. He hurried up into the flat and guzzled down some water straight from the tap, then filled himself a glass up too, and headed through to the bedroom.

Diazepam. Boom. He popped one out of the blister pack and necked it. Whiskey. Boom-badda-boom. He dug that half-bottle out from the back of the drawer under his bed.

Because that was one of the brilliant things about hiding things from yourself, wasn't it? Especially when you'd pretended you'd cleared them out. You always then remembered where they were.

*

Even just after he'd finished it, Frankie couldn't remember much about making his speech in front of that crowd on table one to open the tournament. Applause, yeah. A few laughs. But not a lot else. That pill and the whiskey had both kicked in nicely by then, so the whole thing had passed in a kind of a blur. Had it gone well? Hard to tell. But a few hours later, and no one was bitching, so he was guessing that maybe it had. Thank God then, eh, for all that practice he'd put in.

By five o'clock, thanks to a shedload more water and a couple of nice, icy Diet Cokes, the effects of the booze had worn off completely and he was feeling nicely straightened out and surprisingly unstressed. Well, not that surprisingly really, considering that that pill was probably still doing its thing. But on a level, yeah, for sure. Happy. In control.

He'd managed to chat, in between sessions and watching the various matches taking place, with most of the people he needed to: the announcer, the sponsors and most of the players – apart from Stephen Maxwell, he'd not been able to bring himself to do that. The Topster was on top of his game too, working the club like sodding Jerry Maguire. Only with Aussie surfer hair topping that perfect Mighty

185

White smile of his. Yeah, it looked like the whole event was shaping up to be a proper success.

The best news of all, though, was that Stephen Maxwell – much to Mrs Snaresby's obvious and vocal delight – had gone through in six straight frames on table one. Looking good, then. On form. With no need for any interference from Tam Jackson's lads at all. The same went for the other bent seed, who'd been playing his opening round on one of the tables across at the James Boys Gym, and was winning 5–3. His name was Huw Watkins. A Welshie. Jack had headed over there right after Frankie's speech and had been keeping him informed about all the matches' scores on the blower ever since. Not that Frankie had told him why he needed to know, only that he did.

Yeah, so everything was looking good then, right up until when Frankie ducked back upstairs into the flat, to check in on the phone again with Jack to see that Huw Watkins had finished polishing off his opponent, which he had – and that's when Frankie heard a siren pull up wailing in the street.

Bloody London. Sometimes he wished it would just shut up. He hurried back downstairs to see what was going on. Here all these people were, settling into his club for an evening of serious high-pressure matches, where, apart from the clack of balls, you should have been able to hear a pin drop, but instead you got this.

Ah well, it was what it was, right?, he told himself opening the door, that siren raging even louder. And half the people inside the Ambassador were from London anyhow and would be well used to its Friday-night soundtrack by now. *The best city in the world . . .* wasn't that what Frankie had said in his speech at the tournament's launch party last year? Yeah. Well, maybe he should have warned them it was the noisiest too.

Only – what the hell? – as soon as he stepped outside, he saw that the bleedin' ambulance wasn't here on Poland Street for anywhere else. It was parked up right outside the bloody Ambassador Club's main entrance.

Frankie hurried over. Shit. His heart started racing again. What the hell was going on? Something to do with Tommy? Or Dougie? Something violent? Please, no, not here, not today. Not with all these people inside that he knew.

But right away, on reaching the doors, whatever it was, he saw it was going to be OK. Or if not OK, then not a disaster either, right? Because no one was panicking. Two of Spartak's lads on the door were covering their ears because of the siren, but otherwise smiling, and that was kind of it, and the same went for further inside.

The crowds were still there, watching their various first-round matches. No one freaking out. In fact, the only problem at all was that the crowd round table one – where the tournament's top seed and its only real household name, Adam Adamson, was due to be playing – were looking bored. Why? Because the match there hadn't yet started – Frankie checked his watch – and should have. So why the hell hadn't it, eh?

'Bollocks. Shit. Piss. Fuck. Wank,' said The Topster, hurrying up to Frankie. 'Come on, quick now, Frankie, in here, with me.'

'What the hell is going –' Frankie started to say, but then

realized The Topster was leading him dead ahead towards the players' Green Room.

He could already see the paramedics gathered outside and he couldn't stop that feeling of panic from rising again. But both of O'Hanagan and Riley's players had already got through, so why the hell would Tam Jackson even need to . . . no, Christ, no, he couldn't, because the guys on the door would have been freaking out, right? But what if Jackson *had* done something? What if he'd just decided to move early on nobbling Adam Adamson instead? To get the main obstacle to them winning out of the way? And what if he'd refused to be warned off? What if they'd –

But no . . . the second Frankie stepped inside the Green Room, he saw Adam Adamson was fine – it was his opponent, Damon Reed, who was lying on a stretcher, clutching at his side and groaning.

'Will someone please just tell me what the bleedin' hell is going on?' Frankie said.

'Appendicitis, this lot reckon,' said The Topster.

The nearest paramedic looked up and nodded. Another hideous groan from Reed only seemed to confirm what The Topster had said.

'Good luck, mate,' Frankie told Reed a few seconds later, as they wheeled him out.

'Let us know if there's anything we can do,' The Topster told Reed's manager, who was walking out grimly by his side.

Adam Adamson followed, with his own manager at his side.

'Bloody hell . . .' Frankie said.

'Yeah, and bloody bollocks too,' Andy replied, as soon as they were out of earshot. 'We've got a whole fee-paying audience out there on table one who've not got nothing to watch.' He clawed at his hair in frustration. 'And, even worse, that ITV lot I've been talking to?'

'Yeah?'

'Well, they finally called an hour back to say they would be able to find a slot for it on the evening news.'

'But that's brilliant.' The kind of publicity you just couldn't buy.

'No, that *would* be brilliant,' Andy said, 'it's just they're only prepared to do it if they can film Adam Adamson there in action, on account of him being the only one here most of their viewers will have heard of.'

Frankie felt his stomach lurch. 'Christ, you mean the match Reed's meant to be playing in now?'

'Yeah, the TV crew have just finished setting up. Only now they've got nothing to film except an empty bloody table.'

'But isn't there a reserve?' Because that's how it worked. There was meant to be someone on standby, right?

'Well, there was, but he's pissed off home, hasn't he?' Andy said. 'Because he thought he wouldn't be needed. And now he's not answering his tossing phone.'

'Shit it.'

'Shit it, indeed. Unless, of course . . .' Andy said, a sudden twinkle in his eyes.

'What?'

'Just wait here a second, mate. Leave it to me.'

Frankie felt suddenly exhausted. He gazed around the

Green Room, at the sofas and chairs, the posh new TV, silver American fridge and the coffee machines. It all looked so real, this thing that they'd built. It was gutting they were now going to miss the bloody news.

'Just follow my lead,' Andy hissed, stepping back into the Green Room, and holding the door wide open, so down the corridor they could still see the empty table and part of the gathered crowd.

'Eh?'

But Andy just held a finger up to his lips. Then Frankie saw the ref who'd been due to officiate Reed's match being led down the corridor by Spartak, who steered him in and checked his watch, before walking back up the corridor towards the gathered crowd. The referee looked Frankie up and down.

'But you're the gentleman who made the speech,' he said in confusion. 'You're running this tournament, aren't you?'

'Er, yeah . . .' Where the hell was all this going? Frankie looked to The Topster for guidance, but got nothing from him.

'But you're also a registered member of GLOPSA?' said the referee.

'Eh?' Frankie pretended he hadn't heard. He looked to The Topster again.

'The Global Professional Snooker Association, yeah, of course he is,' Andy grinned.

'Yeah, of course,' Frankie said, turning back to the ref with a shit-eating grin of his own. 'What of it?'

'And, as I explained, he is actually registered to play

today as well,' said The Topster. 'Only we had some late entries, so he kindly stepped aside.'

'But you can confirm that you have registered officially for this Tier Two tournament?' the referee asked Frankie.

'Er . . . yeah.' Frankie nodded at Andy. 'Just like he says.' As if there'd be any other reason why he was here in the Green Room.

'Yeah, which means he's still also officially available to us as a reserve,' said The Topster.

'Exactly,' Frankie said. Christ, he couldn't believe what he was hearing. The Topster was actually planning to have Frankie go out there and play. Frankie stared daggers at him, feeling sick. He might have been playing better than ever, but he was still strictly second rate compared with all those lads out there.

But maybe it didn't matter, eh? Because who cared how much he lost by? So long as the TV crew still ran that slot, then the humiliation would be worth it, right?

'And it's Frankie James, right?' said the ref.

'Yeah.'

The ref slid a folder out of his bag and quickly leafed through its pages. 'Only your name's not down here at all,' he then said.

Oh, bloody brilliant.

'Ah, that's my fault,' said The Topster, suddenly clapping his hand theatrically across his forehead. 'Oh, God, yes, I must have forgotten to post it.'

'Post what?'

'His registration. His fee. Owed to you guys, to GLOPSA, yes, I remember it now. It's still there sitting on my desk.'

'So your client here *isn't* registered for this tournament?' asked the ref, looking more and more dubious now.

'Well no, but, or rather, yes, he was *meant* to be, but . . .'

But the referee ignored him. Brilliant. A stickler for details. That's all they needed. Frankie gritted his teeth, thinking of the TV crew still sitting out there.

'Are there any other actual officially registered reserves here?' the referee then said.

'No,' said The Topster.

'Then the match can't go ahead. And, under such circumstances, GLOPSA regulation 16c states that any other remaining player should get a bye.'

Meaning bye-bye to their slot on the evening news too. Because Adam Adamson was the only player the TV crew wanted to see.

But then a slow hand-clapping started out in the main club. Andy didn't look remotely surprised. In fact, he just smiled as he checked his watch, like it might actually be something he'd planned.

'Look, it just seems wrong,' said The Topster, 'to punish all those people waiting out there, and waste the time of that TV crew too, all because of my stupid mistake, not his.'

The clapping got louder. Frankie spotted Spartak, peering back down the corridor at him, clapping himself. Looking quite the little cheerleader, in fact. The ref's cheeks started to pink. The Topster spotted it too and moved in for the kill.

'Look, is there any way we can . . . just overlook this hiccup for now?'

'Well, that really is most irregular . . .'

'What if I guarantee to have that paperwork and the

192

cheque here by close of play? I can cab it back to my office and be back here even before the first session's done.' The Topster could do that? It was possible, Frankie supposed. '*And* his GLOPSA registration documents,' The Topster said.

Hmmm, the ones that didn't exist . . . but The Topster's smile never wavered. And, as the sound of slow clapping got louder and louder, the ref swallowed awkwardly and then snapped his folder shut.

'All right, fine,' he then said, 'but I really will need those documents tonight.'

'Good man, good man, and you'll get them,' grinned The Topster. 'You're a trooper, mate,' he added, before firing Frankie a big thumbs up and telling him, 'Game on, mate. Game on.'

*

As it turned out, humiliation didn't even come close. Frankie's opponent, Adam Adamson, won 6-0. A donut-ing. But it wasn't all bad. Frankie at least managed a couple of thirty breaks. Enough to stop him feeling like a total plum.

Well, almost, anyway . . . the only penguin suit he'd been able to find in time to wear – something that the ref had insisted on – had been the Old Man's from back in the seventies. *What's all this then? Val Doonican night?* some wag in the audience had shouted the second Frankie had stepped out . . . someone who'd sounded horribly like Detective Inspector Snaresby, to Frankie's ears, at least.

Still, Frankie had got plenty of home support too, to stop him feeling too bad. Xandra had even got a warning off the ref for being overly enthusiastic on his behalf. He'd earned himself a few scowls too, mind, followed by jeers. Tam Jackson being chief amongst them, of course, the prick.

Meanwhile, Adam Adamson had been a total gent, not just in agreeing to the late change of opponent. As he'd shaken Frankie's hand at the end of the match, he'd told him that, with a bit more practice, he might soon end up playing him again. Just as importantly, he said he loved the idea of the Soho Open and was already planning on entering it again next year.

But the main thing was the TV crew. They shot their piece and it went out live. Meaning the Soho Open was truly now out there in the world.

14

If the first few hours of the tournament on Friday had gone by in a bit of a blur, the effect only got worse for Frankie over the next two days. Nothing to do with pills and booze this time, though. More like the insane amount of stuff he ended up having to do.

By the time Saturday evening came round, and with it the quarter-finals, when Xandra asked him how he was coping, he told her he might as well have been in the middle of a bloody tornado, needing every ounce of muscle power and concentration at his disposal just to stop himself from getting blown clean off his feet.

But it wasn't all bad. Frankie was already getting bags of good feedback from the sponsors and punters and players alike. The ripples from the TV slot had gone out wide. A couple of newspapers had followed up in their Saturday morning editions, with more promising to do the same on Sunday. *The Big Breakfast* had been in touch with The Topster as well, saying they'd have the winner on next week, if whoever it was would play along with some kind of suitably whacky Channel 4 comedy snooker idea they'd cooked up.

Equally good, or at least a bloody relief, The Topster had

somehow managed to come up with that paperwork for the association. Frankie still wasn't exactly sure how, but he'd hazard that somewhere along the line fraudulent behaviour and a photocopier had to have been involved. Just as well it had all been settled, though, because Frankie had already appeared in the press following the TV feature, earning him a phone message from Sharon, of all people, telling him well done, after she'd spotted his name in the *Guardian* over her poached eggs on toast.

The only dark clouds still hanging on the horizon – or at least as far as the tournament was concerned – were Stephen Maxwell and Huw Watkins, Riley and O'Hanagan's men. They were still progressing steadily towards the final in their separate halves of the draw, which wasn't a problem in itself, in that none of their opponents had yet needed to be warned off. But what would happen when they did come up against the other top seeds – including Adam Adamson – they were likely to face? Frankie dreaded to think. Tam Jackson and his lads had become a permanent feature at the Ambassador, like gargoyles in a church, all of them permanently scowling and clearly primed to play their part in steering their bent seeds into the final whenever the opportunity finally arose.

But even they were nothing next to the booming, crackling thunderhead of a storm cloud that was building up for Frankie on Monday night. The press was already full of it, the *Sensation* exhibition that was due to open on Thursday, and it was all Frankie could think of too.

Was there any way he could get out of it? Short of suicide, he couldn't think of one. But then, just as he was sitting down on Saturday night – to watch Adam Adamson play his quarter-final that might just take him through to meeting Stephen Maxwell in Sunday's semis – Frankie got a message from Spartak that finally brought with it a ray of light.

*

'There's a kid outside,' Spartak said, getting Frankie up from his seat just moments before the quarter-final's first session began. 'Says he's got a message for you.'

'What kid?'

'Said you knew him. Name of Little Terry?'

Frankie grimaced. Terence Hamilton's nephew, then. Dougie's little cousin. Shit it. What the hell was he doing here? Frankie followed Spartak back through the crowd and outside, listening to the announcer introduce Adamson and his opponent to a warm round of applause. Spartak pointed out the kid, who was waiting a little way down the street. Yeah, it was Little Terry, all right, all dressed up in baggies, like a refugee from Manchester, '89.

'And what can I do for you, then?' Frankie asked, walking up.

'Got something for you, haven't I?'

'From her?' He meant Viollet.

'Nah. Not this time. From him.'

Dougie, then.

'Well, then?' Frankie asked.

Little Terry stuck out his hand. Cheeky little toerag. On the make again. Frankie shook his head, digging into his pocket and peeling him off another twenty from his clip.

'And I bet you still haven't got any change either,' he said.

''Fraid not.' The kid couldn't help grinning, just like before. He handed Frankie the phone. A Nokia. Like what Grew had been banging on about.

'It got Snake on it?' Frankie said.

'Yeah.' The kid looked surprised Frankie had even heard of it.

'Nice.'

'And it's yours to keep,' said Little Terry. 'Compliments of the boss.'

'Double nice. And that's it, is it? Just a gift.' Frankie doubted it.

'Nah, he told me to tell you to hit autodial one.'

'Auto-what what?' What the hell was he talking about?

Little Terry rolled his eyes. 'Give it here. You're as rubbish as my dad.' He punched in a couple of digits, then handed it back.

'Cheers,' Frankie said, but already Little Terry was walking away, tucking that twenty safely away into his baggy jeans' pocket.

'Ah, good, Frankie James,' a voice answered on the third ring. 'My little cousin found you all right then, did he?'

'Yeah, but listen, no offence, OK, but I'm right in the middle of –'

'A quarter-final. Yes. Or the start of one, anyway.' Meaning he had the place being watched, or someone actually there inside.

'So how can I help you?' Frankie said, walking round the block, out of sight of the club, and slinking back into the shadows of a doorway between two shops.

'Well, it's just, you see, I was thinking,' Dougie said,

'going back to that first conversation we had, about you carrying on making Tommy Riley feel like he'd got you on a nice tight leash . . .'

'What of it?' Already Frankie didn't like the sound of where this was going.

'Well, it's just I wouldn't want it to ever feel so tightly held that you felt you needed to obey him instead of me. Or indeed feel any loyalty to him over me whatsoever.'

Christ, had he been talking to Listerman? What was he going to tell him next? That if he did, he'd soon find himself torn apart?

'And I know Viollet was kind enough to show you,' Dougie said, 'our *friend*, there in the warehouse basement, who'd rather let us down . . .'

Frankie's heart thudded, even at the thought of it.

'But what I don't know,' Dougie went on, 'was if she also explained to you that it wasn't only our friend who ended up down there . . . but also, sadly, some people he was very close to as well . . .'

Frankie's heart thudded even harder. Family. He meant family. Or friends. Or both. Not just Jack, then. But Slim. Xandra. Even the Old Man inside. He meant whoever he fucking well pleased.

'You're not going to have a problem with me,' Frankie said.

'Good. That's just what I was ringing up to check. I just wanted to remind you of your . . . responsibilities.'

'And if I do do it all?' Frankie said. 'Just like you want?'

'Well then, I'll be happy.'

'Happy enough to give me that pistol back?' Screw it. It was all Frankie could think of. He might as well ask.

Silence on the end of the line.

'Happy enough to think about it,' Dougie said. 'Or at least perhaps set a timetable around when that might become a real possibility. So long, of course, that in the meantime you continue working for me.'

'And Riley?' Frankie said. Because surely Dougie could see that too? How Frankie couldn't just switch sides. Openly, like that.

'Oh, don't you worry about Riley. He's not going to be a problem for much longer. I've already got all that worked out.'

'You have?'

'Oh, yes.' Another chuckle. Seemed like Hamilton was turning into quite the comedian. 'You see, that was the other little thing I wanted to talk to you about.'

'Go on.'

'We're going to frame him.'

'*We?*'

'Yes, Frankie, that's right. You and me.'

'For what?'

'For everything. For the whole Royal Academy job. We're going to plant one of those stolen art pieces right there in his office for the cops to find, and then call them, so that it looks like it was Tommy who was behind it all along.'

*

Another day, another gangster . . . Forget a dog with two owners, Frankie was beginning to feel more like a tennis ball getting battered back and forth. And not by some Brit like Tim Henman either. Nothing so polite. More like Pete Sampras. Bosh, bash, bosh. Surely, sooner or later, he'd just pop?

Sunday morning, 7 a.m., and it was Tommy Riley's turn to give Frankie a call. Or Mackenzie Grew, anyway, who was then waiting right there outside the Ambassador Club in his red Jag come 7.30, when Frankie walked out through the doors.

No banter between them this morning. Frankie just stared straight ahead. It was the drive back from the dog track on Friday that was partly to blame. The fact Grew, who was meant to be Frankie's mate as well as one of Tommy's top boys, hadn't even tried speaking up for him when Tommy had told him his plan for fixing the Open. But it was more than that, it was Dougie Hamilton too. And that gun and that threat of the basement. And him using them to make Frankie switch sides. Frankie couldn't get it out of his head either, how *he*'d be the one responsible for getting Tommy in the clink. Not that Tommy would know. Oh no, Dougie had assured him of that. Because what use would that be for Dougie, having his new full-time lackey a marked man before he'd even begun properly working for him? And then, of course, there was the small matter of wrapping up the tournament too. Frankie still had that to deal with. And with the semis and final all taking place later today. Yeah, he really had time to spare for this ride now, didn't he? Not.

'So what's this then?' Frankie said, as the Jag pulled up in a posh Chelsea street.

'Tommy's new gaff.'

Frankie looked up at the building they'd parked outside. Bright white in the morning light. Four storeys high. Leafy green trees. Security gates out front.

'What happened to his old place?' The way he'd heard it, Tommy had always lived up round Warren Street, where he'd been born. Not that he'd ever been invited there himself.

'Oh, that's still there, and his Mrs with it . . . but this is where he's going to be spending more of his own *personal* time from now on.'

With her then. With Chenguang.

'Surprised he's not painted it purple then,' Frankie said, not looking back to see Grew's reaction, as he got out of the car and slammed the door shut.

He got buzzed in through the gate by a person or persons unknown when he said who he was. A bunch of slick-looking cars parked up in the flagstoned courtyard the other side. Mercs. Beamers. Nothing as classy as at Dougie's riverside pad. From round the side of the house, he could hear the sound of drilling and shouting, and taking a quick dekko he saw it was a right old mess. Cement mixers. Builders. Laying down what looked like a tennis court.

Walking again round the front of the building, Frankie swallowed the bile in his throat back down as he gazed up at the massive sandblasted edifice, rearing up into the blue sky. He had to keep cool. Just because Tommy had sent for him, it didn't mean he'd somehow got wind of what Dougie had planned – did it? Nah, there was no bloody way, right? Yeah, just keep calm. No getting away from it, though. He did feel a bit of a twat about that snide joke he'd just made to Grew about Chenguang. He'd have been much better off remembering to re-pin that corsage she'd given him back onto his suit. No such thing as too much luck, as they said.

The six-foot lump of battle-scarred muscle that was Tam Jackson opened the front door. Not even a hello. But, again, no point in reading too much into that either, eh? Frankie followed him inside. A big reception area. Chandeliers. Sofas. A wide staircase spiralling up. Nice. Nice and cool. Nice and cool and classy too. Nothing like Tommy at all.

The nearest place like this that had any connection to Tommy Riley that Frankie had ever been to was Tommy's high-end brothel – or Private Members' Club as Tommy preferred to think of it – over in St James's. But this felt more homely. Less to do with grubby money. Not even a reception desk with a girl taking payment for various sexual services. Not that Frankie missed it. That kind of thing had never been his style.

'Through here,' Tam grunted, opening a side door.

A freshly painted staircase led down. A *tap-tap-tapping* noise echoed up from below. The sound of more machinery vibrating through the walls. What was it with gangsters and basements? What was wrong with roof terraces all of a sudden? Surely they'd have had a much better view?

But, nah, Frankie took that back as he reached the bottom of the stairs and walked out into the basement that was midway through being converted. It was bloody epic. Brilliant. Cool.

'Yeah, now that's what I'm talking about. *That's* the kind

of reaction I want to see on someone's face when they walk into here,' Tommy said, grinning over at Frankie from where he was sitting in a raised-up bubbling jacuzzi, with Chenguang in a purple bikini on his left and a similarly attired buxom young blonde lady on his right.

'Not bad,' Frankie said, looking round. 'Not bad at all. Well classy, in fact.'

And it was. Even with all the dust sheets and half-plastered walls. A six foot deep, fifteen metre long hole had been carved out into the ground. What would end up being a pool, no doubt. Corinthian columns had already been set into place at metre-wide intervals around its perimeter.

'Like the last days of Rome, eh?' said Tommy, getting out of the jacuzzi and pulling on a purple robe. 'Only this here's London and it's only the start.'

Frankie noticed Whitney, the Doberman, sitting over by the back wall, where a grey-haired bloke in overalls was working on a decorative alcove set into the plasterwork there. The source of that *tap-tap-tapping* noise.

'That's Matteo, that is. A proper Italian artisan. Used to work in' – Tommy mimed inverted commas with his fingers – 'professional artistic reproduction.'

A forger, in other words.

'Yeah, there's nothing that's ever been made that he can't reproduce.'

Frankie noticed something white around Whitney's hind legs.

'Is she,' he said out loud, before he could stop himself, 'wearing a nappy?'

'Who, Whitney? Oh yeah. Pampers. She's on her period, isn't she?' said Tommy. 'She's being a right grumpy cow.' Tommy sat down at a table with a coffee pot already laid out steaming on it, alongside a plate of fresh croissants. He pointed Frankie to a chair. 'Right,' he said, 'quickly fill me in on how the whole tournament's going then. Tam here recorded your little spot on the telly for me. Well stepped up, son. Well done. That took proper bollocks, that did. Good lad.'

Tam glowered at Frankie, clearly irritated by the praise he was getting. But Frankie didn't give a toss about that. He sat down and helped himself to coffee and shoved down one of the croissants too. Him and Riley talked for half an hour, with Frankie bringing him right up to date on everything, how happy the sponsors were, as well as the fans. Frankie talked Tommy through how much money he reckoned they'd probably made an' all, and what promises they'd had from their business partners regarding further collaborations next year.

'So the long and the short of it, then, is it's a goer,' Tommy concluded when Frankie was finally done. 'And there's nothing else I need to know?'

'Yeah, Tommy,' said Frankie, hating him all over again for the fact he'd fucked it when he hadn't needed to. 'And, no, there's not.'

For a couple of seconds, Tommy just watched him, and it even crossed Frankie's mind that he might be about to call the whole fix off, but then he waved Tam over.

'Right, time to get moving then,' he said. 'We've got the builders prepping in here for laying the pool's foundations next week,' he explained to Frankie. 'But meanwhile you two lads better get back to the Ambassador, to make sure everything there's still going according to plan.'

*

And there's nothing else I need to know? Frankie got back to the Ambassador Club at just gone nine, feeling sick, with Tommy's words still ringing in his head.

Instead of going straight into the club, he headed straight upstairs instead. He was sweating like a pig again, and again not just from the weather. He stuck on his stereo loud, just wanting to lose himself, but hardly had the energy to strip off his clothes and get into the shower. He suddenly wished he'd never done it, this whole sodding tournament. Everything he'd said to Tommy, about how well it had all been going, none of it, *none of it*, might mean a thing after tomorrow night.

He pictured the Old Man, there in Brixton nick. But not in the Visitors' Room, not where he always met him, but instead in his cell. Only then it wasn't his dad's face he was looking at, at all. It was his. Because what if he got caught? What if Bram's plan went wrong? He'd been so busy worrying about getting tripped up by Tommy, or ending up in Dougie's friggin' basement, that he'd shoved all this to the back of his mind. About how he was going to be doing a heist. A *heist*, for God's sake. One that might leave him inside for the rest of his life.

And suddenly he felt like the walls of the shower cubicle were closing in on him and he bit down so hard on his knuckles to stop himself from shouting out and getting heard by Xandra and Maxine in the room next door that he ended up watching blood run down his forearm and spiral down the drain. 'Depeche Mode,' the radio DJ said as he lurched back through to his room. '"Barrel of a Gun."' Yeah, that couldn't have been more apt if it had tried.

By the time he'd got dressed again, Xandra and Maxine had already left the flat to help get the club ready downstairs for today's two semi-finals, which were due to kick off simultaneously on tables one and two at ten, before tonight's final began at six. They'd left the radio on. That 'Candle in the Wind', by Elton John, was playing again. Written for Marilyn Monroe, according to Xandra, it had now been adopted by a grieving country for its dead Princess.

Frankie took the first diazepam with water right here in the flat, sipping it like vodka. He did the second in the alley round the back of the club ten minutes later with an actual bottle of vodka, guzzling it down like water and nearly chucking it right back up straight away. But he didn't. He kept it together. Then breath mints. More coffee. A walk around the block. Until . . . *sliiiiiide* . . . oh yeah, he felt it kicking in good.

And that's how the last day of the inaugural Soho Open went for Frankie James . . . the same as how it had started . . . in a bubble . . . in a blur . . . if anyone noticed, he didn't know . . . didn't care . . . didn't give a shit about anything much, truth be told . . . not about what went down in the semi-finals . . . though, yeah, he'd be lying if he said it didn't make him smile . . . O'Hanagan and Riley's boys, Stephen Maxwell and Huw Watkins, both losing and losing big time like that . . . one of them to Adam Adamson and the other to a lower ranked player called Bo Wang . . . and without Tam Jackson and his boys even being in the building to do anything about it . . . and he didn't give a shit either about the fury in O'Hanagan's eyes as he was forced to watch . . . and he didn't give a shit about the final either . . . or the permagrin on Riley's face as he turned up and saw neither of his boys was even playing . . . or about how he then ended up staying and watching all the same in between Chenguang and his mum . . . or about how good a match everyone said it was . . . or about Tommy's little speech which he still did at the end . . . or him cutting his ribbon and handing over the keys of the Beamer he'd put up as a prize to Adam Adamson . . . or about the congratulations Frankie got himself after that . . . from The Topster, Kind Regards, Jack, Tiffany, JoJo, Listerman, Riley, Chenguang, Grew, Jesús, Slim, Xandra, Maxine, Ash Crowther, Sea Breeze, Darren, even Tam . . . or the look Tommy gave him as he left the building, the look that told him in no uncertain terms that he'd be seeing him soon . . . no, Frankie didn't give a shit about any of that either when it was happening, or afterwards . . . when all of it, *all of it*, sank into a blur . . .

15

Other than that Faithless tune, 'Insomnia', still going round and round and round his head, the only proof Frankie James had that he'd been in the Atlantic Bar the night before, completely off his chops, was that when he woke up and stumbled through to the kitchen of his flat at just gone four on Monday afternoon, there was a nice little card there from Xandra and Maxine, telling him thanks for all the rounds he'd brought them there and that they hoped by the time he woke up he'd have slept it all off OK, as well as thanking him once again for putting them up in the hotel for their treat, and letting him know they'd be back to help with the monster tidy up downstairs tomorrow afternoon.

Another message was waiting for Frankie on the Nokia phone Little Terry had given him. It told him where to meet Bram, Rivet and Lola. It told him when.

*

Really? Like, seriously? Honestly? Are you having a fucking giraffe?

But Bram wasn't joking. No wide smile split that great

209

scarred melon of a head of his. Meaning he must be dead serious. Or as dead serious as a seven-foot geezer wearing nicked Thames Water overalls, bright-yellow waders and a Second World War gas mask slung around his tree trunk of a neck ever could be.

The four of them – Frankie, Bram, Lola and Rivet – were hunched up in the confines of that single-storey maintenance building at the end of the alley at the back of the Ambassador Club. They'd pulled up outside it two minutes ago, at just gone midnight, in a white Transit with fake plates and a just as fake 'Thames Water' stencil plastered down its side. Rivet had backed them right up against the maintenance building's door. A quick look round to check that no one was snooping, and out they'd all bundled, with Rivet working the maintenance building's lock in three seconds flat.

Inside it was windowless and stank of damp. The bright LED head torches the others were already wearing clicked on one by one, showing flickering glimpses of the little room they now found themselves inside, as well as the gas mask that Bram had just stuffed into Frankie's already gloved hands.

'But these things are never going to work,' Frankie said, staring down at it. 'They must be about a million years old.'

'Second World War, actually,' Rivet said.

'Yeah, I was being sarcastic,' Frankie hissed. 'You should look it up in the dictionary. You'll find it between . . . crazy . . . and . . . er . . .' Shit, what else *did* you find it between? Bastards? Lunatics? Psychopaths? Grrrr. What other word for nutter was there that came after 'S'?

210

'Wing nut?' Lola suggested.

'Yeah. Yeah, exactly right. Wing nut.' Beaten in an English vocabulary test by a professional criminal ex-heroin addict from Amsterdam . . . it hardly boded well for Frankie's chances of success for the rest of tonight.

She smiled at him, pleased with herself, but waveringly so, maybe because the penny had just dropped for her too that what they were planning – or rather what Bram was planning – was liable to get them all captured or killed, or quite possibly both.

Bram signed something to Rivet.

'He says they have newly fitted charcoal filters in them, leaving them perfectly sufficient for our purposes.'

'Yeah, well they'd bloody better. Because you know what? Since coming into contact with Dougie Hamilton and you lot, I've imagined my demise occurring in a number of scenarios – but never once through being overpowered by the stench of pure shit while dressed in something that might last have been sported by Dame Vera friggin' Lynn.'

'OK, but no need to be so grumpy about it,' Lola complained.

But Frankie *was* grumpy. In spite of almost a whole bloody box of paracetamol, his head was still pounding from his excesses of last night. He was not in a good mood. Vodka? Had it been vodka he'd stuck on after leaving the club? He could still taste something worse. Maybe tequila. Maybe vomit too.

He couldn't remember anything after doing the last of those pills and that vodka in the alley . . . just glimpses, blurs. Christ, he couldn't even remember for certain who'd bloody won. Had he made a dick of himself? Been hammered while he'd still been in the Ambassador? Who knew? Only time, he guessed, would tell.

He pulled on the head torch he'd been issued with in the back of the van, clicked the switch and shone its beam over the locked sewer access door set into the building's mildewed back wall.

He shivered at the thought of what lay in wait beyond. Couldn't help himself. He hated confined spaces. Got well claustrophobic. It was bad enough in here already. He shone his torch around. It couldn't have been more than ten by ten. And horrible with it. A little table, two chairs. A funny-looking little phone. A little washbasin. Little hooks with helmets on the wall. Little signs telling you don't do this and do do that. It was like a goddamn freakin' clubhouse for moles. Even though they were still up on street level, they could have been miles underground.

'Two minutes,' Rivet said, taking a metal T-bar off a rack on the wall.

Frankie could almost hear the seconds ticking down in his head. Timing. Hell, yeah. That's what this was all about. They'd gone through it all after The Saint had come to get him and taken him back over to the riverside pad. Not just once, but ten times. Old Bram here had a schedule and reckoned that, so long as they kept to it exactly, it would get them all in and out of the Royal Academy alive and in one piece.

'Ala-fucking-kazam,' Rivet said, turning the T-bar in the outsized keyhole in the centre of the access door, its click echoing round the room.

Abracadabra. Alakazam. The perfect Houdini move. Was that really what this was all about for these bastards? Some kind of a game? It certainly looked that way to Frankie, the way they were smiling, the glint in their eyes. They looked more like pill heads reaching the front of a club queue. Mad for it, they were. Either that, or just plain mad.

'Spoo-ky,' Rivet hissed, peering down into the dark, as he pulled the T-bar out of the keyhole again.

He sniggered so hard that Frankie thought he might actually have meant the pun. It was shit enough for even Tommy Riley to appreciate. Shit being the operative word here, of course, as the reek of London's bowels began guffing up at them from the hideous Victorian netherworld lying in wait for them beneath.

Frankie finished heaving himself into his waders and pulled his backpack on. Inside was a bunch of stuff he'd be needing in a bit. Cloths to wrap the artworks in . . . the ones he'd been busily memorizing for the last two hours. And what else? Oh, yeah, clean gloves for wearing inside, so he didn't damage the merch. And a balaclava just in case, even though Bram said the CCTV should go down with the rest of the alarm system. *Should.* Yeah, Frankie remembered the way Rivet had said it. And, last but not least, a brand-new pair of British Knights trainers – British Knights! the cheapskates! – for wearing once they hit the RA, because right up there at the top of Bram's Happy Heist Hitlist was that they'd be leaving no poopy prints for the rozzers to follow back down into the sewers.

'One minute,' Rivet said, checking his watch.

'Can you just stop that?' Frankie said.

'What?'

'The time thing. The countdown. I mean, apart from it being deeply fucking irritating, and if anything *adding* to the bloody stress of all this, it doesn't even make sense.'

Rivet looked offended. 'How so?'

'How in that when you get to zero in around thirty seconds time, it's not really zero at all, is it? Not as far as the – I don't know, *wider mission* – is concerned. It's just zero for this little bit of it and then you're going to have to start the countdown all over again for the rest of what we've got to do.'

'He's got a point,' said Lola.

Rivet folded his sinewy arms across his chest. 'No, he does not. I'm partitioning.'

'Partitioning?' both Frankie and Lola said at once.

'Precisely. I'm dividing the *wider mission* into bite-sized, manageable pieces, each of which I've assigned an individual countdown to keep us all on track.'

Frankie turned round to face Bram. 'And you agree with this, right?'

'Agree with it? It was his idea,' Rivet said.

Bram nodded.

'Come on, Frankie.' Rivet patted him on the back. 'Just trust in the plan.'

Trust in the plan . . . trust in the plan . . . Frankie peered past Rivet into the gaping hole the other side of the sewer access door. The rusted hoops of the top of a ladder showed against a backdrop of dirty, damp red brick. Yeah, Frankie would trust in the plan all right, if only because it sure as hell didn't look like it was God's jurisdiction down there.

'Oh, and Frankie. Keep a hold of this key, would ya?' Rivet said. 'We'll be needing it to get up out of that manhole the other side.'

Frankie took it, stuffed it into his pack. Bram groaned as he scraped the top of his head on the ceiling and his torch beam swung around maddeningly for a second or two. It didn't exactly add to the overall ambience of the place. More like reminded Frankie of that crazy old show, *The Prisoner*. In fact, maybe that's what all this was. Some kind of drug-induced fantasy? An after-effect of the diazepam? Or maybe it was even still last summer and he was off his head in Ibiza with Jesús, Balearic Bob and Grew – and everything that he thought had happened since had been nothing but a dream? Jesus – real Jesus, this time – he'd give both his left and his right nut for that.

'OK, *muchachos*, let's go,' Rivet said. Then through the hole he went.

'And you are really, really sure about all this?' Frankie checked one final time, turning to Bram, kind of hoping that a reason might have just this very second occurred to him to call the whole thing off.

But no such luck. He was grinning again. Madly? Or out of confidence? Or perhaps he just got off on this. Like that Hannibal in *The A-Team*. Maybe Bram just loved seeing a plan come together and really could be trusted after all.

'You next,' said Lola.

Oh, great. So now he was second in line. What was it they always called the poor bastards at the front of the column in those Vietnam movies? The ones who always ended up treading on a mine, or getting machine-gunned or machete'd in half? On 'Point'. Yeah, just brilliant. What a fucking honour. Not.

He turned to tell her as much and to suggest that he bring up the rear, but she simply screwed up her face and quickly waved him on.

'Just get going and quit shining that torch in my eyes,' she said. 'From here on in, we're going to need all the night sight we can get.'

Ah, screw it. At least going up front with Rivet meant he'd get this journey over with first. Frankie turned his back on her and stepped through the doorway and stared down the vertical shaft that Rivet had descended into. But, God, the stink, the stink. Whatever you do, don't breathe through your nose.

The top of the little guy's head was ten feet down already and showing no sign of slowing. Jesus, how deep did this thing reach? Well, fuck it. Here goes nothing. Frankie swung himself around onto the ladder and followed the rungs down, his torch beam tracking the Tetris of wet brickwork as he went. Left him feeling horribly out of body, out of mind, like he was nothing but another slow-falling brick himself, like none of this was real or could be real, and was just part of some crazy computer game dream, in which he was doomed to be trapped forever. He fought the urge to scream.

Be cool. Be cool. This will pass. Jesus, please, just let it be so. And don't fight it. So what if it feels like a game? Run with that. Yeah, whatever gets you through. That this is just some dumb video game . . . where everything you can see . . . the bricks . . . the rungs . . . none of this is real . . . and this isn't you, it's just a game character . . . nothing really bad can happen to you . . . nothing bad at all . . .

His heartbeat slowed. Christ, he suddenly realized how much it had been pounding. Was that what this was? A panic attack? A friggin' heart attack? He hauled air into his lungs. In, out, in, out. Bloody hell, had he not been breathing at all? He even risked breathing in through his nose. And could it be . . . ? Yes, the stench seemed to be fading. Because of what? He was getting used to it? Christ, a new low indeed. Getting used to *this* . . .

'Wowzer,' Rivet said from below, his voice echoing up, suddenly sounding like a character on a TV playing in another room.

Frankie had gone down fourteen rungs already. Fifteen . . . sixteen . . . shit, he'd caught that counting bug off Rivet . . . seventeen . . . eighteen . . . when *ouch*. His knee jarred. Looking down, he saw he'd reached the bottom. A flat black brick floor. Looking up, he saw Bram's giant plastic yellow butt about to squish into his face, and quickly stepped back out of the way.

He tensed, half expecting to crack his head against a wall, but instead he found himself stepping backwards through a red-brick arch. He felt the space around him opening up, almost before he saw it. And Rivet wasn't kidding. Wowzer, indeed.

The main sewer tunnel was huge, way bigger than he'd been expecting. Its roof was cylindrical. A half-pipe, like the skater kids rode under the Westway. Only upside down, of course. And dripping with piss. The whole thing was at least twenty foot in diameter. The sewage channel running beneath it was dry, thank God, not the thick slick tarry gloop sliding past, like Frankie had dreaded. It was black and kind of shiny and almost looked spotless in a weird way. You could've driven a Ford bleedin' Mondeo through it and not even got a spot on the wheels.

'You OK?' Rivet asked.

'Uh-huh. Cold.'

Rivet checked his schematic. Keeping his torch beam down to stop him from blinding them, Frankie turned to check that Bram and Lola were behind him, and saw that they were.

'Twenty minutes,' Rivet said, setting off along the raised walkway that ran up alongside the sewage channel.

Frankie followed, dead ahead, Rivet counting down a minute over what felt like about the first hundred or so yards. But then the going got slower with each step. Wet slime on the ground. Twice Frankie nearly came a cropper. The second time it was only Bram grabbing him by the shoulder that stopped him lurching off their ledge and into the tunnel below. He'd started spotting little flashes of movement all around. Rats.

'Whoah, check it out,' Rivet called back, pointing down into the now frothing, bubbling, slow-flowing channel below.

'What the fuck is that?'

'A fatberg.'

'I refer you to my last question.'

'An iceberg . . . only made of fat.'

'But fat from where?'

'Fat that's been flushed?'

'Flushed?'

'Down the john. Or poured down the drain.'

'*Poured?* There's no fucking way *that* was poured any-where.' Frankie couldn't take his eyes off the disgusting thing. 'How about you guys go collect a sample?' Frankie said. 'You know, to remind you of our little trip.'

Bram flipped Frankie a sign. A universal one that even he recognized. A middle digit pointing upwards, nail-side towards him.

'Yeah, fuck you too, Bram,' Frankie said.

Bram grinned. The stink was almost overpowering now. It wasn't just the reek of fresh shit either. That was more like just the icing on this whole disgusting cake. Frankie was going to need more than a soak in the tub to get rid of this. More like a hose down. Hey, maybe he should suggest that this is what they should do next? Move from impersonating water board employees to joining the fire brigade.

Concentrate, dammit. Just focus on what's ahead. And ignore the damn squeaks of those rats. He followed his feet. One step at a time. Rivet called out another minute. And another, as the tunnel began curving slowly round to the right. At least he thought it was curving. Hard to be sure. Time felt weird down here. Breathing, everything, felt out of synch.

A breeze. Frankie felt that too now. How weird was that? Here, underground. But, according to Bram, this system they'd just entered ran for hundreds and hundreds of miles. From all around came the sound of dripping water. *Plink-plink, plonk-plonk.* Like some pisshead on a piano late at night. Frankie shivered, pulling the zip of his hoodie up tight to his throat. He pulled his hood up too as something unspeakable splashed onto his head.

'Gross,' he muttered.

'What?'

'Nothing.' Frankie's own voice was echoing now, like he was on a mic. He was half tempted to start belting out 'One nil to the Arsenal' to the tune of 'Go West' by the Village People. But, for one thing, he doubted any of the others would get the joke – even though it was *really* good, because they were actually heading west. And, for another, the further he looked down that gaping black tunnel ahead – and now here to the left and to the right as they approached what looked like a junction, with great brick arches separating the four tunnels where they met – the less funny any of this seemed. And not just here, the bloody horror of all this, and the stink now rising stronger by the second as that cold wind picked up again . . . but what was waiting for them at the end of the tunnel, at the top of the ladder they'd go up.

He nearly walked smack into Rivet's back as he stopped dead in front of him. Frankie could hear water – or liquid, anyway – running clearly now. He looked down into the channel crossing theirs at a right angle, but at a lower level, and yeah, sure enough, there it was, the sludge, an actual active main sewerage channel – and the stink hit him then too, like a shovel to the face. Even Frankie's tarnished old ex-smoker's nostrils snapped shut like fucking mussels, with a mind of their bloody own. He jerked his mask onto his face, but within four or five breaths, it had steamed up so much he couldn't see, so down it came again.

Rivet consulted his precious schematic again for a

few seconds, before heading right, so that they were now following the course of the new 'wet' channel. Typical. And gross. The old pongometer stepped up sharply pace by pace. Like it wasn't even air they were breathing, more some kind of foul, gloopy liquid instead. Bile rose up inside Frankie. Shit. What was happening? Was he about to puke?

He started breathing through his mask every few seconds, then taking it off so he could still see. Rivet was doing the same. Frankie's whole body was sweating now, his heartbeat gibbering ten to the dozen. Breathe in, breathe out, fucking shake it all about. Frankie wasn't exactly the world's biggest classical music fan, but even he recognized the tune that Rivet was now whistling. 'The Hall of the Mountain King', from *Peer Gynt*. Frankie still remembered listening to it at primary school with his eyes shut, after his teacher had terrified the shit out of his whole class with tales of murderous trolls.

'Half a mile,' Rivet grunted back.

OK, cool, so just think on that. Half a mile. Sod all. A tenth of what you run nearly every bleedin' day. Half a mile was all it would take and then they'd be there, according to Bram's time schedule, coming up under the RA, with the hardest bit of Bram's precious bloody plan already under their belts. So long as they didn't get lost, of course. Oh yeah, because there was still the possibility of *that*.

Frankie flinched as something showered down from above. Dust. He glanced up at the tunnel's arched roof, the torch beam on his head tracking wherever he looked. So what the fuck had that been? The street? A lorry? The number 14 bus? For the first time, he wondered where the hell he was. Well, down in a sewer. Obviously. But where in London? Which street? He tried to work it out as he carried on walking. But everything seemed back to front and upside down. Thank God for Rivet's schematic, because Frankie might as well have been stuck down a tunnel on the moon.

'Five minutes,' Rivet said.

But then all Frankie could hear was his heart in his ears, pounding and pounding away. They reached another junction, and this time branched off along a – thank God for that – dry channel.

Rivet's footsteps carried on crunching up ahead. *Crunching*. Looking down, Frankie saw the ground wasn't slimy any more. Ten yards on and hang on. Aye-aye. He caught a blast of cool, clean air wafting down from the tunnel ahead of him on the breeze.

But that's when he heard it too. A low rumbling noise. So low that at first he thought it was his stomach. But it rose, and kept rising. First Frankie's feet and then his whole body started to vibrate. Rivet must have felt it too, because he'd stopped dead in his tracks and was reaching out with his right hand to support himself against the tunnel wall. Frankie did it too, adrenaline rushing through him. The whole wall was buzzing, felt like something was trying to break through. Oh, shit. What the fuck was happening now? He'd have tried shouting out, but he knew there was no point. But then, just as fast as it had come, the noise began fading, and then went. And as Rivet turned to face him and grinned, Frankie too worked out what it must have been.

'The metro,' Rivet said, at the exact same time that Frankie said, 'The Tube.'

'Then I guess this must be our stop,' Rivet said, consulting his schematic a final time, before shining his head beam at the glint of a metal ladder rising up through a vertical tunnel in the ceiling ahead.

16

'Shhhh,' Rivet hissed down.

He'd reached the top of the ladder, but instead of opening the manhole cover he'd come up against with the hook handle tool Frankie had just handed him, he remained stationary, with his radio earpiece clamped into his ears.

'Twenty seconds . . .' he said, ' . . . ten . . . zero . . . Jesus, where the fuck is he?'

Frankie peered back down the ladder from where he was holding on, his torch beam lighting up Bram's huge, ghoulish face. Any sign of nerves? Nope. Just the usual blank slate.

Then a crackle of static from above.

'OK, we're good to go. The alarm's down,' Rivet hissed. 'But time's still of the essence. The alarm company will probably be sending maintenance out tonight, not tomorrow like we were hoping. Our priority's still to get in and out of there as quickly as we can.'

Frankie watched him shuffling around up above him for a second, then heard the clank of metal on metal, as he wedged the hook handle tool into the manhole cover's pick hole. A squeak. A grunting of effort. A curse.

'Damn thing won't fucking budge,' Rivet growled.

Frankie felt a flash of hope inside him. Because if they couldn't get out, then they'd have to turn back, right? Without it being his fault either, meaning there was nothing that Dougie could do.

More grunting. Another curse.

Please, please let it be jammed.

But Rivet was stronger than he looked.

'Bollocks,' Frankie muttered, as he heard the lid finally give.

A rush of cold air. Light. Bloody hell, actual moonlight flooded down from above.

'What did you say?' Rivet asked.

'Er, brilliant,' Frankie said. 'I said brilliant. You know, for getting it open. Well done, man. Good on you.'

Rivet was already moving. He slithered up through the opening and disappeared from sight. Frankie climbed up the ladder after him and poked his head out and looked around. The sewer exit was in the corner of some kind of an enclosed outdoor space that was thick with plants. High, windowed walls jutted up on every side into the moonlit, starry sky.

'Turn your goddamn flashlight off,' snapped Rivet, who was already crouched in the shadows of a nearby wall. 'You look like a goddamn lighthouse.'

'Yeah? Well, I feel more like a bloody rabbit,' Frankie said. And not a happy little bunny either. More like one of those poor little bastards from *Watership Down*, doomed to get its head chewed off by a dog.

'Rabid?' Rivet said, screwing up his face, as Frankie clicked off his torch.

'Yeah, that too.'

Frankie hauled himself up out through the hole and crawled over next to Rivet. He could hear a squeaking sound coming from somewhere nearby. Couldn't see what it was.

'So are we in the right place?'

Rivet smiled grimly. 'Of course.'

Yeah, right. Because of the goddamn plan. Rivet turned his back on him and shuffled up beside the nearest door. A jangle of keys, or picks, or something Frankie couldn't see. Rivet started breaking in.

A grunting noise behind them. Frankie turned to see Bram's head sticking up out of the manhole. But that was it. He just stayed there. Then started flailing one arm around and going purple in the face. Shit a brick. He was stuck. His massive shoulders were still wedged tight inside the hole.

He signed something at Frankie, one-handedly. Didn't take a genius to work out that it was probably 'Help'. Frankie crawled back over and took a hold of him under the armpits – well glad he'd already just pulled his gloves for heading inside on – and started to pull. Nothing. Bram didn't budge an inch. From down below he heard the sound of muffled shouting. Must have been Lola pushing from her end. First bit of luck Frankie had got all day, not being the one down there having to deal with that. He hauled harder, but again it was no good. The big bastard really was wedged tight.

'Shit,' Frankie said, 'I reckon we're just gonna have to leave you here until you lose a few pounds.'

Bram looked furious for a second. But then his eyes started to water. His whole face went purple. He even started to shake. For a second, Frankie thought he was literally about to explode with rage. But then he realized he was actually laughing. Or trying to, at least.

And a good bloody thing too, it turned out. Because that's all it took – a little shuffle of those thick ribs inside that enormous body of his – and suddenly he was moving. *Come on, come on.* Frankie continued to heave, half expecting him to actually *pop* out of there any second now like a friggin' champagne cork – and, oh yes, wagon or no wagon, if he made it back safe and sound after all this, he was going to get just as bloody leathered as he had done last night as soon as he got home.

Frankie flopped back as Bram finally came free. The two of them crawled over to where Rivet now had the door ajar. Frankie could still hear that sodding squeaking sound from somewhere out here nearby.

'What the hell is that?' he hissed.

'The bunny,' Rivet told him. 'Quick, go get it.'

'You what?'

'The bunny, man. The bunny. Over there on that drainpipe,' he said, pointing. 'Right in front of that sensor just there.'

Frankie sighed. Could this get any weirder? He crawled over to where Rivet had said – and, sure enough, there was a toy rabbit wedged up against the drainpipe. And, not only that, it was the source of the squeaking too. Its legs and arms were rotating either side of the pipe it was wedged behind, like it was desperately waving for help.

'You got it?' hissed Rivet.

'Yeah, I bloody got it,' Frankie hissed back, jerking the bunny free and fumbling around in the moonlight until he located a switch up its arse and shut it down. What the hell? So much for thinking this couldn't get any weirder. He stared open-mouthed at it in his hands and saw now that it was one of those Duracell Bunnies off the TV ads, the ones that just went on and on and on. And what's more it was wearing a Blackburn Rovers football strip of all things. Had to be some kind of limited-edition toy.

'What the fuck is this doing here?' Frankie said, wriggling back over to where the others were waiting.

'Just bag it. It mustn't be found.'

'Why? What's it done? Robbed a bank in Toy Town?'

'Just fucking do it,' Rivet snapped. 'It's done its job now anyhow.'

The first time Frankie could remember him losing his temper. Okey-dokey. So things were getting serious now. Frankie did as he'd been asked.

'What job?' he said.

Rivet ignored him. Frankie saw that Lola was smiling. Bram too. Or more like beaming in his case. Kind of with pride.

'Just tell him,' Lola said. 'What does it matter now?'

'It's what triggered the alarm.'

'What? For real?' Frankie looked between them, but yeah, it looked like they were serious, all right. 'Your fifth columnist . . .' Wasn't that what they'd called their inside guy?

'Yeah, the guard, he stashed it there and switched it on . . . and cleared away just enough of the foliage there so it was in view of the sensor . . . but wouldn't be seen by anyone looking out.'

And so it had then kept triggering the alarm over and over again, until the inside guy's boss became convinced that the whole alarm system was on the blink . . . and so had switched it off, just as Big Bram's plan had required.

'It's clever,' Frankie finally said. 'Funny.'

'Clever *and* funny. You hear that, big guy? Uh-oh,' Lola said, holding out the palms of her hands like she was sitting in front of a fire. 'Feels like the big man's starting to blush.'

'OK, well, enough of this jibber jabber,' snapped Rivet, 'let's move out, people. Now. Let's go.'

He waved them through. On the other side of the door was someone's office. A desk and chairs. Wooden panelling. Artworks on the walls. Bram went first, then Frankie, then behind him someone cried out in pain. Both him and Bram turned to look. It was Lola. She was sprawled on the floor, clutching at her leg. She must have tripped over the door frame on the way in.

'Shit,' Frankie said, crouching down beside her to support her as she struggled to sit.

'It's my ankle.' Her face was screwed up in pain.

Rivet knelt down and gently took her foot in his hand. She groaned.

'OK, I'm going to try turning it, just gently,' he said.

Another groan. She was gritting her teeth.

'Without taking these waders off, I can't tell how bad it is.'

'I'll be all right,' she said, 'just get me up.'

Frankie helped her, but the second she tried to walk, even with him still there supporting her, her leg gave way beneath her and she gasped out again from the pain. She managed

229

to move a couple of paces, but only by half hopping and putting the minimum weight on her right leg.

'Easy, easy,' Rivet soothed, 'let's just sit you back down.'

From the way he said it, the look that passed between them, Frankie suddenly got it: the two of them were one.

'I'll be OK, dammit,' she protested, but her face was just one great big grimace now.

'No,' Rivet said, 'your ankle's screwed. With a bit of luck it's just a bad sprain, but it could even be fractured too. Either way, there's no way you're going to be able to do what we need you to do.'

'But, I –'

'I'm serious.' He was holding her hand now, looking her hard in the eyes. 'In fact, if you're going to get back at all by the time we need to, at the rate you're going to be moving, you're going to have to set off now.'

'Then who'll –'

Bram was crouched down by them too now. He interrupted her with a hurried set of signs.

'OK, yeah, that'll have to work,' Rivet said. 'Frankie, old bean,' he said in a cod English accent. 'I'm afraid it looks like you're up.'

'Up where? Shit creek? Tell me something I don't know.'

Rivet nodded up towards the top of the building. It made no sense.

'But all the pieces I'm meant to be getting are here on the ground floor.'

'Me and Bram will handle that. We need you to go upstairs instead and do what Lola was meant to do.'

'No way.' God knew Frankie didn't want to be here in

the first place, but at least he'd had a chance to learn his part in this as well as he could, the pieces as well as the route. But now what? They wanted him to wing it? And go wandering off into this labyrinth of a building? No friggin' way.

'We got no other choice.'

'But why me?'

Bram signed.

'Bram's too big to get through it,' Lola said.

'And I'm too short to reach it,' said Rivet.

'Reach what?'

'The hatch.'

'What hatch?'

'The one that leads out onto the roof.'

'And why the fuck would I be going out there?'

'To scatter all this shit that's in my backpack.'

'What shit?'

Rivet ignored the question. 'And photograph it,' he said.

'With this . . .' Lola grimaced in pain as she pulled out a small camera – Viollet's camera, Frankie saw.

'What, we're collecting evidence of our own crime now, are we? Oh, that's just brilliant,' Frankie said. 'What say we all have a nice little group shot of ourselves waiting out here before we all go in?'

Another flurry of signs from Bram.

'Just take the camera,' Rivet said. 'There's no time to explain.'

Frankie gritted his teeth.

'Just point and click,' Rivet said, demonstrating by taking a quick snap of the wall. 'And do it right,' he warned, jamming the camera into Frankie's hand. 'Because Dougie's going to be looking at these photographs too.'

Rivet helped Lola off with her backpack.

'Swap,' he said, handing it over to Frankie.

Frankie peeled his own off his back and made the trade. Rivet unfurled another rolled-up piece of paper, this time showing the floor plans for inside. An arrowed route ran from here where they'd be entering the building just like on the one he'd been given to study. Only instead of leading to the main downstairs galleries, this one led upstairs.

'It'll take you up through the permanent galleries,' Lola said. 'Where the route ends, that's where you'll find the sky-lights leading out. Oh, and make sure to leave them open. As obviously as you can.'

'And the . . . *shit* . . . you want scattering? Any particular instruction with that?'

'No, just leave it up there where it can all be found. Be creative, huh? Make it look arty. Mysterious. Have fun.'

'Fun . . . Yes, ma'am.' Might as well get this over like a good soldier, eh? Because they sure as hell weren't planning on giving him the big picture now.

'And watch out.'

'What for?'

'The guards. There might not be any. Our guy on the inside says he'll do what he can to keep them away from where we need to be, and especially from the *Sensation* exhibition, but you need to keep wary, in case there is some-one doing the rounds in the permanent galleries upstairs.'

'OK, let's get these damn waders off,' Rivet said. 'Let's get this thing done with, OK?'

17

'I'll come with you as far as these back stairs,' Rivet told him. 'But then you're on your own. As soon as you're done, get back here as fast as you can.'

What? Like instead of just chilling out up there for a while and maybe indulging in a little amateur astronomy?

'Sure,' said Frankie, 'I'll see you back here.'

Rivet just stared at him for a second, maybe picking up on the sarcasm even in what he had said. Then he pulled his balaclava down and Frankie did the same. Rivet stood with his ear pressed up against the office door and listened. Then Frankie heard that same tinny jangling sound as before and the door lock gave a click. Rivet pulled the door gently ajar and peered out.

'All clear,' he said. 'Ten minutes. Let's go.'

Frankie checked his dad's Rolex. He could just about make out the luminous hands. Funny, but this whole countdown thing made much more sense when it was leading to you getting the hell out of here instead of in.

Rivet was already through the door. Frankie followed him into the short corridor that lay beyond. It was carpeted. Nice and quiet. If only the rest of the building was like this.

But it wasn't, was it? More like polished wooden floors and floor tiles. Frankie remembered the click-clack of footsteps echoing all around the last time he'd been here.

Rivet moved fast, passing the doorways to what Frankie guessed were other offices left and right. The corridor terminated in a T-junction. Rivet hung a right. Didn't bother consulting his floor plans. Probably already had the whole damn thing memorized. Frankie checked his own black hoodie pouch for the schematic Lola had given him with his route on it. Lose that and he'd be lost too.

Frankie felt a pat on his back and turned to see Bram gazing down at him and giving him a giant fat thumbs up.

'Thanks, big guy,' Frankie said. Then he turned and walked through the door.

He felt his stomach churning like he was going to barf as he stepped out into the main reception. His legs felt suddenly light, like they were about to give way. He remembered being back at primary school again, only this time the Christmas play. He couldn't have been more than seven. He'd been a shepherd and he'd had to give the closing speech. This felt just like that. Like stepping out on stage. Like he was being watched, being judged. Like every single step he took could go wrong.

His British Knights trainers squeaked as bad as those rats down in the tunnel as he made his way to the stairs. He kept to the shadows where he could, skirting the perimeter. Another memory. Dougie Hamilton this time. That security guard telling him to pick up his rubbish. Just about right here where Frankie was now.

He looked up as he reached the bottom step and counted

at least two CCTV cameras up there in the corners of the room. Impossible not to imagine some uniformed thug's eyes widening at the other end as he spotted a movement and zoomed in. But as he covered the first few steps, neither camera tracked him. Meaning – please God – Bram was right and the cameras were just another part of the same security system that his wheeze with that Duracell Bunny had already blitzed.

Squeaketty-squeak . . . Frankie followed the staircase, zigzagging up. He pulled out the floor plan and quickly orientated himself. Yep, he needed to go left now. That corridor over there. The same ghoulish pale-blue lighting as downstairs was operating up here too. Frankie reached the double doors leading into what was marked on his map as the first of the galleries exhibiting the academy's permanent collection, whatever the hell that was.

The top half of the doors was made of see-through glass. More of that pale-blue light beyond. And, shit. Frankie's heart jumped like it was about to do an *Alien* out of his ribcage. His hand froze on the door handle. Someone was there. A man's silhouette stood less than ten feet away. They were staring right at him. Don't fucking breathe.

But then he did. And not just breathed, laughed. Because it wasn't a person, was it? It was a bloody statue. He slowly turned the door handle and the door gave. Not locked, thank God. He pushed it slowly open and stepped inside. Yes, up close he could see that the figure who he'd thought was eyeballing him was Roman and made of stone. Jesus, he even had a friggin' discus in his hand. As Frankie's eyes grew more accustomed to the light, he saw the room was full of sculptures. All part of the Academy's permanent collection, no doubt.

He checked his floor plan again, this time risking using his head torch. He took the second of the two doors on the far wall leading out of here. This one was unlocked too. He stepped through into another gallery. All paintings, this time. With a couple of benches right bang in the centre of the room – directly below the skylights he now needed to bust out through.

He hopped up onto the nearest one and reached up. Bollocks. No good. He was still a good two feet away from reaching the skylight's frame. He used his torch again to check it over. No latches. No catches. No way he could see to open it from this side. But that was OK, right? Because Rivet had said he had to make it obvious that they'd come in and out through the roof. Fine. Then the best way was just to smash the shit out of that glass. But with what? Because it looked well thick. Probably reinforced.

He looked desperately around. Rivet might not have been here in person, but he sure as hell was in spirit. Frankie could practically hear him hissing another one of his bloody segmented countdowns into his lughole. There were plenty of paintings, of course, that he could have used to try and crack the glass. But they all looked well old and the same no doubt went for their frames. Even if he could manhandle one of them up there good enough to swing it like a club, it would probably crack and disintegrate well before that reinforced glass.

The only thing that looked remotely solid enough to break through with was the one thing on display in here that wasn't a painting. It was a great big lump of what looked like stone on the other side of the room. He ran over and read the label underneath it. The *Taddei Tondo*. And, yeah, you know what? It might just do it. It was certainly heavy enough. If he could just get it back there onto that bench, he might be able to swing it up and smash the shit out of that glass.

He reached for it, but then stopped. The date next to its name on that label caught his eye. The name of the geezer who'd carved it too. Michelangelo. Fuck a duck. As in *the* Michelangelo, right? As in the same fellah who carved *David* and the bloody Sistine Chapel ceiling. Oh yeah, Frankie's old art teacher, Mr Garcia, had taught him plenty about him. About how he was possibly the most talented artist who'd ever lived.

And no, no way could Frankie bring himself to use it like he'd just planned – even if he could lift it. He didn't even think about it, he just stepped back. It was one thing stealing a Virgin Mary made out of elephant poo, but using a Michelangelo as a battering ram would have been totally out of order, right?

But if not that, then what? Again, he imagined Rivet's voice counting on down. He stared desperately around. There had to be something. And then he saw it. Half hidden in the shadows, over there in the corner. A fire extinguisher. Nice and solid. Should be well up to the task.

He jerked it out of its cradle and ran back to the centre of the room, hauled one bench up on top of the other and carefully clambered up. Plenty close enough now. He could even see his eyes glinting back at him from his balaclava in the reflection of the skylight glass. He got a good grip on the extinguisher and swung it hard. Nearly came a cropper too as it bounced right back at him. Just about kept his balance. Definitely reinforced then. He planted his legs wide and steady and gave it all he could . . . and this time with a horrible squeaky sound, a little crack zigzagged out from the frame across the glass. He hit it again and the crack grew wider. The third time, the whole pane shattered, raining down glass all over him and onto the floor.

Had that been noisy? Shit, he couldn't tell. Noisy enough to hear on one of the floors below if anyone was about and listening down there? Better pray not. He lowered the fire extinguisher by its hose gently onto the floor and reached up and broke the remaining shards of glass free from the skylight frame with his gloved fingers.

Time to move. He flattened the little backpack Lola had given him as tight as he could onto his back and then reached up and took a grip on the frame. What if someone was up there? He got a horrible vision of guards and cops just squatting there waiting to catch him, their beady little eyes already glued to his exposed fingertips, reaching out to haul him up.

Steady, Eddie, he slowly pulled himself up. Thank Christ for all that work down the gym, because at least he had the muscle to do it. The first thing he felt was the temperature drop as he hauled himself up. Cool air. God, it felt good. Like a glass of cold water. Relief hit him next. No one was here. Just a long, wide flat roof. Straining now, as he heaved his torso on out, he quickly shifted his position and hooked his knee up onto the frame. His heart lurched as he nearly lost balance. But then he was up. He was through.

So what now? Keep low. That was for sure. Because there were taller buildings here. Way taller. Windows and balconies all around. And so what if it was the middle of the night? This was London, the city that never bloody slept. Anyone who looked out or stepped out would get a bird's-eye view of him if they only looked his way.

Bollocks. He rolled onto his back. A sky full of stars. It would have been beautiful if he hadn't been so sodding scared. Right, time to see what goodies Lola had packed for their little adventure. A tuna sandwich, perhaps? A Penguin? A Twix? No such luck. He unzipped her rucksack and tipped its contents out onto the roof by his side and just gawped. What the hell? Was he dreaming? An arrow. Rope. Crampons. He felt like he was playing some surreal version of the friggin' *Generation Game*. What next? A cuddly pissing toy? Oh no, he'd already found that downstairs. Oh, but here was the pièce de friggin' résistance too. A bunch of black-and-white postcards of Houdini himself.

Just the usual kind of stuff a gal packed whenever she went on an art heist then. It made about as much sense as some of the art pieces in that *Sensation* exhibition down below. But then maybe that was the point? A crime to match the target. He remembered that band from a couple of years back. The KLF. Wasn't that what they'd been called? The same ones who'd dumped a dead sheep outside the BRIT awards after pretending to shoot the crowd? The crazier the publicity stunt, the more attention it got. Meaning maybe there was method in this madness. Bram and Dougie's method, through and through.

But what the fuck, no matter, hey? At least Frankie knew what to do with it. Scatter it, right? Wasn't that what they'd said? Well, scatter it he would. Like a solid bloody pro. Or more like an exploded aircraft, actually. He just got up and half ran, half bounded across the roof, dropping the items willy-nilly. Then he remembered what Lola had said. Make it look weird . . . mysterious . . . arty. OK, fine. So be it.

He got creative with the rope, tying it round the periscope hood of an air vent, before lowering it down the side of the building, carefully between the lines of windows so it couldn't be seen from inside. It didn't even reach the ground, coming up maybe ten feet short. He could imagine some copper just standing down there and staring and scratching his head and wondering if someone really could have climbed up and then back down with all those stolen works.

Frankie couldn't help smiling at the thought. He grabbed the postcards of Houdini next and arranged them in a pentagram, using little sticks and stones he found in the guttering to hold them in place. He looked around, satisfied. The whole thing looked like the product of a deeply disturbed mind. Not so far from the truth either. He needed to get out of here before he lost his marbles for real.

Shit. The camera. He'd nearly forgotten. Snap snap. He did it quick.

Gripping on to the frame of the skylight, he then lowered himself back down, his muscles warming to the task this time, already limbered up. He climbed down off the benches. He thought about moving them back to how they'd been before. But no. Leaving them like this was fine. It would just look like whoever had nicked the exhibits from downstairs had used the benches to get back up onto the roof.

Right, time to scarper. He hurried over to the door. Then stopped. Something was bugging him. But what? Something not right. He turned and slowly looked back round the room. At the paintings . . . the *Taddei Tondo* . . . the benches . . . No, nothing wrong there. But then he saw it. The fire extinguisher he'd used to smash his way up through the skylight. The one he'd taken off the wall.

He ran back to it and snatched it up. Too risky to leave it. Any copper worth their salt would ask questions. What was it doing there? Christ, they might even be able to see from the CCTV tapes before the system had gone down where it had been before. Next thing they'd be asking was whether the dents on its rim might have been made by someone using it to bash the shit out of the reinforced glass. And how come someone would need to do that from in here if they were breaking in from outside.

He stuck it back in its cradle and hurried back to the gallery door and quickly got out his map to orientate himself. He checked his watch. Shit, he was late already. The CCTV above his head still looked dead, thank God. No lights or movement. But he needed to get out of here fast.

He reached the landing at the top of the main staircase in under a minute. Come on, come on. Another two minutes, and you'll be there. Inside those lovely, cold, dark, shit-smelling tunnels. But then what? He pictured Dougie Hamilton's face. Frankie still didn't trust him as far as he could spit.

He didn't even see the guard, just ran straight into him at the junction of the two corridors leading out onto the landing at the top of the main stairs. Their two heads cracked together. Both of them stumbled and fell.

18

'Ugh,' the guard called out.

Shit. Frankie had landed underneath him. Not a small lad either. Had to have weighed fourteen stone. Frankie fought to get his arms free. But the guard struggled back, grabbing at Frankie's wrists, trying to pin him down. Frankie twisted left, then right. That did the trick. Overbalanced the bastard, sent him rolling hard against the wall.

But straight away the guy was coming back at him, grabbing at him, air hissing between his gritted teeth. Frankie twisted himself round again. He jerked his knee up. Yeah! Got him too. Right in the nuts. Drove him back against the wall. Pinned him with his foot. But not for long. The guard grabbed hold of Frankie's leg with both hands. Frankie felt the panic rising. Christ, he was going to get caught. No, no way. Both his legs started kicking out automatically, desperate to get away. Then the guard's grip suddenly slackened. Shit. Frankie saw he'd been kicking him right in the face.

Blood was pouring from the poor bastard's nose, but he wasn't moving. Frankie felt sick. Shit, what had he done? He scrabbled round and leant over him. No. Please no. Hamilton had made him many things, but please, not *this*. Not a killer. But still nothing, the guard's head just lolled over on its side facing the wall.

Shit. What now? CPR? Frankie couldn't just leave this bastard to die. A memory . . . back in the school yard, laughing with his mates doing some first-aid course with plastic dummies as their victims. Breathing. Yeah, that's right. He had to check the guard's breathing first.

He leant in close, holding his own breath, listening. Please, please, please. Nothing. He couldn't hear a thing. Frankie reached to open his jaw. But shit. It was only now that he got a good look at the guard's face. And recognized it. No bloody doubt about it. But from where?

The main entrance. Christ. Yes. Here. Just downstairs. This was the same bloke who'd pulled Dougie up for littering. Shit. That same long curved scar under his throat. Frankie pulled his balaclava up off his face onto the top of his head. Taking a deep breath, he gripped the guard's nose with his left hand just like he'd been taught at school, and took a deep breath and leant in.

'Whoah!'

Frankie's turn to cry out. He reared back before his lips had even touched the guard, like he'd been stung by a bloody wasp. Because the guard wasn't dead. Nothing bloody like it. He was staring right up into Frankie's eyes. At Frankie's *face*.

Frankie was scrabbling back now, up, stumbling back. Shit. Tits. Bollocks. Wank. The guard was still staring at him, his mouth opening. Arrrgh! What the hell was Frankie meant to do now? Tie him up. With what? The only sodding bit of rope he'd had was dangling down the side of the building. Anyway, it was too late. The guard was already nearly fully conscious. He was trying to get up. Two more seconds and he'd be grabbing for Frankie. They'd be locked in a tussle again.

Run. The thought hit Frankie like a thunderbolt. Nothing else for it. Apart from battering the bastard again, only this time on purpose. And no way was Frankie doing that, right? Even if it meant getting caught. Right? *Right.* This guy had done nothing wrong at all. Dougie. He was the one who needed beating. He was the bastard who needed to pay.

Frankie turned before he could change his mind. He nearly tripped over something on the floor. The guard's radio. He snatched it up. He sprinted across the landing and scarpered down the stairs. He turned back halfway to see if the guard was chasing after. Nothing. No sign of him at all.

Frankie kept on running, retracing his route. Maybe the guard was concussed? Meaning maybe he wouldn't remember Frankie's face? Or work out which way Frankie had gone? Here's hoping. Or else Bram's whole ruse about having come in and out through the roof would be blown. Only a matter of time then before the cops figured out how they'd really got out. And then what? They'd check the sewers . . . and then that maintenance hut for prints . . . and none of them had been wearing gloves in there. And what about the truck? What if there was CCTV out there on the street nearby when none of them had got their balaclavas on? Christ, what if they'd been captured on it going in from the van?

First things first. He had to get back to Rivet and the others and tell them what the hell had just gone down. And *before* that guard alerted the others. If he hadn't already. And shit, Frankie couldn't understand it. He had the guy's radio, but why wasn't he shouting out? Because there was no one else there? Because he was the only guard out here on patrol?

Frankie grimaced. Let's just pray to God that's true. And not just that . . . oh, Jesus . . . Frankie's balaclava . . . he remembered it now . . . it was still halfway up his face . . . He jerked it down, wondering again how good a look at him that guard had just got. Enough to describe him? But maybe even worse than that. Enough to recognize him? From when he'd been here with Dougie? No. No way, right? Right? Think back. Did he even really look at you that time with Dougie? No. You didn't speak to him either, did you? No. At least Frankie was pretty much sure. So, no, he was safe, right? But what if he *did* remember him and *did* pick him out from the CCTV footage they probably still had of that day? Then they'd not only see it was him, Frankie James, but that he was with Dougie Hamilton too.

Frankie's lips curled into a smile. Couldn't help himself. Because, oh yeah, now he saw it . . . God really did have a sense of humour, eh? The same poor sucker Dougie had humiliated and put in his place was now going to get Dougie and Frankie caught and this whole gig rumbled. Oh yeah, if ever an irony had been sweet, it was this.

The door to the office they'd first come in through was shut when Frankie reached it. And locked.

'Rivet? Bram? It's me,' he hissed, rattling the handle.

He glanced back over his shoulder, half hoping to see one of them coming, dreading it would be that security guard or one of his mates instead. The door handle he was holding suddenly shifted. It opened and Rivet looked out.

'Thank fuck,' Frankie said. 'I thought you'd split.'

'Bram already has,' Rivet said, pulling him inside and shutting the door after them, 'and Lola set out the same time you left. The state she's in, it's going to have taken her at least until now to get back.' Rivet's torch beam settled on Frankie's face. 'Shit,' Rivet said. 'What the hell happened? Did you fall?'

'If only . . .'

'What do you mean?'

'I got hit.'

'By who?'

'A guard.'

'What? You're serious?'

'No. I just punched myself in the face for a laugh.'

'But . . . where?'

'Upstairs. I think he's still there. Coming round . . .'

'You mean you –'

'Hit him back? More like kicked.'

'Kicked?'

'Look, it was complicated. We were both lying on the floor.'

Rivet was just gawping at him, for once at a loss for words.

'But sod that. Listen, he's not going to be down for long. I couldn't see anything to tie him up with or I would have. Meaning we'd better get the fuck out of here. And fast.'

Rivet was still gawping, no doubt running the maths, trying to work out whether his whole precious mission had now been compromised or not. Frankie looked around the room. There was a pile of cloth-wrapped parcels by the door which led outside into the little courtyard. Whatever Bram hadn't been able to carry then.

'Wait,' Rivet said. 'What did he look like?'

'Eh?' Frankie stared at him. Oh, he was still talking about the guard. 'Look like? Fucking sore. Well, by the time I'd finished with him, anyway.'

'No, I mean it. Describe him.'

Frankie did.

Rivet looked surprised. Then smiled.

'And definitely a curved scar . . . right here, under his neck?'

'Yeah.'

Rivet's smile became a grin.

'But aren't you worried about him raising the alarm?'

'No, at least I don't think so. Look, I haven't got time to explain now. Let's just get us and this shit down the sewer and get out of here, just in case I'm wrong.'

*

It took them maybe twice as long to work their way back through the sewer tunnels as it had done to reach the RA. There were the parcels, for one thing. And Lola, for another. They caught up with her about two thirds of the way back. She was being supported by Bram. He'd had to abandon two of his cloth-wrapped exhibits, meaning Frankie and Rivet then had to go back for them once they'd got Lola safely up into the maintenance hut.

248

Safely. Hah. As they sat there in the torchlit dark, Frankie felt anything but. The fact was all he'd been able to think about since he'd left the RA was his passport sitting there behind the bookcase in the flat where he always kept it hidden. Because the only place he'd feel safe right now was abroad. Oh yeah, he could feel a little impromptu holiday coming on and fast. And maybe a permanent one too. Certainly high time he got on his horse like one of them cowboys and pissed off over the horizon until the heat died down. At least from abroad he'd be able to check the news and see if the cops really had fallen for Dougie's little wheeze. Or if instead they'd already arrested Bram, Rivet and Lola – and were coming for Frankie next.

'So we getting out of here then?' he said.

They had all the stolen exhibits stacked up neatly by the door that would lead them back out onto the street and the van that would still hopefully be waiting outside. Lola was slumped in one of the small metal chairs, clutching at her leg. Her skin looked pale in the torchlight. Bram and Rivet were leant up against the wall either side of her, with Bram just gazing steadily at his watch. It was taking all Frankie's willpower not to just shove past them and rip that door open and run.

'All in good time,' Rivet said, tapping his watch.

'Another bloody schedule? More com-part-fucking-mental-ization?'

'Exactly so. Three minutes,' Rivet said.

'Fine. So now would you mind telling me what the fuck all that was about back there? All that stuff about the guard and why he wasn't going to set the alarm off?'

The others exchanged looks and Bram signed something.

'Because if he's who we think it is,' Rivet said, 'he won't say shit.'

'And why's that?' But, even as he said it, Frankie guessed the answer. 'Because he's him, isn't he? Your inside man. The one who put that Duracell Bunny there?'

Rivet mimed shooting a target with a pistol. 'Bullseye, Frankie. You got it in one.'

'That fucking bastard,' Frankie said.

'Who?'

'Never bloody mind.' Dougie, that's who. Frankie was already running the whole incident back through his mind. Him and Dougie in the RA entrance hall. That guard coming over and ticking Dougie off. Then Dougie taking off those bloody great Aviator shades of his and the guard backing down. And why? Yeah, Frankie got it now. Because the guard had just that second recognized Dougie, without his shades on, as the man he was working for on the sly, because of that gambling money his kid owed. And he'd have wanted the whole encounter over as soon as possible so it wouldn't distract anyone's attention on CCTV. Because if there'd been any sign of recognition or familiarity between the two of them . . . well, were the guard at any point to somehow get fingered in all of this, then that might have left him and Dougie linked.

'Nah,' Rivet went on, 'he won't say shit – other than maybe he fell. The last thing he'll want is the cops paying him any attention at all.'

'And all that other stuff? The stuff on the roof? I worked it out, by the way.'

'Worked what out?'

'Why you had me scattering it up there.'

'We thought you might.'

'It's the diversion you were telling me about, the one that'll stop the cops looking for how else we might have got out.'

'And the one that the press will fascinate over too, making sure this story runs and runs.'

'Hence the postcards,' Frankie said. Something else he'd worked out. 'To go with that Houdini headline Dougie's friendly hack's going to write.'

'Exactly, they'll provide the perfect kindling to get this little publicity bonfire of ours up and running.'

'You'll love what I did with the rope then.'

'What?'

Frankie quickly explained and Lola cracked up, even through gritted teeth.

'Very good.'

'Yeah, it wasn't long enough to reach another building, or the ground . . . just enough to perplex. And along with the crampons . . . well, it's inspired. I don't think that sly old bastard Houdini could have done any better himself.'

Bram grinned.

'Shame we didn't have a tightrope balance, really,' Frankie said. 'I mean, imagine what they'd make of that.'

'And the photos?'

Frankie handed the camera over.

'Yeah, all safe and sound.'

Rivet clicked through the images on the little screen and nodded, clearly pleased.

'Who you gonna send them to?' Frankie asked.

'Oh, the usual suspects. The *Evening Standard*,' Rivet said. 'And *The Times* and the *Guardian* and the Beeb, ITV and Channel 4, and, I don't fucking know, maybe even Bruce Forsyth, huh? Anything to get the word out . . .'

'And, sure, they're not going to buy it forever,' Lola said, 'they'll measure the rope and find out that wouldn't have worked . . .'

'And draft in some climbing expert who'll then tell them that the crampons couldn't have worked either . . .'

'But who cares? The more unanswered questions they get, the better. Especially when a couple more friendly journalist friends of Dougie start adding more grist to the rumour mill.'

'Like maybe we zipwired, or used a fucking helicopter to get in and out of there . . . hey, that would have been funny,' Lola grunted, 'we should have taped out a helipad "H" up there.'

'Or maybe they'll just think we travelled by demonic portal,' Frankie said, remembering the pentagram he'd outlined up there instead.

'Or I don't know what,' said Rivet, 'and who the fuck cares what dumb-ass schemes they come up with that we might have used . . . so long as they don't get the shitty truth.'

'The sewers we've just climbed out of . . .'

'Quite so.'

Lola groaned. She was still clutching at her leg.

'You know, she needs to see a doctor,' Frankie said.

'And she will.' Rivet checked his watch again.

'I can call one once we're back at mine,' Frankie said.

'Yours?' Rivet said.

'Well, sure. I mean it's less than fifty yards away,' Frankie said. But, yeah, maybe he got Rivet's apprehension too. Because there was still plenty that could go wrong between here and there. Even this late, they had to be careful. There was still the possibility that someone from one of the nearby streets might be putting out their rubbish in the alley bins. Or, more likely, some junkie, dealer or hooker turning tricks might cop a load of Frankie and the others waltzing past with their stolen modern masterpieces in hand. And, even covered up with these cloths as they might be, someone watching might put two and two together and decide to make a phone call to trade information to try and claim a reward.

'Enticing as the thought of a bourbon and a game of pool is,' Rivet said.

'Snooker,' Frankie said.

'Right. Yeah, as enticing an offer as that is, it'll have to wait. OK, time,' Rivet said, pushing up off the wall, the camera still in his hand.

Have to wait? What the hell was he talking about? Frankie watched, confused, as Rivet unlocked the door and edged it open. A slither of light brightened. Such a shock after the dark of the tunnels that for a second Frankie thought someone must be stood out there with a torch shining in. But no cop's shout came. Just the low growl of a car driving by. The light faded with it and Rivet pushed the door wider and slipped out, whispering at them to stay put. Ten minutes later and he was back, with a new black gym bag in his hands.

'We're good,' he hissed, ducking back in, and patting the bag. 'And, even better, we've been paid. Mr Hamilton liked the photos very much.'

Well, at least someone was getting something out of this. Frankie reached for the packages to start help carrying them out to the van, but Bram rested a restraining hand on his wrist.

'What?' Frankie said. He made to reach for the parcels again, but Bram just shook his head, not slackening his grip.

'OK, Frankie,' said Rivet, 'it's been a blast . . .' He smiled at him, holding out his hand.

'But what about the –'

'Artworks?' Rivet asked.

'Yeah.'

'Not our business. Next stop for them is that club of yours, but where they're going after that, I neither know nor care.'

Frankie looked from Rivet to Lola and Bram, then back again. Looked like they all felt the same way about that. Meaning Dougie probably hadn't told them the stolen pieces were to be stored at his long term then. Looked like him and Viollet clearly hadn't trusted their hired art thieves enough for that.

'But hey, don't look so sad,' Rivet said, shaking him warmly by the hand. 'They're not expecting you to carry them all by yourself. They said there'll be somebody along to help you right away.'

As Rivet stepped back to help Lola up from her chair,

Bram stepped in. He shot Frankie that wide, cracked smile and gave him a hug. He signed something in the flickering torchlight.

'What did he say?'

Lola grinned and patted Frankie on the shoulder as Rivet helped her past him towards the door.

'That if you ever get tired of working for Dougie Hamilton, you should consider coming and working for us.'

I don't work for Dougie Hamilton. But the words never made it out of Frankie's mouth. Because what was the point? Here he was, in the company of three career criminals, wearing a balaclava, and being left to stand guard over a pile of stolen art that he'd just helped steal from the RA. At just what point did he consider himself *not* a criminal these days? Who cared whether he'd been blackmailed into this or not. He was still *owned*.

He watched them go. Bram shut the door behind him, leaving Frankie alone. An engine started outside. A diesel. The van they'd driven here in? Frankie kept his gloves on because he was still paranoid about the cops maybe working out their real route, even if the guard he'd had his scuffle with wasn't a problem any more. He kept his balaclava rolled up on the top of his head too, right down to his eyebrows, his paranoia about the possibility of CCTV in the street outside still high too.

His eyes kept flicking from the door leading back down into the sewers to the door leading back outside. He pulled up a chair by the sewer door, close enough so he could listen for anyone coming up. Hear anything and he'd have to run, taking as many of those artworks as he could.

But the first noise he heard was from the other door. Another engine pulling up outside. Then voices. The click of the lock. Then the door swung open. A pair of wide shoulders squeezed in. A glimpse of the screwed-up eyes of the owner.

'Turn that fucking torch off,' said The Saint.

19

'A-chooo!'

'Are you *sure* you don't want me to get you some bog roll?' Only, like, the fifth time that Frankie had asked.

'No, I'm fine.' The Saint wiped his great big red strawberry of a nose on the sleeve of his suit jacket, leaving horrible wet streaks on its black shiny material. 'It's just my farting hay fever,' he complained. 'You sure you not got any flowers in here?'

'Certain. Anyhow, this place is meant to be pretty much bloody hermetically sealed, isn't it?' Frankie said, looking round the basement of the Ambassador, where they'd just finished stacking the last of the stolen works of art.

'*Her*-what?' The Saint scratched at the thin ginger stubble on his head.

'*-metically*. Look, it doesn't matter,' Frankie said. 'Are we done here now? Can we just –'

The Saint's phone rang. 'Shut it, scrote,' he warned Frankie, answering it. 'What? Eh? No, I can't hear . . . The reception . . . it's . . . What? Bloody thing. No. Listen. Wait.'

The Saint trudged upstairs, still muttering into his mobile phone. Christ, Frankie was glad Xandra and Maxine were safe in their hotel. Imagine bumping into this great Lurch in the middle of the night here? You'd think you'd woken up in an episode of *The Addams Family*.

Frankie stared around him, under the cool white lighting. He was exhausted. Not just physically either. Though, Christ, he was that. Those tunnels had taken their toll on him, all right. But, mentally, yeah, that was even worse. He was done in. Could sleep for a week. That phrase about drooping eyelids? He'd always thought it was a cliché. But he really did need a couple of matchsticks to prop his up now. Either that or a stiff drink to kick-start the old circulation. Yeah, sod it. He set off upstairs. Time for a quick visit to the bar. Not like he'd be falling off the wagon, really, either, was it? Not seeing as he'd not actually been on it all bleedin' weekend.

'Ah, good, you're here. Now open those sodding doors.' The Saint was standing by the bar, in its little pool of yellow light, with its phone still clamped to its ear. 'Yeah, boss, he's coming now.'

Boss. Meaning Dougie was here? Right outside the club? The club where the art was being stashed? On the same sodding night it had been nicked? Well, this just got better and better, didn't it? Maybe Frankie should just speed up the inevitable and stick a flashing neon sign up outside telling the cops exactly what they'd just done? Could that make it any easier for them to nail them than it already was?

Frankie walked past the bar, only just managing to resist ducking behind it to pour himself a quick shot of Jameson's, and into the gloom of the club beyond, where he'd kept the lights off. Weaving his way in between the banks of seating, he opened the front door and stepped aside to let Dougie in. But it was Viollet who came though first. All dressed in black, as per usual. No smile, but her eyes flashed with amusement as she looked him up and down.

'Nice look,' she said.

He only remembered then, he was still wearing the bright-yellow waders he'd put back on for the return journey through the sewers. Her nose wrinkled up, as she took a couple of steps further back.

'Nice smell, too,' she said. 'Not.'

Well, that, at least, made Frankie smile. Her joke, not her revulsion. 'I'd never had you down for a *Wayne's World* fan,' he said.

A bob of those dark eyebrows. The nearest he'd maybe ever get to any actual intimacy with her again? More than likely. What was it she'd called him and her? *Past tense?* Yeah. A shame, though. Because all Frankie could think about now was tomorrow. And where he might be by then. And with who. Again he pictured his passport, up there in the flat. Because sticking round here wasn't going to be getting any easier, was it? He was a potential target for everyone from Hamilton, to Riley, to the cops now.

'Who's Wayne?' a man's voice asked.

Dougie. He'd at least had the common sense to wear a hat like he'd done at the Royal Academy that day. Suited and booted too, in spite of the late hour. Looked like he'd just got back from a day's grouse shooting. He looked Frankie's shit-spattered fishing waders up and down.

'Catch anything, did you?' That nasty little smile of his twitched at the edge of his thin lips.

259

'Everything you could have hoped for.'

Dougie glanced from Frankie to Viollet and back. 'I'll be the judge of that,' he said.

'This way.' Viollet strode past Frankie and led Dougie down into the basement.

Frankie stayed put. Or, rather, he didn't. He marched straight behind the bar, the siren call of that whiskey way too strong for him now. He plugged a tumbler up under the optic and pushed it once, twice, three times.

'You want one?' he asked The Saint, who was watching him, dead-eyed, from where he was standing sentry just along the corridor at the top of the basement steps.

'Nah, I'm driving,' he said.

'Oh, yeah,' Frankie said. 'I forgot what an upstanding member of the community you were.'

Frankie poured himself another whiskey, and gazed back into the twilight of the club. The banks of seating, dividers and competition tables were all due to be taken down and out tomorrow, and things put back as they were. He smiled, thinking about being out there on table one, up against Adam Adamson. He remembered the clapping crowds. It had been all right, hadn't it? And not just that, not just his little dance in the limelight, but all of it, the whole sodding thing.

But then his smile faltered. Because that was then, wasn't it? And this was now. And it didn't matter how well all that might have gone, because here he was back where he always seemed to find himself. Right in the shit.

Outside he caught a couple of notes of 'Candle in the Wind' playing from a passing car. And, yeah, suddenly it kind of made sense to him, why so many people seemed to like it. Because it was about this, wasn't it? About life. About the nasty nitty-gritty at its core. About how no matter what you tried to build, it was only ever a matter of time before first it, and then you, got snuffed out.

'Well, it seems like congratulations are in order,' Dougie said, walking over to the bar, with Viollet hanging back behind him, her face half hidden in the shadows.

'A toast, I think, is in order,' he said. 'Bar keep, would you mind doing the honours?'

Bar keep, the cheeky little prick. For a second, Frankie remembered how it had felt, besting Dougie two years ago, when he'd come here and crashed his car. Even with The Saint and Viollet here, and with all that would come his way if he did, wouldn't it maybe, just maybe be worth it, rushing Dougie now and wiping that snide little smile off his pasty little face?

'Sure, no problem,' Frankie said, 'so what'll you be having?' Yeah, the sensible option. Just keep the bastard sweet, then see if you can get what you want, and then get him out of here as fast as you can.

'Oh, I think champagne's in order. You do serve champagne, I take it?'

Frankie ignored the slight and cracked open a bottle. Moët. Two glasses. One for Dougie, which he pushed towards him across the bar top now. One for Viollet, which he slid her way.

'And yourself?' Dougie asked.

Funny, but even though he'd felt only two minutes ago like he could have done with another five, ten, twenty shots, the thought of it now just brought bile rising up to the back his throat. He took a bottle of iced water from the fridge instead.

'The boss just told you to drink,' said The Saint. 'So fucking well drink a proper fucking drink.'

'I don't,' said Frankie, pushing his whiskey tumbler back out of sight.

'Yeah, but you just –' The Saint started.

'No, that's all right,' Dougie cut him off, handing Viollet her glass. 'Far be it from me to interfere with a man's moral code.' He raised his glass first to Viollet, then Frankie, then The Saint. 'To a great night's work.'

'A great night's work,' said The Saint, before glaring at Frankie. 'Fucking say it,' he snapped.

'A great night's work,' Frankie said. He walked round the bar and handed Dougie his set of keys for the basement door. 'I was wondering if now might be a good time to ask you when I might get that pistol back.'

'I bet you were.'

'And?'

'Well, before we can even think about discussing when and how and if that might happen, first there's something else we need to do . . . with this . . .' He nodded at Viollet, who only now stepped forward into the light. She was carrying something. The Digley piece. The little dog.

'What?' Frankie said. He already didn't like the sound of whatever this something else was, or the glint in Dougie's eye.

'We need to take it on a little walk . . .'

'Do what?'

'Well, I say *we*, but I really only mean you,' Dougie said. 'Oh, and The Saint here too, obviously. Just to make sure it's done right.'

And, oh yeah, OK, now Frankie saw what this was all about. The rest of tonight's work. Framing Tommy. And that's what they were going to do it with, was it? This sodding little stuffed dog that The Saint now had gripped by the scruff of its neck? Because that's what Dougie was sending him and Frankie off to do now – plant it in Tommy's office.

'Stitched up by a piece of taxidermy,' grinned Dougie, taking another deep glug of Moët. 'Oh, I do hope Tommy sees the funny side of this, I truly do.'

*

Frankie and The Saint drove in silence in The Saint's black cab. Or at least with them not speaking. More bloody Streisand playing, mind. Her warbling this time in bloody French.

Frankie shifted uncomfortably on the plastic Tesco bag The Saint had made him sit on. Frankie had already got changed out of his waders and into jeans, trainers, a hoodie and a baseball cap, but he still hadn't had time yet to shower.

He stared at the stupid wrapped dog on his lap, with the stupid words on its stupid sign still visible through the stupid bubble wrap. 'R.I.P.' Yeah, Frankie knew the feeling. Or at least he might do by tomorrow, depending on how tonight went. Because this really was it, wasn't it? Him stuck between two gangsters going *tête-à-tête*, as the good Lady Babs might have sung it herself.

Tommy's office up above his lap-dancing club, Whistling Gussets, was so close to the Ambassador that they could have walked there in ten. The Saint got them there in six and parked up in the taxi bay outside.

'See?' he grunted. 'Told you this mode of transportation had its perks.'

'Yeah, aren't we lucky?' Frankie said.

'Oi, you can park that,' The Saint growled.

'Oh, I thought we just had?'

'And that. This is a sarcasm-free zone from here on in. Get your serious face on. We're not here to muck about.'

Easy for The Saint to say. He'd clearly been born with his serious face on. Getting out the cab, though, Frankie was finding keeping a straight face harder and harder. Maybe it was the alcohol. Or nerves. Or maybe it was even that ruddy little dog making everything feel surreal. Not just its stupid little sign, but its stupid little paw now, sticking out of the bubble wrap so that Frankie had to tuck it into his jacket to stop passers-by seeing it. Not that there were many of them about. Or many sober ones, anyhow. Thank God it was the middle of the night.

Whistling Gussets had shut hours ago. Its neon sign, showing a pair of kicking, stripy can-can legs, was switched off. The same went for the lights in all its windows facing the street.

'This way,' Frankie said.

'Eh?' The Saint had been heading for the main entrance.

'The tradesman's . . .'

'Huh-huh.' The Saint grinned.

Brilliant. So sarcasm was off tonight's humour menu, but vintage gags were in? Frankie stopped by a dark doorway halfway down the alley.

'Surprising,' said The Saint, examining the door.

'What is?'

'I'd have thought Tommy would have had better security than this.'

'They look pretty state-of-the-art locks to me.'

'Shows all you know.' The Saint rammed in a crowbar he pulled out from under his jacket. A cracking noise. The whole door frame split. 'Don't matter how good a lock if you're not even trying to pick the bloody thing.'

The Saint fumbled for a piece of paper in his pocket.

'Quick, read that, would you? I haven't got me glasses.'

'What is it?'

'The alarm code. One of Tommy's cleaners was kind enough to furnish us with it. Either that, or Dougie was going to have her son's bollocks fed to him in front of her. But so it goes.'

Frankie read out the numbers.

'The alarm's behind the bar,' said The Saint, setting off.

Another empty, twilit club. Floor-to-ceiling poles glistened in the glow of the emergency exit signs. A smell of disinfectant and spilt beer. They found the alarm box behind the bar just next to the fridge. The Saint shoved him roughly aside and knelt down, rummaging again for something in his pockets. He took his phone out and put it down on the bar top, then dug again, this time pulling a pen torch out and shining it onto the alarm's keyboard.

'Jesus,' he said. 'Whatever muppet shut up shop didn't even remember to switch the piggin' thing on.' He scrunched up his piece of paper in disgust and stuffed it back into his pocket.

'Okee-cokee, then . . .' He got up, looking around. 'You've been here before, I take it?'

'Yeah.'

'Nice birds, are they?' He was staring at the dance floor. 'Is it just tits they show, or gash as well?'

'I don't know about any of that,' Frankie said. 'Last time I was here, I was up meeting Tommy in his office. Top floor.'

'Then be a good chap, would you? And get me up there, *tout suite.*'

Frankie led him back across the dance floor and on down the corridor to the side entrance they'd come in through. A steep staircase led up . . . and up . . . and up . . . Christ, Frankie's legs ached – tonight's drama had already gone on way too bloody long. But, come on, you're nearly there. Just one more Task of Hercules to go, right?

The last time Frankie had come here to see Tommy, these stairs had been crawling with punters shuffling back and forth between the main bar downstairs and the private lap-dancing rooms up here on the higher floors. Frankie could still remember how nervous he'd felt about coming up here to talk. Well, more like beg really. To ask Tommy for his help in clearing Jack's name. But not just nervous. He could see that now. Young. Wet behind the ears. Hopefully he'd got sharper since. Hopefully that still might get him out of even this fix.

Either that or he was screwed.

'Nice smell,' said The Saint.

'You what?' Frankie thought he'd misheard.

'Of the birds,' The Saint said. 'You know, their perfume.' He sniffed loudly. 'You can really smell it in the air. That and, you know . . . their fanny,' he added. 'You can really get a whiff of that too.'

'You're not married, are you?' Frankie said.

'Nah. Never met the right girl.'

'Funny that . . .'

'Oh, right, I get it,' said The Saint as they reached the top of the stairs. 'More jokes, is it? I'm not gonna tell you again.'

'Just trying to lighten the atmosphere,' Frankie said.

'Well, don't.'

They finally reached the top floor. Two doors. The one on the left had a fluffy pink star on it.

'What's that, then?' asked The Saint.

'The girls' dressing room.'

The Saint tried the door handle. Locked. He reached for his crowbar, but thought better of it.

'Nah,' he mumbled to himself, 'no time for that now.'

For what? Frankie hardly dared imagine, though a quick and deeply disturbing image did briefly enter his mind, of The Saint happily powdering his face in there, wearing nothing but a feather boa, as he played at dressing up.

They both stopped outside the second door. It didn't look anything conspicuous. More like the entrance to a caretaker's room. The only thing giving it away was the hefty-looking keyhole, indicating an even heftier lock behind.

'Right, now, where's that key?' The Saint mumbled, digging round in his pocket.

'Another gift from our cleaner friend?' Frankie asked.

The Saint ignored him. He checked all his other pockets before blowing out a long sigh.

'Fucking bollocks, I've only gone and lost it. And my bleedin' phone. Must have left them both in the car.'

Frankie wished Rivet was here. They could do with his particular skill set around now. 'I don't suppose you've got a –'

'Set of picks?' asked The Saint. 'Nah, never needed one.' Without warning, he half picked Frankie up by the scruff of his neck and deposited him a foot to the left. He then stepped back to give himself room, before kicking the door just below the lock with the heel of his size twelve boot. Two more thunderous kicks and they were in, with the door hanging open and its state-of-the-art lock mangled like it had been battered with a sledgehammer.

'Nice,' said The Saint, peering inside but not stepping forward. 'Very nice indeed. I always did think Tommy had good taste.' He glanced slyly at Frankie. 'Well, get on with it then.'

'You not coming in?'

'Nah. You see I knew Tommy at school, didn't I, just like I did your dad.'

'And . . .'

'He was always one for the . . . what do you call it?' The Saint stared at Frankie blankly.

Frankie stared blankly back.

'You know,' said The Saint. 'Like James Bond . . . all that sneaking around and spying on people shit.'

'Espionage?' Frankie hazarded.

'Yeah, that. And you know what?'

'What?'

'I wouldn't put it past the sneaky fucker to have a camera in there. Hidden away, like. Separate to the system these mugs forgot to switch on downstairs. Something he could then show the cops.'

'Ah, so what you're saying is . . . it's OK for me to go in there and maybe get filmed, but not you.'

'Exactamundo.' The Saint rewarded Frankie's keen thinking with a brief sliver of teabag-coloured teeth. 'So crack on then, scrote. And make sure to stick it somewhere obvious. You know what the fucking plod are like. Half of them couldn't find their own pissin' noses in a mirror.' The Saint jerked a balaclava down over Frankie's head and grinned at him through its lopsided peepholes. 'Now don't say your Uncle Sainty don't ever look after you, eh?'

'Right,' Frankie said, his voice suddenly muffled, as he straightened up the balaclava so he could actually look out of both eyes. 'Thanks.'

Walking into Tommy Riley's office, he half expected to see him sitting here behind his desk, with a cigar clamped between his lips and an Al Capone-style machine gun in his boxer's fists. But no. Nothing doing. *Somewhere obvious . . . somewhere obvious . . .* Frankie just wanted this done with. He crossed the room to stick it on Tommy's desk.

'Oh, and make sure to unwrap it,' The Saint called in after him. 'I know it's not traditional, like, with presents. But we really want Tommy to get the joke. Or get that it's on him, anyhow. Even if he don't know who's played it. Before they bang him up.'

Somewhere obvious . . . oh, and funny too . . . Frankie spotted it then. The perfect bloody place. Unwrapping the little dog, he put it in the corner of the room. There was a clear line of sight from there to the open office door, and outside he heard The Saint first chuckle, then laugh out loud, a deep, rich belly laugh that Frankie wouldn't have believed the miserable old bastard capable of.

'Perfect,' said The Saint. 'Nice one, scrote. Wait till I tell Dougie. He's going to fucking shit.'

20

Turned out The Saint hadn't been right about Dougie Hamilton's reaction to hearing where Frankie had left the little dog. He didn't actually shit himself. But Frankie reckoned he really might genuinely, actually have done a little wee in what were his no doubt posh designer Calvin Klein pants. He really did laugh that hard.

'You left it in his dog's basket?'

'Whitney's basket? Yeah,' Frankie said.

'Whitney? Tommy Riley's dog's called Whitney?'

Dougie snorted with laughter again. Something little boy-ish about the way he did it, though. So much so that, for a second, Frankie could almost picture him bouncing on his dead dad's knee as a kid. Maybe this bellend wasn't quite such the corporate wall of concrete he made himself out to be. Maybe he might even agree to returning that pistol after all? Might he even have it on him here now? If not, though, well . . . Frankie needed to get out of here as fast as he could. His heartbeat was already pounding at the thought. Because who knew how long Dougie's good mood would last? Not long, he reckoned. Not long at all.

'Er, listen . . . I hate to bring it up again, but that pistol?'

271

he said, stepping in between The Saint and Dougie, who was sitting on a black leather armchair.

But other than to flick Frankie a brief, annoyed glance, Dougie pointedly ignored him. He was still dressed in his immaculate tweed suit, leaving Frankie worrying that tonight's business was far from over, as he'd feared.

'He put it right there in the middle, boss,' said The Saint, having to park his enormous frame on the sofa in Dougie's Maida Vale mansion flat living room, he was still chuckling so hard. 'With its little "R.I.P." sign pointing up at the ceiling. You couldn't bloody miss it, boss. The cops are bound to take a picture of it too, yeah? For evidence, like, and to show him. My God, I'd kill to see his face.'

'Oh, that is *too* good.' Dougie's eyes were shining like he was high, the same way Jack always used to look whenever he'd done too much gear. 'Oh, God, I can't wait to tell Viollet about this when she gets back.' His voice suddenly hardened. 'Talking of which . . . where on earth is she?'

This last question was to Barry, the same beardy, Sasquatch-faced twat with the bat who'd clobbered Frankie in the Cobden Club the same afternoon this whole hideous episode in his life had kicked off. He'd brought the Louisville Slugger here too. Had it propped up in full view next to the white baby grand piano he was currently leaning back against.

'Well, she said she was heading down the shops,' Barry said.

'The shops? At this time of night?'

'She said she wanted cigarettes. Said she'd find a twenty-four-hour garage.'

'Why didn't you go for her?'

'I offered, but –'

'She doesn't even smoke,' said Dougie.

'But . . .' Frankie remembered her smoking all right, lying there in his bed.

'Were you about to say something?' Dougie said.

'Er, no,' Frankie said. 'It's just that, er, the only garage round here that'll still be open is a good couple of miles' walk away.'

'Huh.' Dougie checked his watch. 'She'll probably be back soon then. And talking about timing . . .' His smile was gone and he was glaring at The Saint. '. . . what the bloody hell took you two so long to get back? How the hell did it take you nearly two hours? It's less than three miles away.'

'Some bastard slashed our tyres,' said The Saint.

'They did what?'

'All four. Front and back.'

'Who?' His eyes narrowed suspiciously. Something about this he didn't like at all.

'If I knew that, I'd be wearing their bleedin' skins as a coat,' said The Saint. 'They scratched the shit out of the paintwork too. Scrawled some gang tag on it. West End Massive, or some such shit.'

'Hmmm.' Oddly, the gang thing seemed to calm Dougie down a notch. 'Yeah, well, next time make sure you call. That's why you've got the phone.'

The Saint said nothing. His veiny cheeks pinked.

'Christ, I can read you like a book. What, you broke it, did you?' Dougie said.

The Saint scratched at his head. 'Uh, more like lost it, really, boss.'

'Bloody hell, sometimes I don't know why I bother. I'm just trying to bring this whole game into the modern era, but here I am still lumped with dinosaurs like you.' He sighed heavily. 'But I suppose at least there's still some things you're good at . . .'

'Yeah?' The Saint's yellow teeth flashed.

'Yeah, fucking grab him,' Dougie said.

Oh, shit. The Saint didn't need telling who exactly it was Dougie meant. Dougie already had his pistol out – that same sodding pistol that Frankie had risked coming here to get, instead of getting the hell out of Dodge while he still could have – *should* have, fuck it, he was screwed.

Dougie levelled it at Frankie's head. Not that he needed it. The Saint already had Frankie's arm halfway up his back and was slamming him up against the wall, spreading his legs, all nice and professional, like. Frankie would have fought back, but . . . well, Dougie wasn't the only one aiming a gun at him, was he? There was the little matter of the sawn-off shotgun Barry had just pulled out of his black gym bag too.

Lowering the gun, Dougie got to his feet, whipped a cheap-looking phone out of his jacket pocket and punched in a few digits. 'Yeah, is that the police?' he said. 'I want to report a robbery.' He walked out through the living-room doorway and into the hall. 'Yeah, a great big bloody robbery,' he went on, his voice fading, '*and* I want to tell you who did it . . . no, it doesn't fucking matter who I am . . .'

By the time Dougie came back into the living room, Frankie was already trussed up like a turkey, gaffer-taped to a brown wheelchair that smelt vaguely of stale piss.

'I take it you're not planning on giving me that back then?' he said, staring at the Browning Hi-Power pistol that was still in Dougie's hand.

'What, this?' Dougie looked down at the pistol, as if surprised to see it there. 'Oh, yeah, you're going to get it, all right.' He mimed popping Frankie in the head. 'Just like I promised. But only after I've had you tortured first, to see what you really know about your brother's involvement in Susan's death.'

He put the phone he'd just made his anonymous tip-off with on the edge of the grand piano's keyboard, then slammed the lid down. Again and again.

'Oh, don't worry about the noise,' he said, turning to Frankie. 'These old mansion blocks were built to the very highest standards. Walls three feet thick. Whoever the neighbours are, they won't hear a peep. No matter how loud anyone screams.'

Anyone . . . it was obvious enough from the way he said it and the smile on The Saint's face when he did who was going to be screaming and who was going to be making that person do it.

'Yes,' Dougie went on, 'you see, that's why Dad decided to snap this flat up when he was dying . . . so he could be nice and peaceful, right to the end.' Standing behind Frankie, he took hold of the wheelchair's handles and wheeled him slowly over to the window. 'This was his chair. Or was meant to be,' he said. 'He didn't really get to use it much, he was so sick by the end.' He stopped just in front of the window which led out onto the balcony. Frankie could see his half-reflection staring back at him, with the city of London glittering out towards the horizon beyond. 'But I'll tell you something for nothing,' Dougie said. 'He didn't half love this view.'

Frankie thought about it. About trying to convince Dougie again that he'd done nothing wrong. That Jack hadn't either. But he'd tried that before, hadn't he? Back in the Cobden Club. And all it had earned him was a smack from this twat over here with the bat. He thought about begging too. But he knew that would do him just as little good.

Christ, he'd really fucked this up, hadn't he? Should have just run when he'd got the chance just now when The Saint had parked up downstairs. Shouldn't have pushed his luck, coming up and hoping to get that gun and then get away. Because now his luck had run out.

He felt like crying, but no, fuck that. Not in front of this bastard. Not yet. But what then? Wind him up good and proper. Get him to let off some real steam. Yeah, why not? If he was going to be tortured, he'd rather be concussed when he was. Plus, the longer he dragged all this out, the more chance he'd maybe have of someone finding him here. Even though he couldn't for the life of him think how.

'I never believed you, anyway,' he said.

'About what?'

'Anything, really. You giving me back that gun. Or doing anything other than deciding to fuck me up, once tonight's job was done.'

276

'Oh, yeah?' Dougie asked, clearly not believing him. 'And why's that?'

'Because you're just like your father, aren't you?' Frankie gave him his very best smile. 'A lying, toerag cunt.'

'You –' But Dougie couldn't even get the words out. It was like he'd been punched in the guts. Hard to tell from a reflection, if someone was turning purple, but Frankie reckoned he probably was.

'Oh, and thick as well,' Frankie said. 'I mean, I'd kind of guessed you might be, on account of you only being a solicitor and not a barrister, and you *still* thinking I know anything about Susan's death' – he stared him hard in the eyes, praying for the last time he might finally see this was true – 'but I didn't actually know for sure until you made your little call to the cops just now that you really are dumb enough to still think you've won.'

Dougie spun the chair round to face him. Oh yeah, proper purple, he was. Chenguang would have no doubt thoroughly approved.

'Won? *Won?*' Dougie shrieked. 'What do you know about winning? You're dead, you know that? Fucking dead! And not only that, but in these last few days of your pathetic little life, I've used you, *used* you like the fucking lowly, insignificant pawn you are to knock out the fucking king.'

A mobile phone started trilling. Dougie jerked it out of his suit jacket pocket.

'Well, go on, then,' Frankie said, 'aren't you going to answer it? Because then we'll see who's the pawn in all this. Then maybe you'll realize I ain't quite so stupid as you think and might actually still be useful to you alive after all.'

Because, oh yeah, Frankie knew what was coming. For once, he was one step ahead of this prick. Which was why he'd come up here, hoping to get that pistol sharpish, knowing it was the last chance he'd ever get.

'Yes,' Dougie said, clamping the phone to his ear, 'this is him speaking . . .'

Frankie watched as Dougie went a deeper and deeper purple, enough to make even a rock band jealous. He would have enjoyed it too, other than the fact he was now almost puking at the thought that it might well prove to be the last thing he ever saw.

'And you're sure? A hundred per cent sure?' Dougie stared, just stared at the phone for a second, then hurled it across the room and it exploded against the wall.

'Something wrong, boss?' asked The Saint.

'Of course there's something fucking wrong. *Everything*'s wrong. My source . . .' He was growling, actually growling. 'My source has just told me that the police raided Tommy Riley's office on the back of my anonymous tip-off.'

'And?' The Saint was frowning. He clearly couldn't understand how this was not a good thing.

'Only that little fucking doggy wasn't there.'

'But we put it there, boss. *He* did . . .' The Saint was pointing a fat, pudgy finger at Frankie. 'I watched him do it. I watched him myself.'

'Well, it isn't there now.' Dougie's face had shifted up a gear, from purple into puce.

'But how?' said The Saint. Then his eyes lit up. 'Someone must have moved it, boss. Gone in there after we . . .'

'Yes, yes!' Dougie screamed. 'Of course someone fucking

moved it. And the same bastard then put that fucking dog, along with all the other stolen art pieces, back into the fucking Royal Academy!'

The Saint just gawped. His brain couldn't process it.

'All of which means,' Dougie said, staring hard into Frankie's eyes now, 'that someone fucking betrayed me to Tommy Riley, didn't they? Someone told him not only about the whole robbery, but how I was planning on framing him for it too.'

Frankie jammed that smile back on his face. 'Meaning maybe instead of you killing me,' he said, 'we should just sit down and talk about this instead.'

*

Frankie's head was pounding. His nose was broken, along with two of his fingers on his right hand, from when Dougie had finally lost it back there in the living room a few minutes ago. So much for hoping that Dougie might decide he was more useful to him alive now than dead. Seemed like he'd decided the opposite. As well as still wanting him tortured to see what he knew about Susan, all Dougie wanted now was revenge.

After Dougie had finished beating him, The Saint had wheeled Frankie through into here, a back bedroom of Dougie's apartment, with a blood-stained bed and sound-proof foam padding nailed to the back of the door. Looked like he wasn't the first lucky visitor who'd been there.

The Saint was currently standing over the dressing table whistling something that sounded horribly like 'Send in the

Clowns', while slowly sharpening a vicious, curved Bowie knife on a whetstone, before he got stuck in.

Frankie flexed his arms, again and again, trying to loosen the tape he'd been tied to the wheelchair with. His heart was stuttering, his face wet with sweat. He'd pissed himself too. A whole fat bladder full of it. Dougie had already told him exactly what was going to happen . . . first the torture . . . then a nice slow death . . . then Dougie and his crew would be going after Jack and the Old Man . . . and Tommy Riley too, of course.

Unless Tommy somehow got to him first. And Frankie prayed with every atom of his fucking being that he would.

'You really shouldn't have done all that, you know,' said The Saint, gazing at Frankie in the dressing-table mirror. 'Messing up his plans like that.'

Maybe not, and certainly not now it had turned out like this. But it wasn't exactly like Frankie had had any other choice, was it? It all came partly back to what Listerman had said, about people working for more than one master generally ending up getting ripped apart. Because he'd been right, hadn't he? Right from the get-go. No matter what Frankie had done, or how he'd tried wriggling or playing the two of them off, from the second Dougie Hamilton had set himself up against Tommy Riley, Frankie would have had to betray one of them eventually. The only real question had ever been *who*?

But it hadn't just been what Listerman had said that had made up his mind, but what the Old Man had told him that last time he'd visited him in Brixton too . . . *if you do have to choose between them, then you choose based on who you think you can trust the most, and who can get you the furthest . . .*

Frankie had hated Tommy for his decision to wreck the Soho Open, but at least he'd done it to Frankie's face, not behind his back. Whereas Frankie had never believed for a second that Dougie would ever let him have that pistol back. Nah, that stone-faced weasel had been lying to him right from the start.

Frankie had finally cracked in the basement of Tommy's new Chelsea pad on Sunday. Before that, when it had just been the robbery he'd been working on for Tommy's rival, he'd been able to square it with himself. But after he'd found out about Dougie taking Tommy down too, he'd had no choice. *And there's nothing else I need to know?* Well, yeah, there had been. And he'd told Tommy all about Riley's plans, all the hows and whys of the heist, and about Dougie then planning on planting one of the nicked art pieces in Tommy's office for the cops to find.

Frankie could pretty much guess how certain matters had proceeded from there. Getting the dog out of Tommy's office before the cops took a dekko would have been easy. Christ, Tommy had even made it easy enough for them to plant it there in the first place, by leaving the downstairs alarm off. Getting the other pieces out of the Ambassador would have been simple too, because Frankie had given Tommy the spare keys.

But as for the rest of what had happened . . . well, some of that Frankie was less sure of. First up, he'd expected Tommy to just nick the art from the basement and keep it for himself. But, OK, he kind of got why he hadn't. Because that gear would have been hard to shift and he'd not invested in other works by the same artists like Dougie and his partners had. And, yeah, he also got why Tommy might have wanted it to look like the whole heist had never happened. Because otherwise, after that tip-off about him having been involved, the cops would have been watching both him and his business interests too closely. Something Tommy would have wanted to avoid at all costs.

But what Frankie really didn't get was *how* the hell Tommy had managed to get all those pieces back inside the Royal Academy before the cops had got there? Sure, he'd bought himself the time to do it, by slashing those tyres on The Saint's black cab. And a nice touch too, adding that gang tag. But how had he *actually* done it? As in broken back in?

'I always wonder what people like you think about?' said The Saint, finally turning round.

'What people?'

'Soon to be dead people. People what is fucked.'

'Oh, those people . . .' Frankie felt sick, but he still tried to smile. Maybe there was still some way of talking The Saint out of this? After all, the two of them had almost been co-workers, right, this last couple of weeks.

'You know, about whether you made bad choices along the way,' said The Saint, 'or whether, if you could go back now, what you might do different.' He shook his big fat head. '. . . because, really, the second you double-crossed Dougie by grassing him up to Tommy like what you done, surely you knew this couldn't end well?'

But, no, Frankie hadn't known that. He'd thought he'd

got it covered. That was the point. He'd been banking either on getting that gun and getting away from here before the news of the 'non-robbery' got through, or on Tommy 'sending in the cavalry', as he'd put it, to pluck Frankie from Dougie's grasp. Only problem with the latter being that Frankie had told Tommy he'd reckoned that he'd be meeting up with Dougie tonight over at that old warehouse on Narrow Street. Where the bloody cavalry might well be arriving right now. Not that it would do Frankie any good. Tommy probably didn't even know this flat he was in now existed.

'So what's it going to be, then?' The Saint dug into his leather travel bag and pulled out a claw hammer and held it up alongside the glistening Bowie knife. 'Hammers or knives?'

'I don't suppose you've got a feather duster in there too, have you?' The joke didn't even sound funny to him. He remembered the bloke in the basement of that warehouse. More meat than person. And that was it, wasn't it? That was going to be him. He felt his stomach clench and his balls try and climb up into his stomach. Oh, God, help me. Someone help me, please.

The Saint leant down and peered inside his bag, before coming up grinning. 'No, scrote. I'm afraid you're all out of luck.'

'I don't suppose either that there's any point in reminding you again about how you were once mates with my dad?'

'Well, you say mates . . . the truth is, I never really did like him . . . always felt a bit jealous.'

'Jealous?'

'Yeah, because of your mum. I always thought he was punching well above his weight where she was concerned.'

'You knew her?' Even now, even here, the information made Frankie's heart thunder even faster than it already was.

'Oh, yeah . . . but there's no time to get into any of that now, we've got a job to do here, and it's getting late.'

'What about money?' Frankie said. 'I've got money . . . I can –'

The Saint shook his head, looking disappointed. 'It always comes down to money, don't it? That and –'

'Just *please*,' Frankie said, because, yeah, he already felt like he was back there, down in that other basement two years ago with Terence Hamilton, with that Stanley knife flashing in his hand . . . and no way was he going to get lucky enough to get away from something like this twice. 'Just *please* . . .'

'That and begging,' said The Saint, tearing off a strip of duct tape and smoothing it down across Frankie's mouth. 'There. Much better. Now no more of that silliness, eh? Because we're all professionals here.'

No! I'm not! Frankie tried screaming through the gag. *I'm not a professional. I run a fucking snooker club.* But even as he was gnawing at the tape, desperately trying to mumble it, he knew what The Saint would say: *That means you are a professional. You were the second you took that on. Just like your Old Man before you. Just like anyone who comes anywhere near Riley or the Hamiltons, or tries to grab a sweet piece of that Soho pie.*

'But, even so, I am genuinely sorry it's all come to this,'

said The Saint. 'Times are you've kept me almost amused as we've been doing our little drives here and there . . . but then again I do understand why the boss doesn't want to do it himself. I mean, don't get me wrong, I'm not saying he doesn't like getting his hands dirty – because if push came to shove then he would, like through there just now with you, and he enjoyed giving your brother a right battering down that pub alleyway last year as well . . . got a right sweat up, I can tell you.'

So it *had* been Dougie behind that assault that had put Jack into hospital. Frankie hauled at his restraints, but the tape was still too tightly bound.

' . . . but he has got such pretty hands, see,' The Saint went on, 'I mean, you've seen them, right, all manicured, like . . . you could almost say they were intelligent hands, couldn't you? And not the sort to be sullying themselves with this sort of grunt work, not when there's old lags like me with rusty old chisels like these . . .' He pulled a number of other blood-stained implements up out of his bag and clanked them down on the dresser. '. . . that are more than capable of getting the job done.'

As he weighed the knife and the hammer again in his hands, Frankie tried twisting, turning in the chair. Tried to rock it, tip it over. Nothing worked.

'Anyway, don't say I didn't warn you . . . to get out.'

Frankie didn't need the tape off of his mouth for The Saint to read his expression as he leant in.

'Oh yeah,' he said, 'out there in the sticks, when I said you should piss off on holiday and soon, I meant it, I really was giving you the nod . . . a chance, you know, because of

285

all the times we'd spent together . . . and you clearly liking Barbra Streisand so much, an' all.'

The Saint put the knife down, his decision made, and gave the hammer a little practice swing. Bile sluiced up into Frankie's mouth – he only just managed to swallow it down. But what was even the friggin' point? Choking to death on his own spew would probably be a hundred times better than what The Saint had in mind.

'Now, Dougie was very explicit, I'm afraid,' The Saint said, leering, 'well, when I say that, what I actually mean is that *you* should be afraid, heah, heah, heah . . . he said that I should really go to town on you . . . or not even town, really, think of it more like several small villages first on the way into town . . .' His dark eyes glistened at how clever he'd just been. '. . . yeah, Dougie wants this to take as long as possible . . . and look . . . he even wants me to keep a record.'

He pointed at a clipboard with a lined piece of A4 on it, and next to it, another little digital camera like Viollet's. Viollet. Where was she? Did she know this was going on? Probably. No, more like definitely. The bitch.

Frankie jerked his head back, looking up. A banging noise had just come from next door. Loud enough to hear through that soundproofed door. Pretty fucking loud, in other words.

'Well, well, well . . . what's all this then?' said The Saint. 'A last-minute reprieve? A stay of execution? I wouldn't count on it with that one. Nah, he's sure what he's about. Never changes his mind. More like, he's just lost his temper again. Smashed that fucking piano up into firewood with that bat, I shouldn't wonder.'

More banging. This time a frown settled on The Saint's face.

'Don't move,' he grinned down at Frankie. 'I'll be back in just two ticks.'

Pop.

Frankie heard the noise the second The Saint opened the door. Then *pop-pop*. Two more. The Saint just stood, still grinning, for a second. Then his eyes rolled back into the top of his head and he fell backwards, crashing onto the floor.

'*Hola, Señor Frankie,*' Jesús said, flashing him a perfect white smile as he stepped into the room and over The Saint's dead body, all in one lithe, fluid motion. He'd got a pistol with a silencer in his right hand and he slowly scanned the room. 'All queer,' he yelled.

'*Clear . . . clear . . .* for the hundredth time of telling you, the ruddy word is *clear*!'

Mackenzie Grew rolled his eyes at Frankie as he strode in, his white suit spattered with blood, and leant down and checked The Saint's pulse. 'Yep, nice shooting, Jesús. Right between the fucking eyes. Dear Mr Jimmy Flanagan is officially a goner. Couldn't have happened to a nicer bloke.'

'Well, fuck me, if it isn't General Custer,' Frankie finally managed to say, as Grew pulled the tape off his mouth.

'Custard?' said Jesús. 'Like in cakes?'

'No, Custer,' said Grew, rolling his eyes again, 'you know, as in the bloody cavalry?'

Jesús's turn to roll his eyes at Frankie now. He tapped his forefinger at the side of his head. 'This Grew, he *ees loco, sí?*'

'*Sí*,' said Frankie. 'Bloody *sí*.'

Grew started to untie him. 'Christ, what's that smell?' he said.

'Me,' Frankie admitted. 'I pissed myself.'

Grew glanced across at the various torture instruments The Saint had got lined up. 'Can't say I blame you, son. Can't say I blame you at all.'

'And Dougie?' Frankie asked. Had he still been next door when the boys had come through just now?

'Oh, you needn't worry your pretty little head about him no more,' Grew said. 'I just used his head to turn that lovely white piano of his a most alarming shade of red.'

'And I shot that other asshole,' Jesús grinned. 'Right through *hees* knees, before I *feeneesh heem* with *hees* bat.'

So the Sasquatch had got squashed.

As Frankie stood up shakily, Grew pulled a clean white towel out of The Saint's bag and started dabbing at the blood on his lapels. 'What?' he told Frankie. 'Quit your gawping. This is Paul Smith. New season. The longer you leave it, the worse a stain gets.'

'How?' Frankie said.

'Well, I've always said that lemon juice and white wine's the best for getting blood out.'

'No. You. Him. Here. Now. How?' Frankie said.

'How. Did. We. Know. You. Were. Here?' Grew grinned back.

'Yeah.'

'The sex bum,' said Jesús, popping a yellow Gummi Bear into his mouth.

'What?'

'He means sex bomb.'

Frankie just stared.

'The Saffa, son,' Grew said. 'That girl everyone's frightened of, or in love with. Or everyone except me.'

He couldn't mean . . . 'Viollet?'

'Ah, she said she'd met you.' Grew shot him a sly glance. 'Maybe more than just *met*, though, eh, looking at you now?'

And, suddenly, Frankie saw it. Why she hadn't been here when him and The Saint had come back. Why she'd slipped away. Because Frankie wasn't the only one who'd been playing both sides, was he? Viollet Coetzee must have been too. And it was her who'd told Tommy where to find him, here in the Maida Vale flat, instead of the Narrow Street warehouse.

Yeah, without Viollet Coetzee, he'd be dead.

21

'Oh, I do wish I could have been there, to see little Dougie's face when he got that call from whoever his tame pig is, to tell him that there'd been no heist,' Tommy Riley said. 'Was it a picture? Would it have made me laugh, Frankie? I bet it bloody would.'

'Yeah,' Frankie said, remembering what The Saint had told Dougie, 'you'd have laughed till you shat.'

'Easy on the language, son,' said Tommy, wagging his finger disapprovingly. 'Ladies present, an' all that.'

'Sorry, eh?' Frankie said, nodding across at Viollet and Chenguang, who were swimming in parallel up and down the pool.

Frankie was sitting with Tommy, Tam Jackson and Tommy's nephew, Darren, at the breakfast table in the basement of Tommy's new Chelsea pad. And, boy, what a change a week made. The building work had all been finished in here. Concrete foundations in. Water on top. Light rippled across the white ceiling and the Corinthian columns and alcoves on the walls. Opera played gently through the sound system. Maria Callas instead of Babs. Yeah, things couldn't have been more different if they'd tried.

Then there was Frankie himself. The bruises on his face had died down. His nose had been reset. The only sign left that he'd been in any real bother at all was the splint on his right hand still keeping his fingers there straight.

Other scars, mind, they wouldn't be so easy to heal. Frankie could still picture him, The Saint, standing over him with that claw hammer swinging down. And Dougie too, or rather what was left of him and the twat with the bat . . . that whole blood-spattered, bone-splintered mess of a living room . . . Grew might have got a clean-up squad in there to wipe the whole place down like none of them had ever been there, but Frankie was still waking up sweating every night, like he'd never even made it out.

'Do you want to know what's really funny, though?' Tommy said, stroking Whitney, who was lying by his bare feet, chewing on his robe's purple cord.

'What?'

'Show him, Tam.'

Tam shoved the morning's papers across the table to Frankie, nudging the silver tray of peach brioches Darren's way, who quickly snaffled two up.

'Turns out that exhibition of his didn't need any extra publicity at all,' Tommy said.

Frankie scanned the front page he was pointing at. A picture of that Myra Hindley piece Sharon had told him about. The article below talked about the protest and the outrage it had provoked. But the publicity it had generated had clearly worked its magic. The exhibition itself had got itself record attendance figures. Oh yeah, all those artists on show in there, it looked like they'd already gone global after all. Frankie wondered who Dougie Hamilton's silent partners had been. Because they'd all be making out like bandits by now.

'I've been meaning to say thanks, by the way,' said Frankie.

'Oh, yeah? For what? Saving your life?' Tommy lit a cigar.

'Yeah, of course that. But for the tournament too. For calling off the fix. Before it was too late. Before everyone involved smelt a rat and its reputation got shot to bits.'

'Ah . . . that . . . well, that was just a little reward . . . for you tipping me off about what Dougie had planned.'

Frankie nodded slowly. 'Yeah, but, you see, I've been thinking about that too.' He stared into Riley's eyes. 'Because you must have known already, mustn't you? About what Dougie was planning? *And* about him having recruited me? *And* about him planning to frame you? You must have already known all that, *before* I told you, on account of the fact you already had Viollet working for you.'

Tommy sucked smoke deep into his lungs. 'Ah yes, but only just. She switched sides quite late in the day, see. After Grew had made her an offer she couldn't refuse, to stop working for that prick and to come work for me.'

Frankie glanced across at Viollet, who was now drying herself off on a lounger at the far side of the pool. Was it money she'd switched for? Or did Riley have something on her? Just like Dougie had got on Frankie? Either way, it was funny, though, wasn't it? Especially after what Dougie had said about chess. Because all that time he'd been fixating on toppling the king, he should have been watching his queen instead.

'So why didn't you tell me?' Frankie said. 'When I admitted what I'd got myself caught up in? Why didn't you tell me then that you already knew?'

Tommy smiled, blowing a thin plume of grey smoke up towards the spotless ceiling. 'Well, because then I'd have had to admit that I'd been testing you.'

'To see which way I'd flip?'

'To see where your loyalties truly lay.'

'To see if you could trust me?'

'Which I can.'

Frankie remembered his last meeting here, that day before the heist. When Tommy had asked him, *And there's nothing else I need to know?* Thank God, he'd changed his mind and told him everything he knew. Because if he hadn't, well . . . he'd probably be as dead as a dodo by now. Or a Dougie. Or a Saint.

'And that's another reason why I decided to call off the fix in the tournament,' Tommy said. 'You fronting up like that, it got me to thinking, that maybe some people really are trustworthy enough to go into legitimate business with, not like that dishonest, double-dealing, unreliable prick who let Hackney track go to the dogs . . . '

'An unfortunate turn of phrase,' Tam said.

'Eh? Oh, "to the dogs" . . . hah hah, good one, Tam, nice spot . . . get it, Darren? Get it?'

'Oh, yeah, Unc. Brilliant.' Darren reached for a third peach brioche, but Tommy slapped his hand away.

'Yeah,' Riley said, 'because, see, you're maybe not like him and more now like a . . . like a trusted . . .'

'Junior partner,' said Tam. 'Very junior,' he added, glaring at Frankie.

'Yeah, more like that,' Tommy smiled. 'So how do you like them apples, then, Frankie?' he asked.

A lot more than ending up like Dougie and The Saint, that was for sure. 'Yeah,' Frankie said. 'Junior partner sounds just about right.' But did it? Sure, at least in the context of the Soho Open. But was that really all Riley was talking about?

'Good. All's well that ends well, then,' said Tommy.

But it wasn't over. Not for Frankie.

'When . . . when whatever it was that happened to Dougie . . . happened,' Frankie said.

'Grew happened to Dougie,' Tommy said, flicking ash off his cigar into his herbal tea. 'But what about it? You want details? Photos?' Tommy grinned like a skull. 'Because you know me, I love a snap or two to keep as souvenirs, especially of people who I wasn't there in person to say goodbye to . . . and that twat even left me a snazzy new little camera.'

'No, it's not that.'

'Then what?'

'Was there a pistol?'

Tommy frowned. 'No, I think Grew used a piano. At least for the *coup de . . . de . . .*?' He glanced sidelong at Tam.

'*Grâce,*' Tam said.

'Yeah, *grâce.*'

'No, I mean did Dougie have the pistol on him? The one I told you about. The Browning Hi-Power?'

294

'The one he was using to blackmail you with? The one with your sticky little prints all over it?'

Frankie had had no choice but to tell Tommy about the gun the same morning he'd told him about Dougie's plans, because right away Tommy had demanded to know why the hell Frankie was working with him. But Frankie still hadn't told him that it was the same pistol that had been used to kill Mario Baotic, because that would have been giving Tommy the same power over him that it had given Dougie.

'Yeah, that one.'

'No, or at least I didn't hear nothing about it.'

'No, boss,' Tam said. 'There was no gun, apart from that sawn-off.'

Was he telling the truth? Was it possible that Dougie had got rid of it before Jesús and Grew had arrived? Could someone else really have come round and taken it away? Frankie couldn't see how.

Tommy stubbed out his cigar and held up both hands. 'A mystery then. But you know what? We can't ask little Dougie now . . . not with him having been . . .' He nodded at the bottom of the pool and crossed himself. '. . . so permanently laid to rest.'

Oh, Jesus, he didn't mean that . . . but, yeah, from the grin on Tommy's face, as he gazed down at the freshly laid pool foundations, it was obvious that he did.

'But you know what, Frankie?' he went on. 'Don't let it prey on your mind too much. Because *if* it ever were to turn up and come into my possession, I'd make sure to keep it somewhere nice and safe and out of sight.'

If . . . the way he said it . . . it sounded more like it already had.

'After all, we're friends, right?' said Tommy. 'And friends always watch each other's backs.' Rising, Riley slipped off his robe to reveal his shiny purple budgie smugglers beneath.

'One last question,' Frankie said.

'What?'

'Once you found out what Dougie was planning, why didn't you just stop it? The whole heist?' Because Grew had already told Frankie about how Bram, Rivet and Lola had never been working direct for Dougie Hamilton at all, but for Viollet. And how, after showing Dougie the photos on that camera and getting their payment, Viollet had then told them where their new loyalties lay. Rivet and Bram had swung back round and taken all that art back in through the sewers into the Royal Academy, where they'd also then cleared the roof. 'Why did you let them go to all the trouble of stealing all that stuff to begin with, if you were only planning on putting it back? Why didn't you just, I don't know, call the whole thing off and make your move on Dougie then?'

'Ah, well, that's because I wanted to see if it was possible,' Tommy said. 'To really get in there, into the Royal Academy, and nick something and then get back out without being noticed at all.'

'What, out of academic curiosity?' Frankie somehow doubted it.

'Not exactly.' Tommy walked over to the pool steps and slowly lowered himself into the water. 'So what do you think of the decor?' he asked, setting off in a gentle doggy paddle towards the far end of the pool.

'Yeah, it's like I said last time I was here, it's classy. Real classy,' Frankie said.

'No, I'm not talking about the fucking columns, son. Here, Darren, hit that bloody switch.'

'Sure, Unc,' Darren said, waddling over to the wall next to the jacuzzi.

A light came on at the end of the pool. It was only then that Frankie noticed it, the curtains covering the alcove there. They slowly began to part.

Frankie just gawped. Because, Christ, was he really seeing what he thought he was? The *Taddei Tondo* . . . the same priceless work of art by Michelangelo that he'd nearly used to bash that skylight in?

'Tah dah!' said Riley. 'Or *Taddei*, at least!'

'Hah hah. You're on fire today, Unc,' chuckled Darren.

Frankie's mouth was still flapping wide. Because, surely, *surely*, he couldn't actually mean that . . . ? No . . . it had to be a fake . . . Yeah, there'd been that Italian bloke here, hadn't there? That forger, Matteo, or whatever he'd been called. He must have just copied the design for Tommy . . . because there was no way that Tommy . . . that the real reason that Tommy had let that whole heist go ahead . . . was to see if he could actually get a fake one in there and then somehow get the original out? No, there was no way. There was no way at all, right?

Right?

Experience book one in the Soho Nights series

If you enjoyed THE BREAK

then you'll love listening to FRAMED

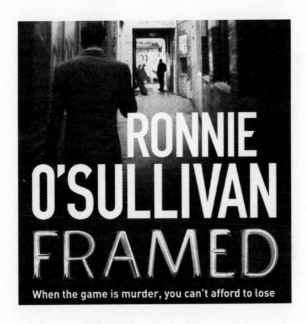

Available to download today

*Experience book two in
the Soho Nights series*

**If you enjoyed
THE BREAK,
then you'll love
DOUBLE KISS**

*The race is on.
The stakes are high.*

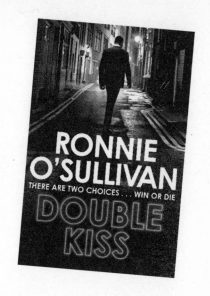

Frankie James thought his troubles were behind him. He's busy running his Soho Club, and his brother's finally out of prison. But when a postcard arrives from Mallorca, he's stopped in his tracks . . . Is it from his mother – the woman who's been missing for eight years?

When the goddaughter of London's fiercest gangster, Tommy Riley, goes missing in Ibiza, Tommy knows there's one man for the job – Frankie James. Just when Frankie was on the straight and narrow, he's now faced with an impossible choice. If he agrees to help find Tanya, he'll be thrown into a world of danger. If he doesn't, Tommy could destroy him.

For Frankie James, old habits die hard. One thing's for sure, playing with this gang is no game. But with everything at stake, how can Frankie say no?

Read on for an extract . . .

1

'It's coming home . . . It's coming home . . . It's coming . . . Football's coming home . . .'

The Ambassador Club was packed tighter than a tube carriage during rush hour. The owner, Frankie James, reckoned there had to be 150 punters in here. Maybe more. Pumping their fists in the air, with their England flags draped down their backs, looking like a bunch of pissed-up, wannabe superheroes all trying and failing to take off.

The hulking, great silhouette of Spartak Sidarov stood wedged in the open doorway, bright sunlight pouring in through the tiny gaps that his massive shoulders hadn't quite blocked out. Frankie's old mate was more used to bossing Oxford Street night club queues, but it was good to have him here today, seeing as how many people had turned up this afternoon to watch the match and how hammered most of them already were.

A good job too that Frankie and Xandra had put the hardboard covers on the club's twelve snooker tables that morning, while Dave the Shock had been installing the two big wall TV projectors he'd picked up from the Rumbelows clearance sale. Because none of this crowd were here to play.

The whole room stank of smoke and spilt booze. There wasn't a ball or a cue in sight.

The tabletops were littered instead with overflowing ashtrays and pint glasses, and a young woman called Shazza was now curled up on table six and snoring like a drain – Frankie kept half an eye on her.

Everyone else's eyes were glued to the screens. England one, Switzerland nil, with just ten minutes to go. It was the first match of Euro 96 and the action was taking place right here in London, just up the road at Wembley. With the whole world watching. Or at least that's how it felt.

'Come on, boys. Keep the bastards out,' Frankie muttered under his breath, swilling dirty pint glasses one after the other through the glass-washing machine behind the bar, his shoulders tightening up as the Swiss surged forward again.

He'd put a hundred quid down at Ladbrokes on England to win. But not just this match, the whole tournament, three weeks from now, at odds of 7-1. A win would mean Frankie could escape Soho for a nice little holiday.

He hadn't had a day off since Christmas, not once in the last six months.

He glanced back at the photo montage his mum had stuck up here on the wall between the optics. Back when her and the Old Man had still been together, and they'd all used to head off down the Costa del Sol along with a bunch of other families from round here. His mum was right there in the middle, her beautiful smile suspended in time, as she hugged her two precious boys – Jack and Frankie. Frankie couldn't have been more than thirteen.

Frankie was rudely brought back to the here and now by loud cheers and shouts of encouragement. Up on the screen, the clock ticked over to the eighty-three-minute mark. The crowd started belting out the Lightning Seeds' anthem again, even louder this time.

'Three Lions on a shirt . . . neeeeeever stopped me dreaming . . .'

Frankie joined in. It was hard not to. This sodding tune was that damned catchy and the stakes were that bloody high. He grinned across at Doc Slim and Xandra. Both working the bar beside him. Doc doffed his worn leather cowboy hat, looking more and more like Colonel Sanders by the day now that he'd upgraded his grisly grey moustache to a full-blown beard.

Xandra was sporting her new, that-girl-from-the-Cranberries, cropped barnet, along with the panther tattoo on her bulging right bicep that Frankie had sprung for on her nineteenth birthday last month.

Bloody kids. She was only five years younger than him, but he still felt like her dad. He'd even insisted on meeting the tattooist and checking he was properly licensed before he'd let him set to work. But then Frankie had always been older than his years. He remembered his mum always saying that about him, even when he was a nipper.

'Don't give up the day job,' Xandra laughed, mock grimacing and sticking her fingers in her heavily studded ears. She'd already told him she'd heard cows in labour singing better than him on the County Antrim farm where she'd grown up. The bloody cheek.

Then *booooooooo*. The crowd's choral antics switched to

jeers. Frankie's ice-blue eyes locked back on the screen. Bollocks, double bollocks, Stuart Pearce! He'd only just been bloody penalized, hadn't he? For handball. In the box. Shit-a-brick. This was all Frankie needed. England starting off their campaign with a draw.

Pearce's nickname – 'Psycho, psycho, psycho!' – rumbled through the crowd. The Swiss striker, Türkyilmaz – 'Wanker, wanker, wanker!' – stepped up for the kick. Seaman stared him down from the English goal, his dodgy 'tache and slick-back glistening in the blazing hot sun, making him look more like he was planning on selling his opponent some double glazing than blocking an actual shot.

Frankie couldn't watch. It was the same as whenever he watched Tim frigging Henman on the box, tightening up on his second serve at set point. Frankie sometimes felt that maybe he was capable of jinxing it all personally, just by wanting it so much.

He looked the opposite way down the bar instead, at Ash Crowther and Sea Breeze Strinati, who were both hunkered down on their usual stools, with their bent backs squarely to the room, totally wrapped up in the same game of chess they'd been playing since last Tuesday. Or was it the Tuesday before?

Then the whole crowd groaned, 'Nooooooooo!' And Frankie forced himself to look back at the telly. Arse flaps. The Swiss players were celebrating all over the pitch. Practically cartwheeling, the cuckoo clock-fiddling bastards. Gritting his teeth, he watched the replay. Türkyilmaz went left. Seaman right. Leaving it one all now, with less than four minutes to go.

'Bloody England,' he groaned.

'Aye,' Slim grumbled, bumping his hat on the ceiling light as he reached up to fill a tumbler from the optics. 'It's at parlous times like this that one almost wishes one had been born a Kraut.'

'Oi, mate, two pints of Guinness,' some bumfluff-chinned, pumped-up teenage lump in a white Umbro tracksuit yelled across at Frankie. 'Er, please?' he quickly added, clocking Frankie's glare, along with his black suit and tie, and no doubt wisely hazarding a guess that he was the boss man round here.

Dress smart. That's what Frankie's Old Man had always told him. Look like the man and most people will treat you like him too.

He'd not been wrong. Frankie served the lad, who was all smiles and friendliness now. Even gave Frankie a tip, which he bunged in the communal Heinz baked beans can by the till, safely out of reach of any tea-leafing bastards in here. Today's event had transformed the whole of Soho into a pickpockets' paradise, bursting with pissed-up punters, all flashing their cash.

He risked another glance at the screen. Two minutes left, before injury time. With England nowhere bleeding near the Swiss bloody goal. He obviously wasn't the only one getting that sinking, Tim Henman feeling. The cheering and chanting had all but tailed off, an uneasy, muttering half-silence taking its place.

The drinks queue had finally dried up, with the whole crowd now transfixed by the screens. Maybe that was no bad thing either: the Ambassador Club had been non-stop for the last two hours and Frankie was knackered and Xandra and Slim's eyes looked like they were being held open with matchsticks. But, on the upside, at least the till was overflowing for a change. The takings were even better than Frankie had hoped for and he allowed himself a little smile. But, Christ, would he sleep heavy tonight.

'Another drink, boys?' he asked Ash and Sea Breeze.

Ash looked up and scowled. Sea Breeze just scowled.

'Fine, suit yourselves.' Frankie walked back over to Xandra. 'Miserable old gits,' he said.

'Still not talking to you then?'

'No.'

She shot him an awkward half-smile.

'It's not funny,' he grumbled. 'In fact, it's downright bloody rude. I've known them both since I was a kid.'

'And that, old chap, is precisely their point,' said Slim, fixing himself his usual whiskey and soda. 'They've been coming here longer than you. It's like a second home to them.'

'More like the opposite of home,' Frankie said. 'Half the time the only reason they're here at all is to get away from their bloody wives.'

'*And* for my erudite and loquacious company,' Slim said.

'Yeah, I do actually know what those words mean,' Frankie said. Which was at least half true.

'They just feel like they should have been consulted, that's all,' said Slim.

He was talking about the TVs. The Sky Sports signs outside. The new customers.

'This is a business,' Frankie said, 'and a business –'

'Needs to make a profit,' Xandra and Slim parroted, both of them rolling their eyes.

Frankie felt himself flush. Christ, had he really been saying it that much? A half-cheer went up from the crowd, then died down. Tony Adams. But the shot went nowhere. Then more muttering and shuffling started up. It felt like no one else in here really reckoned that England were going to score again either. The whole atmosphere was winding right down.

'You two taking the piss doesn't make it any less true,' he told Xandra and Slim. 'We've got to move with the times –' *If we don't want to get left behind . . .* He nearly said that too, but stopped himself just in time. Could already see them starting to roll their eyes again. 'Anyhow,' he said, 'it's not like we're doing anything else that every other bar in town hasn't already done.'

'I think that's rather their point,' said Slim, lighting up a B&H. 'This is an oasis of culture and tradition. Or rather' – he glanced distastefully up at the screens – 'it *was . . .*'

Frankie had had enough. 'Yeah? Well, bad luck. This isn't a charity or a museum. The TVs ain't going anywhere. At least until the final. Especially if England get through.'

'Ah, so there *is* a chance this'll turn back to a proper club after that, then?' Slim said. 'You should have just said. I'll let the boys know.'

A *proper* club? By which he meant a snooker club, which is exactly what the Ambassador Club had been since 1964. And, yeah, a big part of Frankie wanted that too, to keep the tradition alive, but for that he needed money and the plain fact of the matter was that all his usual punters like Ash and Sea Breeze just didn't bring in enough cash.

'It all depends on how the tournament goes,' he said. He meant *his* tournament, not this one. Snooker, not footy – the Soho Open. The tournament he'd spent every second of his free time these last six months trying to set up. 'If that starts to make money, then fine. We'll go back to how it was. But until it does, the TVs stay and this lovely lot' – he pointed at the crowd – 'they stay too. Because it's their wonga that's currently keeping this place alive. And, anyhow, I don't see what your problem is with any of them, they all seem perfectly bloody nice people to me –'

A sudden burst of shouting. A goal? Nah, nothing doing on the screens. Frankie's eyes flicked right. More yelling. Shit. Trouble. A surge of bodies over there in the corner. The sound of breaking glass.

Bollocks! Here we go again. Frankie gritted his teeth in anticipation of more trouble coming his way, just when he didn't need it. The story of his fucking life.